SLIPPING ON KARMA PEELS

WHISKEY WITCHES PARA WARS BOOK 5

F.J. BLOODING

Whistling Book Press

Alaska

Copyright © 2021 Frankie Blooding

Printed in the United States of America

Published by Whistling Book Press

Whistling Book Press
Alaska
Visit our web site at:
www.whistlingbooks.com

Other Books in the Whiskey-Verse

Shifting Heart Romances

by Alivia Patton & F.J. Blooding

Bear Moon

Grizzly Attraction

Here's the reading order to make it even easier to catch up!

https://www.fjblooding.com/whiskey-verse

Other Books by F.J. Blooding

Devices of War Trilogy

Fall of Sky City

Sky Games

Whispers of the Skyborne

Discover more, sign up for updates and gifts, and join the forum discussions at www.fjblooding.com.

WHISKEY MAGICK & MENTAL HEALTH

S ign up to learn more about our books and receive this free e-zine about Whiskey Magick and Mental Health.
https://www.fjblooding.com/books-lp

To
Ginny and Linda
who made me feel like a sister again.

That last attack on Troutdale had shaken Paige. DoDO had managed to get through her defenses, through all of them. The ones on the town. The ones on the house. They'd killed friends and co-workers. They'd nearly killed the kids.

And they'd done that by murdering hundreds of other people, using *souls* as bullets.

Half the town was in mourning – either the dead or fighting for those in comas. They were planning funerals. Lots of them.

And all Paige could do was sit there at her desk and plan a war, for more funerals, more deaths. It didn't feel right.

She'd met with the major power players. They'd voted to go to war—and Dexx had proposed in the middle of the vote for war. Blessed Mother, that man's sense of timing sucked.

The most powerful people in the country weren't responsible for actually making war happen, though. The real reason she and Dexx had been in that meeting was because *they* were supposed to make the war happen.

But it wasn't as easy as snapping her fingers. It wasn't as

simple as making a declaration. This war would be in the yards of the American people. So, whether they all agreed to this or not, everyone would be involved, and Paige had to do everything she could to... minimize the cost of innocence.

Though, would it matter in the end? By the time actions created consequence, would she still care?

She had to hope so. But at the same time, she didn't know *how* to start this war. There was a right way and a million wrong ways. If she started this on the wrong foot, without the real support of the people she was fighting for, without enough people to fight, without enough resources to support things... There were so many ways to lose this.

She met Dexx's gaze across from her desk. "What are we supposed to do?"

"Well, we can't give in." He looked away from her and let his head fall back, but the chair didn't have a high back, so he was forced to sit up again. "This is..." He shook his head. "I just got my alpha back."

Paige's office was quiet without her full staff. But a few people did wander past her door at random times, reminding her she wasn't entirely alone.

She knew what Dexx meant. He'd spent the last year inside and outside of real time trying to get away from Bussemi in order to reclaim his bond with Hattie. He'd managed to get his spirit animal back, but he hadn't taken care of Bussemi. Alone. "We're fucked." That man *alone* was too powerful. If several generations and reincarnations of Dexxes couldn't take that sorcerer out, then who could?

He raised his eyebrows. "I *did* take care of Mario. He would have been a problem— he *was* a problem. A big one."

Dexx was right. He had, but the cost had been high. "And that's good." But taking care of Mario hadn't helped them with DoDO at all. If anything, DoDO was growing in power. "I miss Cawli." More than she wanted to admit. She'd grown more than a little dependent on him and his magick, being able to shift shape on a whim? That had been... awesome.

They were gearing up to fight a war. A real one.

That was terrifying. *Talking* about going to war and then actually doing it were two wildly different things. She looked around her office, taking in the art Ishmail had picked out for her. He was a good chief of staff and a better assistant. She still missed Willow and felt incredible guilt for her death—

But that wasn't the point of *this* moment. She needed a focus point. "Okay. Who are the big bad guys we need to face here because we have more than one."

"Oh, to yearn for the days of old when we only had one villain," Dexx said, clasping his hand to his chest.

She gave him a look that told him to take this more seriously. "Love you." Her tone told him to shut up.

He grunted with a smile, acknowledging both sides of her statement. "Bussemi." He held up a finger. "Walton." He held up another finger. "People supporting them?"

Paige shook her head. What she needed was a crime board so she could figure out what was missing, what to focus on, and what they needed to ignore. She grabbed the tablet of art paper Rai had left—that girl was really getting good at drawing—and taped it to the wall. This way, if someone came in who didn't have clearance, she could take it down quickly. She'd have to come up with something better, but for now? This would do. "There's also a demon who can touch my magick. Threknal."

"He can what?" Dexx got out of the chair forcefully and followed her to the wall. "When were you going to tell me about that?"

She didn't answer his question because it was obvious. They'd had a lot going on. "I'll make a call to Mama Gee and see if there's something she can help with. She's the one who caught him the last time. I really shouldn't have..." She looked at Dexx out of the corner of her eye and grimaced. "…released him."

He frowned at her with a look that said he *wanted* more information, but he shook his head. "We do *not* need someone like him on the battlefield when we're already stretched thin."

She really appreciated him not pressing her for more details. "We need armies." They had one. Sure. But… they needed *more*. Serious ones. Not just paras willing to fight with tooth and claw or humans ready to defend their land with personal arsenals.

"Okay. How do we get those?" Dexx asked, running his fingers down her back as he studied what she wrote on the paper.

She was jotting down everything they needed in randomness. She'd compile it into to a prioritized list later. "I need someone who understands war." That wasn't her and that wasn't Dexx. "Without that? We lose before we even get started."

"Who are we going to get for that?"

"I don't know." But she had a few ideas. She wasn't willing to lose just yet.

I have few fears in life.
　　Kids are one of them.

So, okay. I realized in that moment that, as a full-grown thirty-something woman, a preteen shouldn't scare me in the slightest. I was still bigger than that little punk. I was definitely smarter than him, and I smelled better.

But this little... a-hole didn't know when to f-ing *stop*. And *that?* That annoyed the piss out of me.

Time for a little karmic placement.

That eyeroll-worthy little twerp picked up yet another one of my bars of soap, scraped it across his snotty nose, and then put it back. That was the third one in a matter of minutes.

Look, I'm not allergic to a little snot. I know that the shelf-life on "gross" isn't long, but when you're just nasty because you can get away with it, I'm going to punch you in the face with your own karma.

With pleasure.

"You want to stop wiping your nose on my soaps, kid?" I asked, sidling up to him with a likeable enough smile. I'm pretty, even at the ripe old age of thirty-two—maybe even because of it—and I know how to sweep men and women off their feet. No matter their age.

But this kid? He glanced at me, shrugged flippantly, then grabbed another soap out of one of the boxes and wiped it up his nose. Then, he looked directly at me with a what-you-going-to-do-about-it smile and put it back.

I just smiled back and winked at him. You know why? Because f-him that's why. I sashayed back to the counter near the side of the occult shop I ran with my girlfriend and grabbed one of my karmic blessing cards. Walking back to him, I palmed the card so he couldn't see it.

His eyes flared as he watched me, maybe taking in my full appearance. Like I said. I'm not bad to look at and I own my sass with my biker boots, fishnets, and ragged black skirt. I like my t-shirts sassy and tight and I definitely wear the bras that make my not-as-young-as-they-used be but-still-not-that-old-so-stop-judging-me tits to stand at attention. I have just enough control over air to be able to manipulate men a *little* more, so I employed that, pushing my wavy dark hair around me.

Yeah. The kid was a little slack-jawed.

I walked past him, leaning in to whisper, "Maybe don't be a complete asshat." I slipped the karmic blessing into his back pocket and kept walking. "Okay?"

Whomper, my personality-enhanced broom, met me at the end of the aisle, peaking around as if he could *actually* see. Though, could he? I didn't know. I'd imbued him with a personality and the ability to walk and move on his own. I hadn't given him eyes or ears. He just somehow managed not to run into things. Magick, man. It was awesome.

I pushed my broom out of the way and back into his hidey-corner near the window. I'd stashed a coat rack there with some material I changed out to suit my moods and the changing seasons and sometimes holidays if I felt like entertaining the notion of celebrating them. It wasn't for coats though. It was so Whomper had a place to watch people and not get lonely.

A lonely broom was a bad, bad broom.

"Stop it," I hissed at him.

He "wagged" his handle, which meant he bashed it around like a tail.

Yeah, giving my broom life hadn't been the *brightest* move of all time.

After getting Whomper stashed back behind the violet material-draped coat rack, I turned to survey my handy work and prepared to laugh my butt off.

The kid grabbed one of my soaps, looking around to see if I was there. He kinda saw me. I know how to hide in my own darned store, all right? Then he smiled and proceeded to wipe that soap up his nose.

I just waited. He'd been karmically marked. I didn't need to do anything else.

He returned the soap to the box and turned toward his mom.

She bumped into the glass tower display and a large black candle fell and whacked him on the head, cracking and breaking on the floor.

"Jerimiah Anderson," his mother screeched.

I could be judgmental about that. She'd bumped the table. She'd made the candle fall and hit her kid. But I *knew* she hadn't *really* been what had knocked the candle onto the kid's —Jerimiah's—head. His karma had.

The kid's face turned red. "It wasn't me, you cow. You hit me."

I glanced at Whomper with an excited grin because things were about to get good. That kid was putting out some *nasty* karmic reactions.

My broom quivered in what I took as excitement and then poked his stick out around the material for a better view.

"You do *not* get to call me that," she said, gripping her purse straps and looking around worried.

That wasn't a good sign. That typically said, "abuse in the home," or even that she was scared of her own son. Huh. I had a spell for that.

It could also just mean that she'd raised a walking temper tantrum and didn't want to get judged. Yeah. I had a spell for that, too.

"I'll call you whatever I want. Now, pick that up." Jerimiah took a step back, his foot finding one of my geode balls. He twisted his ankle and stumbled into the basket that held them. They then rolled out, making it even more trip-worthy. He bent down to catch himself as he tipped over but put his hands on the soap box shelf.

And dumped them all over the floor.

His eyes lit up with bristling anger as he held up his arm. "You cut me!"

Definitely abuse in the house. I'd step in and handle this soon, but not quite yet. I wanted that blessing to kick him around just a *little* longer first.

"How could I have," his mother asked, her voice small yet assertive, "when I was standing over here. Now, clean up your mess before—" She glanced around and leaned in. "—people see."

"I am *not* cleaning this up," he said belligerently.

And then proceeded to step on one of my bars of soap—a black and yellow bar that had been imbued with elderberry and five finger grass. Yeah, my karmically blessed customer had just slipped on my Fuck You Karmically soap bar.

It was a gag gift. The real title was on a removable sticker. When the bar was gifted, the sticker was removed to reveal the other name. May You Be Blessed. It was a best seller.

He slipped and fell on his backside on top of the geodes and bars of soap and the broken candle.

The mother took a step back, her eyes widening in what I read as fear.

Okay. *Now* it was time to step in. "Watch my back," I whispered to my broom.

His excitement died and he was now *very* solid as he stood on broom bristles of anger.

I stepped around the corner as Jerimiah growled low and long and got to his feet. "Oh, my," I exclaimed with a chipper smile. "What a mess." I wanted to rub that in.

Jerimiah spun on me his face angry. But it melted away a little as he brushed off his pants. "Yeah, uh, Linda hit me with a candle, and I fell."

"Linda, huh?" So, maybe not his mom. Step-mom? Rough. I looked down at the candle in question. The thing was *huge*. The part of me who understood insurance was concerned about a head injury. The witch side of me just enjoyed the fact that he'd been whacked pretty good. "You broke my karma candle, dude. Do you realize what that means?"

He frowned, staring down at it. "Linda owes you a lot of money? She broke it."

"On your head, obviously," I muttered, but screwed my smile back in place. "You've been blessed. Congratulations." I wiggled my fingers and did a little dance.

Narrowing his eyes, he looked around at the mess, his hands out.

"I know, it doesn't *feel* like a blessing right now, but it is." And if I'd managed to catch him at *this* point in his little a-hole life, I might have saved him a little. "And this?" I knelt down to pick up the soap he'd slid on. "This is my karmic soap. And this?" I pulled some of the soaps he'd landed on. "This is a karmic soap. I believe you wiped your snot all over it. And this one? One of my favorites." I handed him the blue and grey bar. "The karmic scrub? So good. Looks like karma came a callin' for ya, kid."

And it had. There were *other* soaps and candles on the display.

None of those had attacked him.

Which told me even more about this kid. Karma *wanted* to dance with him, meaning that fickle bitch thought he was worth saving.

His hands fisted on either side of his body and he glared at me, obviously at a loss for words.

I'm not saying that because I *knew* he couldn't speak. I'm saying that because he actually *didn't* speak. I'm not a mind reader. I'm just, seriously, not stupid.

I rose to my biker-booted feet and gave him an alluring smile, cocking one hip flirtatiously—not like I was *actually* flirting with the jail-bait boy. I've learned that an easy way to diffuse a situation is through straight up sex appeal. "All of this soap is ruined, unfortunately." I shrugged helplessly.

"Especially now that you've spilled it all over the floor. I don't know which ones are carrying your literal snot."

Linda's eyes widened. "I can pay for the damages."

And then Linda would never be back, and I had a feeling I'd be one of her last chances as her situation degraded. I often was. "Nah. I've got a way for him to pay me back."

"I'm not paying for this," the nincompoop boy said.

I chuckled. He seriously was. I tipped my head to the side. "May you be blessed." I *loved* handing that out, though I had to be careful because of the law of return. Yeah. Sometimes, that came back and bit me in the butt. You might think I'd be a nicer person as a karmic witch? Nah. I'm just as human as everyone else. I just *know* better as I'm doing bad things. Which makes the karmic blow-back worse. "The payment will be... easy."

Linda shook her head and reached into her purse. "Just tell me how much I owe you."

"*You* owe me nothing." Though the woman would be paying later, but not to me. That's kinda how karma worked even *if* I wasn't the one throwing it around like a dish best served cold. "But this sweet little thing?" But what did I want from him?

Hmm. I could employ him, but service would mean I'd actually have to deal with this little gem of a semi-human being. No. I didn't like that idea at all.

Toenail or fingernail clippings came to mind. Those *could* be useful, especially since the boy was *obviously* filled with rage. I could think of at least three potions I could infuse with those alone. But they were *easy* to give and I wasn't looking for ease.

The kid had lustrous long locks of dark brown hair. Taking *those* would serve three purposes:

I'd humiliate him by shaving them off *in the store*.

I'd have a lot of product to use for potions—though I

would have to hurry as hair didn't keep its potency as long as nails did.

And it would have a bigger karmic impact on *him*.

Linda had continued to talk. She was babbling now, and I hadn't listened to any of it. Okay. I was *kinda* listening and the only thing I really gleaned was that she was well-versed in talking herself out of situations that would break her bones. She was a bruises-are-better mitigator. Which, by my experience, meant the kid's father was probably the abuser and the kid was probably a fantastic student.

I met her gaze and held it, ignoring the whiny voice of the boy as he complained about how none of this was his fault and how he should be blameless. "You want to save him?" I asked in a tone that was *below* the volume of the kid.

See, that's something that people who have been abused excel at, being able to hear small sounds in the wake of world-shattering noise.

Linda clamped her lips shut, held my gaze, and nodded.

"You're going to let me," I said under the kid's volume, "take all of his hair."

Thanks to the kid, we now had a small audience. I'd had, I don't know, maybe five customers before? Now, they were all peaking around the shelves and there were *more* of them as if the tantrum was actually drawing them in.

Yeah. That's another reason why I'm not big into the "worship the customer" philosophy and thinking they were always right. Sure. I like money. Paying the bills is great. But I'm not going to turn in a boot-licker just to make a buck. I've already got some pretty low morals. They don't need to be *that* low.

Also, sometimes, I can make a small mint on the pity-buys. Commerce works in mysterious ways. Though, with the current state of politics, I might want to be a *little* more careful. Though... we were in *New Orleans*. The government was *really* going to come in here and take away our culture? Yeah, probably not.

I smiled at Linda. "I don't want your money. I just want his hair."

The kid squeaked a startled, "What?!" and shut up finally.

Linda raised her chin, blinking several times as she thought about this. Glancing over at Jerimiah, she pulled her empty hand out of her purse which settled under her arm. "And that will cover the cost to replace all of this?"

And then some. "I'll even throw something in there to help with your... situation."

Linda met my gaze with the fierceness of the warrior spirit the people in her life had beaten out of her. "Deal," she whispered.

See? I don't just own and operate an occult shop in New Orleans, which is cool by any right. I'm this person. I'm the last resort. I'm the worst "good" choice left.

I give people the power to build themselves back up again.

And this kid's hair was going to help a lot of people. And make me a crap-ton of cash for the business.

"Excellent." I smiled at the other customers on my way back to my cash register where I grabbed the clippers I had stashed there—not because I did this often but because Jerry, the guy who owned the *other* occult shop, had a dog and I was the only one who could actually get him shaved every month. I pulled out my behind-the-counter bar stool and set it out right there in the front window. "Take a seat."

I spent the next probably fifteen minutes sheering that kid's hair. He was *silent* the entire time. But *as* I was doing that, I also turned on my mini-burner and a single serve candle. I had those encased so I could create candle spells for people as needed. You'd be amazed at how much people would pay for a "real" spell that only asked for them to light a candle.

Little effort and big reward equaled lots of money.

When I was done, a few of the customers had managed to clean up the mess Jerimiah had made, stacking it up on the counter as neatly as possible and they—and about five or so *more* customers—were now perusing my book section and trying to figure out what to do with chicken feet. A lot of people thought they were "dark." Look, seriously? I could make a *spoon* dark. Chicken feet were just another protection method. But damn if they didn't bring in a lot of money. About half of it was spent by people who had no earthly idea what to do with them.

And I was okay with that.

But I took a clump of the much quieter Jerimiah's hair off his shoulders—because I was keeping as much as I could— and took it over to the counter. Now, okay. Here's where I go a bit over the top for commercial reasons. Sure, magick needs a little show and tell—not super really, but okay. And certain spells need words—for energy focus, not because the magick itself needs it. But when you're running an occult shop, you want to *find* reasons to *inspire* people to spend money, and the *best* way to do that is if they think you're a real witch.

You know, which I am.

So, I chanted some mumbo-jumbo—it was more of an instruction manual for Linda—and then shoved the hair strands into the soft, black wax. I then reached under the counter and added some wolfsbane, some devil's shoestring. I removed the candle from the mini-burner and turned to Jerimiah. "While this is setting, how about you go get that broom over by that window over there and clean up all this hair." I smiled sweetly at him. "I want all of it."

Jerimiah glowered—at the floor—and trudged in the direction I'd shown.

One of the wandering customers actually helped him locate Whomper. Well, the broom helped a little, too.

Linda was a bundle of fiery nerves as she gripped her purse straps and then released them in quick succession.

So, I told her to go look through the store and find one thing that called to her. "It doesn't have to make sense to you, but if it calls to you, bring it here."

Nodding, Linda walked away.

A man sidled up to the counter with a devilish smile and a flirtatious twinkle in his eye. "I'll pay for the damages."

Oh, the pockets of chivalrous men. "You wanna know how much it costs first?"

He shook his head and offered me a credit card. "I'll take your number."

Okay. So, you might have heard I had a girlfriend earlier, but here's the thing. My barndoor swings both ways. But I was with Veronica. There were moments when I didn't *quite* know why, but those were rare. She made me happy and that's all that mattered.

So, I just smiled and dropped my eyelids as a refusal to his proposal. "My girlfriend wouldn't understand."

He chuckled good naturedly. "I had to try. But I'll still pay for that." He gestured to the pile on the counter.

So, I went through and tallied it all up and gave him the bill.

He didn't even blink. He just paid for it.

I reached down and pulled out an amulet I kept for those rare customers who deserved a special kick of karma. It works both ways. Sometimes, it's a slap in the face—and a punch to the gut. But sometimes—like in this case—it was a pat on the back. I'm not totally *evil*. Judgmental? Oh, yeah. Definitely that.

He accepted it and draped it over his head. "Have a nice day." He saluted with his receipt and left.

The rest of the day flew by. Two *other* customers offered to pay for the damages, but I told them it was already covered. Jerimiah—thanks to Whomper who was a *very* good broom— cleaned up his hair which I stowed away for a rainy day.

And the customers just kept flooding in.

I didn't even realize the sun had set until I felt soft, warm lips caress the back of my neck as Veronica's arms slid around my abdomen, tucking me in close.

Smiling and feeling as though everything was suddenly right in the world, I finished the transaction, the customer beaming at us.

New Orleans was a special, *special* place and I *loved* it.

I turned in her arms, allowing my fingertips to trail along her shoulders before clasping behind her head. "Hey, baby."

"Hey." Veronica pulled her head back to survey the store before turning her swoon-worthy brown eyes to me. "Looks like you have been hit."

Let me just show you my *gorgeous* Veronica. I won't say she's the love of my life. Someone already took that spot, but this woman sure is a close second. She's tall and curvy in *all* the right places. She loves flowy skirts that would totally get tangled up in *my* legs, and she has the most perfect toes for her open sandals. I've got ugly feet. Always have. Her skin is just that shade of brown that reflects light back at a person, making her look like she's softly glowing all the time. And her hair? Damn, that woman makes most people jealous. It's long and full and utterly luxurious. Is it extensions? A weave? I don't know and I don't care. My woman is physically beautiful.

And her soul is too, which is how she claimed my heart.

I released her and moved around the counter. If she was here, it was *past* closing time. So, I made a pass to make sure the store was empty and locked the front door, flipping the sign closed. "Yeah. Pretty much. Don't know what got into everyone."

"I do," Veronica said, her voice tight.

Oh, bad sign. I flipped the middle switch to take out most of the lights and turned around. "What happened?"

The look on her face was grim, like grim reaper grim as she raked her full top lip with her bottom teeth. "The vice president is moving to ratify the Registration Act."

"But I thought Secretary Whiskey had stopped that."

Veronica nodded and then closed her eyes with a sigh. "And she was doin' good, near as I can tell. But... he fired her."

I'd heard that. We all had, but I'd just thought it'd been a click-bait headline. The president couldn't just *fire* people like that. Could he?

Veronica opened her eyes and nodded.

"Shit." What were we— "What do we do?"

"We are meeting."

That was something I heard a ton before, but these "meetings" just meant that she'd be home late and that I shouldn't worry. Which I typically didn't. Much.

"Come with me," she said quietly, offering her hand.

I paused for one second as that request settled over me like a blanket. I met her halfway and took her hand. "You bet." I had no idea what was in store, but I was finally going to get one step closer to figuring it out.

2

I 'm not real sure what exactly I expected, but a bunch of women I already knew sitting around in a circle drinking sweet tea wasn't it. But...that's exactly what was going on here.

I mean, okay, at first, it was great. I was kicking back and drinking and dodging Lilianne's dirty looks. Seriously, I didn't know why that woman hated me so much. I knew she'd run an occult shop once and I just figured I must be doing better because she didn't have one anymore and, well, I did. But for reals? I had no idea.

But, eventually, all I could think about was the fact that Jerimiah's hair was getting older and needed to be used and there were soaps I needed to replace, and that karma candle wasn't going to replicate itself. It—for all that it was a two-hundred-dollar candle—was a big seller. Well, I mean, for a big piece like that.

I was also starting to get a little irritated with Veronica. I didn't know why. She sat on the other side of the room and was doing normal stuff. But the irritation rolling around in me was getting worse.

Thankfully, though, Mama Gee stood in front of the group and banged her big witch stick. I'd called it a staff one time and she'd given me this look that said, "never again," so... yeah. Message received. It was a stick from then on.

The women in the circle turned to her, raising their faces, opening their palms up on their laps.

There's this thing in magick, especially when you're working with other witches, where you create bonds and give your energies.

I wasn't a part of this circle. I hadn't bound myself to them or their practices, so by following suit, I'd just look like a monkey and I'd probably feel like one too. So, I kept my face to myself and my hands folded in my lap.

The ladies chanted around me. It wasn't like in those white-girl witch shows where they all memorized the same chant and repeated it over and over again until someone floated. No. Each woman brought her own kind of chant and rhythm and words. The *intent* was clear. They were stoking a magick "fire" if you will. They were building the energies in the room.

Everyone except Mama Gee and Veronica.

Which just meant they were the ones who were going to *use* that magick.

Veronica closed her eyes, raising her arms over her head and swaying her hips. Every witch had their own way to manifest energy or cast or do magick. My girl danced. She'd been born a dancer—if her grandma's stories said anything. When that woman was sad, she'd dance to feel better. Her energy was low? Dancing. Had a boo-boo? Dancing. Well, and sometimes a Band-aide and some wound cream.

Mama Gee was a singer. She didn't have a mermaid's voice—I'm talking about *Little Mermaid*, not real mermaids because they don't sound the same at all—but her voice held *raw power*. Her pale palms pushed at the gathered magick and with one jerk of her hands, it settled around us in a dome.

Veronica swirled her hips from side to side one more time, her hands flowing opposite of her hips and with one thrust—that would have turned me on if I wasn't so annoyed by her—silence filled our space.

We were surrounded by a shell of magick that muted what we said so no one else could eavesdrop on us, and it was like… it was like putting a pot over your head. If you haven't done that, go do it now. You'll hear it. There's this kind of vacuum of anti-sound *and* everything kind of echoes at the same time. Did you do it? Great. Yeah. The room sounded like that.

The other women stopped their chanting and got comfortable.

That was something I could join in doing. Whomper was with me—I never left home without him—so I had him prop me up. It was a little like having a tree follow me everywhere, but I could ask *my* tree to lean back a little. Which he did.

Mama Gee sat on the chair Veronica pulled out for her. It was homemade, but in a cool way. It looked like it had been woven together with fresh spring branches, and it probably had been. The legs were braided and twisted together. Smaller, suppler branches had been even more tightly woven together to form the seat and back. Witch work was beautiful, and I loved it.

"I have some terrible news," Mama Gee said.

Mama Gee is the leader of the paranormals here in New Orleans. New Orleans was a safe place for us.

Usually.

And we had Mama Gee and her ancestors to thank for that. Well, and the witches she and her people gathered around her.

I admit, I was a little hurt she never once picked me, but I was a tough witch to stay with. People struggled to stand beside me for long because I'm karma walking and sometimes that spilled out. At all the wrong times.

Which was probably why I was irritated with Veronica. She and I was treading dangerously close to the longest time I'd been in a relationship with a single person.

"Paige Whiskey has asked for our assistance."

I'd met Paige once and I liked her well enough, but the kinds of things that woman needed help with were major. This was no small ask.

"She has lost her position of power in the government."

"Whut duz dat mean?" Lilianne asked, her Cajun accent strong.

I'd always thought her accent was just a cover, a character she'd taken up to sell more chicken feet, but it seemed like it was real.

"It means that things are progressing as we'd thought," Mama Gee said, sitting back in her chair with a groan. "It means we're moving toward war."

"But how do we know that?" Edmee asked, her full lips twisted. I didn't know much about her except she loved the color red and always wore it.

"Because of Valfire," Veronica said, raising her chin.

Sidonie—a big woman with a small personality—glanced at me and then back at Veronica, her small, dark eyes narrowed. "I thought that was being handled."

Veronica pressed her fingertips into her forehead until they paled. "Threknal was released."

A wave of exclamations rippled through the circled women.

"Well, *sac a maam*," Lilianne cursed. "How did dat hap-pen?"

I still didn't *quite* know what "sac a maam" meant, but I took it to mean, "What the hell?" I could be wrong. I'd been raised in Alaska, the white-people capital of North America, so I didn't know, really, and it wasn't like I could just be like, "Hey, what does that mean?" each time they threw something at me like that. Half the time, I didn't even know how to repeat what they'd said.

Mama Gee closed her eyes as if fending off pain. "I can only assume Paige Whiskey released him."

"But how?" Lilianne exclaimed, slapping her palms together as if imagining someone's face there. "Is she not the demon witch?"

Okay. So, this was a little interesting. I'd never heard of the woman being called the demon witch before. Sure, there'd been stories here and there from the last time she'd been in the area. But a demon witch?

Which meant that Threknal was a demon. Huh. Okay. But how did that lead to Valfire and how did Valfire—who had a supremely cool name—lead to war?

"I do not know," Mama Gee said, massaging her eyebrows with her finger and thumb.

"So, whut we do now?" Lilianne demanded, gesturing to me like she wanted to punch my face.

What the fuck had I ever done to that woman? But I kept a lid on my retort and just leaned into my broom.

"We need to send someone to Troutdale where Threknal is at," Veronica said emphatically.

"And who, *ma chèrie*," Sidonie asked calmly, "would you send?"

My girl pushed her shoulders back and raised her head high. "Me and Wy."

The circle of women exploded in cacophony. Man, I love that word. It sounds so cool when you say it out loud. Cacophony. Like a screaming murder of crows.

Which... yeah. That was pretty accurate.

Veronica just looked at me through the word explosions, holding my gaze like a Valkyrie in a battle of death.

I had no idea just how big this thing was. I didn't understand why she needed me to go to Troutdale with her unless it was to help her walk in the white-girl world.

It didn't happen immediately. And by immediately, I mean it really took a few minutes. But eventually, everyone's very vocal and very hot tempers simmered.

Gesturing to first Veronica and then to me, Mama Gee nodded. "Capture Threknal. Do *not* go after Valfire. All our hopes ride on recapturing Threknal."

Lilianne shook her head and glared. "Ahnd eef you do fuck dis up—" She made a fist with her hand and shook her head, biting off a curse I couldn't repeat even if I'd remembered the words.

Veronica nodded gravely. "I understand."

I was glad Vee did because I sure didn't.

So, as everyone filtered out and as Whomper walked around getting pets from as many witches as he could—I really hadn't thought I'd given him the soul of a dog, but he really acted like one—I waited for Veronica to stop getting her instructions from Mama Gee. I wasn't so full of myself as to think I needed to insert myself into that conversation. There's a *reason* I've survived to this ripe old age of non-perky-tits.

When Veronica finally *did* manage to break away from her fearless leader, she smiled at me, slipping an arm around my shoulders. "Ready to go pack?"

No, but I could multi-task. "How're we getting there?"

"Plane." Though something on Veronica's face said she was worried.

I knew why. Flights were hard to get after President Flynn had tried and failed to enact the Registration Act. A lot of people's ID's had been flagged. We didn't know if ours had.

We didn't know if we were cleared to board a plane. And if we weren't? Then how? We could drive, sure. That seemed like a very American thing to just think. We could *drive* from Louisiana to Oregon. It'd take us *forever*, but it could be done.

Except that the borders had been kinda closed since President Flynn had done her thing. I would have thought it would have lightened up with acting President Walton, but now it was worse. State borders were practically closed to *everyone*, not just paranormals.

"Who is Threknal and this Valfire guy?"

Veronica leaned over and kissed my cheek. "I'll explain later."

Later turned out not to even be that day. Somehow, we managed to score tickets, which probably wasn't that hard since the airlines were desperate for people willing and able to give them money. And Veronica used her magick to get us through. In this instance, my magick was completely useless. Karma had its place. Lying and cheating to get on a plane? Yeah. Not a great idea unless we *wanted* to get caught.

I thought maybe she'd tell me on the plane, but I was having a hard time containing Whomper. Also, we had to be careful of what we said when others could hear us and the man sitting on the other side of me was *very* interested in what we were doing on our trip.

Whomper had the ability to hide his form, which was important if you were a witch living in secret. He'd shrunk to the size of a pen and hid in my purse, but he ruined the effect by bapping the side, and wiggling incessantly. That broom had a brain smaller than a pigeon, I swear. He didn't quite realize what was at stake.

We landed in Portland without much of a fuss, but when we went to leave, our bags were searched and we were *properly* frisked. Like... the only thing they left untouched were the wildly unmentionables. And it wasn't the TSA that molested us.

It was agents of the Department of Dipshit Offairs, or whatever their acronym stood for. You know how I could tell? They *all* had English accents and wore the same black uniforms.

Leaving with *most* of our things—they'd nearly taken Whomper but they'd apprehended three of my charms—we walked out of the airport and grabbed an Uber. The driver was super chatty about how uncommon it was to get fares out of the airport anymore and how his kids liked to eat but that he'd have to be pretty inventive if this continued. He then asked if we were paranormals and then reminded himself that we couldn't be because we'd flown in and they didn't allow paranormals on flights. Had they ever? Was that a thing that'd been allowed before?

He was a prattler.

We made it to the checkpoint *into* Troutdale where we were once again invited *out* of the car, our stuff was ransacked *again,* and we were asked what our business was there.

Dude, I was seriously *this close* to slapping the next molesting hand with karma.

But Veronica just smiled sweetly and responded with the same story she'd given the DoDO agents at the airport that we were there visiting family. People just relaxed after she spoke to them, which was part of her charm. The Agents of DoDO were a *bit* more resistant, but not entirely.

A beat-up old truck pull up going the wrong way on the exit ramp as our Uber driver was excused and told to return to Portland. An old guy with a big white mustache stepped out from the pickup as our driver drove past him. "Bill." The man actually tipped his hat like in the old days.

Bill—the jerk DoDO agent who'd felt up my skirt—

nodded cordially back. "Sheriff. These two say they have business with Wendy Green."

"We asked them to come," the sheriff said gruffly. "She was attacked. In a coma."

"Oh." Bill's blue eyes widened. "They didn't mention that."

"We're private people," I ground out, trying to make a karmic play on the fact that I hadn't *invited* his *very* personal search of my body.

Bill flicked an eyebrow in response and rested his hands on the rifle slung across his body. "Well, something on them set off our sensors. Just keep an eye on them."

The sheriff glanced at us and then jerked his head to the truck. "Ladies, if you don't mind. Got a lot of stuff to get done here."

I grabbed my backpack and satchel and went to the bed of the truck, tucking them both close to the cab. Veronica did the same.

I rode in the middle and was a little shocked to see a gear shift. Great. So, I kept my knees as close to Veronica's as I could. Reverse was a little too personal for my liking.

The sheriff didn't say anything until we were well into town. "Okay. Who're you really here to see?"

"Paige Whiskey," Veronica said. "I hope that is not an inconvenience."

He shook his head and continued to drive. "Don't know why you didn't just ask for a door."

That was something we could do? "We thought it'd be too..." Needy? High maintenance?"

"Common sense?" He finished with a snort. "Damned world's been turned upside it's head. Next time, just ask for a door."

Noted.

I didn't know what we were going to face, but our world

had definitely changed. For better? For worse? That was still undecided.

But I had a feeling we were the ones who were going to shape that.

Yeah. That wasn't a scary thought.

3

The Whiskey complex turned out to be a business center on one side of the property and a big ol' house on the other end of the gravel driveway filled with cars in the middle of the woods.

Sheriff Tuck stopped at the office building first, shuttling them through as he looked for the Whiskey witch. Huh, that was catchy. It was hustling and bustling with activity, looking a bit like a human beehive.

Whomper chomped at the bit to be released into the wild and to meet *all* the new people, but I wasn't sure all these fine obviously well-paid people were ready for him.

So, after not finding Paige, Sheriff Tuck then led us to the main house.

First of all, can I just say that it's a little weird being shown around town by the sheriff and not being in trouble or being looked at like people are glad it's you and not them? That was just weird.

Secondly, I walked into their "house" and there weren't any TV's going. No radios. No phones. No electronic noise at all.

But there were a lot of people. Kids mostly.

Loud stomps and kidly yelling headed toward us and first one boy and then two others appeared running from a too-furnished living room into the entryway toward us.

"Bobby," Sheriff Tuck barked.

"Sorry," the lead boy cried on his way past and up the stairs almost directly in front of me.

I scooted out of their way as all three of them scuttled by, shouting a quick hello to the sheriff.

This place was weird. And terrifying. Who was watching those things? The kids, I mean.

Sheriff Tuck led the way down the hallway, peering left and right as if to see through the doorway at the end. "Is Paige around?" he called.

"Out back," a female voice answered. "You stayin' for dinner?"

The sheriff grunted.

Stepping into the Whiskey kitchen and dining room was like stepping into a magazine spread of what a country kitchen was supposed to look like. It was big and open, and the appliances were all new. But that dining room table? The L-shaped monstrosity looked like it was supposed to house Congress, not a family.

The kitchen itself was filled with several people—not just women like it would have been in the south. I mean, men knew how to cook and I knew quite a few who were really good at it, but when you went over to someone's house for a get-together, the women were in the kitchen and the men were outside. Usually. Or the women were watching the kids while the men drank beer and barbequed. That's just the way it went.

This kitchen had two women. The rest were either kids doing dishes, or were men helping the kids doing the dishes.

Was this some strange kind of matriarchal commune?

Paige hadn't come off as a commune type of woman when we'd met before.

Whomper hit me from inside the confines of my purse, obviously wanting out.

I smiled and waved on our way through, squeezing my magickally tiny-sized broom inside my wallet-sized purse and following the sheriff out the sliding glass door.

Paige was out there surrounded by a lot of people. She had a burger in one hand and was listening attentively as she chewed. She glanced over at the sheriff and her eyes narrowed in a happy greeting—it's hard to picture, I know, but just try it out and you'll see. It's a thing—but then she saw me and Veronica and they widened again with surprise. She shoved her mouthful of food in her cheek and said something to the woman she'd been listening to, heading over to us.

I hadn't been nervous until that moment. I can't even tell you what set me off. Maybe it was the fact that I was seeing with my own two eyes just how different her world was from ours? I don't know. But a wave of "unease" washed over me.

It could have been the fact that there were a *lot* of kids running around and I was already on edge and grumpy with Veronica for not telling me what was really going on and for staying... You know what? I actually didn't *know* why I was irritated with her. I just was.

"Veronica," Paige said, greeting us and kind of ignoring the sheriff. "Wy. Did you bring your broom?"

I wasn't sure if I should be offended by that or not. "Yeah. Can I let him out?"

"As long as you think it's safe. Does he bite?"

A big bear lumbered into the yard, grumbling. Another came out of the woods behind it—him—her—them.

I hoped they were shifters because I'd grown up in

Alaska, home of the wild wilderness where we took bear encounters seriously.

Before my concern could reach critical levels, though, a few people came up to greet them and they did indeed shift into a tall, curvy blonde-headed woman and a muscular brown-haired man. Both perfectly naked.

And nothing was said about it. No one reacted. No one gawked.

Huh. Maybe there really was something to this being paranormally woke thing. "Uh, no. He should be okay," I said, trying to pull myself back into the conversation. "Just, uh, he tends to hit hard when he's excited."

"Like a dog," Veronica said bluntly, her expression dry. "He's like a really stiff dog whose entire tail is the body."

Paige shook her head and then looked at me expectantly.

So, I opened my purse and pulled back the flap.

He flew right out, growing from about the size of a dragonfly to the size of a real broom in the blink of an eye. With a flourish, he landed on his bristle feet as if to say, "Ta-da!"

"Go play," I told him. "But be careful how hard you hit."

Paige just watched him run off, then gestured with her paper plate. "There're burgers on the grill."

Looking around, it looked like this was pretty normal. "Well, I'm hungry and I'll never turn down meat."

It was a bunch of small talk on the way through the hamburger line. I had a choice of elk, deer, moose, or beef. I, of course, went with moose. That was the one thing I missed the most about Alaska. Moose meat was the best meat.

Though, as hamburger, if people didn't know *how* to add the fat *into* it, it could come out pretty dry and that's what this one was. So, I just added some more jalapeno mustard and an extra slice of tomato to it and called it good.

Veronica led the small talk conversation and we made it successfully through all the little things of kids and school—

why was she even asking about that when we didn't have kids or plans of having kids?—and—

Wait.

I glanced over at Veronica who was a little taller than I was and really listened to her words.

"I love the thought of kids running around our house."

And she looked happy and dreamy like this was an actual thing. But she and I had *had* that conversation. I *knew* what kind of a crappy mom I was. I wasn't subjecting a kid to that again. I'd flunked once and once was enough for me.

The rest of *that* conversation passed without me. Maybe this was the reason I was irritated with her? Maybe I'd just *felt* us slipping further apart, like she was ready to move on with her life?

As a person who didn't stay in relationships long, this didn't hurt. It *actually* felt a little like relief. Being with people for a long time is hard work, and not the kind I'm typically great at. I also super don't enjoy watching people get bitch-slapped by karma-times-three each time they made a tiny dumb decision. That was *my* life, but it was unfair of me to inflict that on others.

So, if kids were Veronica's thing, if this was something she wanted, then I'd let her have it.

With someone else.

But eventually our over-dry burgers were eaten and the time for small talk was at an end. Thank the gods.

"So, what are you doing here?" Paige asked in her blunt manner.

I'd actually expected that sooner. "What do you know of a demon named Threknal?"

Veronica turned and gave me a daggery look.

What? If Paige was the demon witch, then why would I hide any of that information?

"He's why you're here." Paige's brown eyes took on a

hooded feel and her breathing sped up a tick. "He was trapped in the DoDO base outside New Orleans."

"We know that," Veronica said evenly. "What did you do with him?"

"He—" Paige narrowed her eyes, a light dawning them almost bright enough to see. "I released him."

"Why would you do that?" I asked incredulously. "I thought you were the *demon witch*." I totally put a bunch of emphasis on those last two words.

Paige released a frustrated breath. "I had to. I could—" She tucked in one side of her mouth and looked away for a beat. "He was able to touch me."

"Yeah?" I really didn't understand how this was important. I reached out and touched her with my hand. "So can I."

But then something slapped my arm. It *felt* like a hand, but I didn't see one.

Paige clamped her lips closed, looking at me expectantly, her dark eyebrows high.

There was no one else around me. "Wait. That was you?"

She nodded.

But *how*? "So, you—but that was a hand."

"My witch hand." She looked at something beside me as if she could *see* her invisible… hand.

Which, yeah, she probably could. But there was no way *I* could. So, I took a step back.

She shook her head and held up both of her real hands as if in a gesture of "it's okay."

I was catching up, though. Her magick was hands—which sounded kinda dumb, but what did I know? And a demon could touch that.

"He could touch my magick. I had no way of… crossing him over."

That probably hadn't been the only thing going through

Paige's mind at the time, though. "Crossing him over? Isn't that what ghost witches do?"

"Mediums?" Paige asked like she was talking to a kid. "Yeah. Anyway, that's why I called you. You guys were able to capture him before? I don't know how he ended up in DoDO hands. But I need him caught again."

Veronica held up a hand to stop me from speaking even though I hadn't even opened my mouth. "What's going on?"

"A lot of threats. I've got the president and a big sorcerer of some kind who's after my family. I need someone to take on this challenge so I can focus on those two."

Well, that sounded legit.

Paige frowned and pulled out her phone, a look of alarmed excitement flitting over her face for a moment before she looked from Veronica to me and then back again. "Can you take care of this without using DoDO to further contain him?"

I still didn't *quite* understand why *we* were going after *demons*. We... really weren't the hunt-demons-down type of witches.

"Yes," Veronica said. "He's here. We'll capture him."

Paige narrowed her eyes, glanced at me, then folded her arms over her chest. "Why?"

Yeah. I had the same question. Why? What was going on here? I mimicked Paige's stance and turned to my lover.

Veronica gave me a look that said she didn't appreciate me but turned to Paige. "He works with another demon, someone bigger. And I'm trying to stop *him*."

"So, not Threknal." Concern washed through Paige's dark eyes. "Someone stronger."

You know? Normally, my red-flag meter would be through the roof at this point. But for some inexplicable reason, my inside voices were telling me to remain calm and to follow

Veronica's lead because the situation was already being handled. A plan was already in place.

But instead of comforting me, that just made me a bit more on edge.

"Would that one be after me, too?"

"No." Veronica seemed so sure.

But how?

Paige shook her head, but then took a step back. "Okay. Find him. Deal with him." She took a step back, preparing to leave. "If you need anything ask." She then turned and walked toward another group of people.

I grabbed Veronica's attention. "Why *am* I here? Why didn't you bring the one who helped you before?"

"Wy," she said with a soft sigh, cupping my face with her free hand. "I love you."

Which was her way of saying everything from "you're an idiot" to "you're so pretty" to "quit talking."

She took both my arms and nuzzled my nose. "I brought you because you're a karmic witch and the strongest weapon we have."

"Then how'd you get him the last time?"

"Pure luck, baby," she whispered against my lips and then kissed me.

That woman had magick in her lips I felt all the way to my toes.

She pulled back to sink my soul into her eyes. "And I know I won't be so lucky twice. Now, would you just trust me?"

There was definitely something going on here, but I let her take my hand and drag me away to find lodgings. I would be getting to the bottom of this one way or the other.

But when I did, would I have one more reason to let her go? And if I continued to dig, would I just be making it easier for myself?

Or was that what I was hoping for?

Crap. Sometimes being a thinking, feeling, wanting person sucked.

———

Paige left Veronica and Wynonna behind and went in search of Derrick. Acting President Walton had texted her. He wanted to meet. She had to hope it was good news, that he wanted to discuss how to proceed. Maybe he had a new plan for paranormals and Paige could figure out a way to salvage this.

But she knew that wasn't likely the case and getting her hopes up was a bad idea.

Derrick saw her approach and raised his head. "Where to?"

"Ruben's office."

He nodded and cut open a door without any further ado.

Stepping into Pearl's office—Ruben's secretary because creating a door directly to his office was a bit no-no—she was greeted by Ruben's open door. He saw her arrive and flagged her in.

Paige wasn't sure if she should be surprised he still had a job or not. She didn't know how these positions worked. But he gestured for her to close the door behind her. So, she did and took the seat he offered her.

"I don't know what you're walking into," he said, looking at her over his wirerimmed glasses. "Could be good. Could be not. We discussed a bunch of options today."

That didn't sound good. "Including?"

"Giving you your post back." Ruben's eyes were shielded as he looked away as if knowing that wasn't an option.

Or that the sales pitch had been about keeping Paige quiet by doing so.

"Don't do anything that will send us into a war we don't want."

A war *he* didn't want. Well, paranormals wanted equal rights and if the only way to achieve that was through war, then they were happy to meet their obligation. She nodded, though, to indicate she'd heard him.

He studied her, his eagle eyes narrowed and then leaned back, steepling his fingers. "I'm not going to like what you have planned, am I?"

She'd grown to respect this man. When the tides shifted, when the U.S. split, she'd want him on her side. But would he be willing? "If he proposes treating us like criminals again? Probably not." In the time she'd known Ruben, he hadn't appeared to be loyal to the person filling the office as much as to the office itself. Did that make him an ally? If she was getting ready to openly declare war? Probably not.

He nodded and stared hard at his desk. "You'd have thought we'd have been trained by now how to handle something like this. You know, with Black Lives Matter, and all the sex rights." He shook his head, waving a hand to note he understood he'd given the wrong name for that. "Women's rights, voting rights, racial suppression. All of it."

This was one reason why he had her hope. Not her trust or loyalty, but her hope that he could one day earn those. "I think what you're learning is that none of those issues were ever handled correctly to begin with. If they had, you might have a viable answer to our situation."

He nodded his head to rest against the back of his leather chair. "Will we ever find a way?"

"We have to hope we can." Paige had to have faith they could *build* a world where freedoms and equal rights were just common courtesy. But would she and her leadership just make the same mistakes that entire nations had in the past?

"Right. Well," he said, waving his hand to the door to the Oval Office. "He's waiting for you."

Paige didn't sit around for another invitation. She braced herself for the worst and went inside.

The acting president had been meeting with General Tall —McCormick.

General McCormick stood and bowed his head to Paige grimly before leaving. But he paused at the other door and gave Paige a long look that almost conveyed respect before he closed the door behind him.

What exactly did that imply? What was he thinking? What was he intending? If he reached out to her, she wasn't going to slap his hand away. Or was she just reaching? Maybe he'd been trying to tell her to be careful.

Walton smiled at Paige, his expression conveying a note of impatience around the edges. He gestured to the striped couch. "I hope things are going well."

Did he? Really? "We're still working on getting people out of comas and burying our dead, so no. We're not okay." That reminded her. Willow's funeral was the next day. Hers and three others. Fuck. "What do you want?"

He was silent for a long moment, then he threw his arms over the back of the couch, lounging back. "I've dissolved your office and I'm not reinstating it. Any actions you've been trying to put through while you were illegally in your position will be nullified."

Was she surprised? Honestly? No, but she'd been working on good things she couldn't allow to die. "I was given the job by the president and was voted in by the Senate."

"No. You were voted in by the Senate and they hogtied Flynn into taking you." He shook his head. "I'm not going to be bullied into accepting you into our government."

It didn't look like he was too open to creating a real peace.

Well, there was that answer. But what act would draw them actively into war? President Dawn Flynn had been the one who'd allowed the attacks on the paranormals before. Would Walton be so dumb? Or would he be more subtle?

"When the gays first showed up, we didn't create a secretary position for them and invite them into the government. They had to win the votes of the people who were set against them, too. And look at them. They have voter-backed senators and representatives now. Heck, we even ran against one in the last election."

Paige almost fell down the emotional rabbit hole he'd intended her to, to realize that she and the paranormals with her should be ready to fight hard for the right to prove themselves the equal of cis white men, but...

That wasn't right. Just because that'd been the road the people before her had chosen didn't mean that was the path she had to take now.

But she did have to consider *why* they hadn't decided to take greater action. And the reasons were pretty big. Walton had a lot of power behind him. Not just money or influence, but in weapons and armies.

General McCormick and all his experience.

The deck was stacked against anyone opposing the power and might of the government.

And that... pissed her off.

Walton let his arms fall to his lap as he settled comfortably into the conversation. "Same with the blacks and the natives and all the other races. Women."

Irritation hit her as she watched his smug face. She understood what he was getting at. The rules were simple. Anyone could file for their rights and after many decades—or longer—they'd probably win just like those before them.

Had the paranormals *really* been treated any different than those who had come before them?

No.

So what made her different?

The extent to which the government had rounded the paranormals up, imprisoned them, killed them, to the point where they'd even invaded an elven city in a different world.

But *that* had been President Flynn.

"I know what you're thinking, Ms. Whiskey. You can't use *your* status to compare to theirs, claiming injustice. If you do, you have to follow the same path they forged."

Paige bit her tongue. She'd had to do some research to see if going to war over what had happened so far was even possible. And the answer, frustratingly, was no. In U.S. history, people in the minority were routinely incarcerated without probable cause. They were commonly killed or suffered from hate crimes. Yes, DoDO had invaded an elven city. Yes, DoDO had invaded American cities. But DoDO wasn't the U.S. government, so retaliating through an act of war against the actions of a foreign entity weren't... enough. And Walton might hide behind DoDO for as long as he could.

But even *if* he didn't, even *if* he decided to enact these horrible acts onto the people—his people—it wouldn't be *enough* to bring an act of *war* against her country.

What would then?

"I'm putting the Registration Act through the proper channels. It already has the votes, Ms. Whiskey. It will be passed, and it will be enforced."

That was information she had too. She wasn't there for that. She was there to determine if—no, when they were going to war. And that pissed her off more than a little. She couldn't declare war because she didn't like what the government was doing. She'd be... bringing the country to war, possibly bringing down world-wide economies by weakening the U.S. She couldn't do that lightly. "What will happen to my people?"

He shrugged. "If they're criminals, we'll treat them as such. If they're not, they'll go back to work."

"And their rights?"

He paused. "Let's take it one step at a time."

Paige lived in a world of her own creation—Troutdale—where humans and paranormals lived side-by-side and things were great. They didn't live in fear. Shifters could shift in the middle of town now and be "accepted." There had been robe stations put up around the town for that though, so it wouldn't be completely awkward. But the humans didn't fear for their lives. They enjoyed magick and were getting used to their toothed and hooved friends.

She didn't appreciate the fact that this man preferred the power of fear.

"You will not oppose me on this," Walton said, dipping his head to look at her almost coyly. "You have no voice in our government anymore, no voice in our society."

But her voice wasn't silent.

"And you won't go to the media. There's a hush order on all the major media outlets. The news *can be* paid for and they were. Handsomely."

There had to be others. They'd find a way around that, to get the real news to the people.

"Ms. Whiskey," he said, dropping his chin. "Any act to defy me will be seen as an act of aggression."

Like what? A rally? A Facebook post? A meeting? A peaceful protest? Would that be the match? They needed *something*.

"And..." He smiled as if what he was about to say was going to tickle him the most. "This is the last time you will use door magick. You are to stay in your little town. Everyone is officially on lockdown."

Well, now that she knew where exactly he stood on the matter, it was time for *her* to react accordingly. She rose to her feet and nodded. Then, without saying anything further, she walked out of the Oval Office, said nothing to Ruben on her way by, and left Washington D.C. and all her hopes for a peaceful solution.

If they were going to take this to war, they needed one hell of a match.

And she wasn't certain Walton would give her that. He'd push for oppression, sure. But would he give her what she needed to start a war *and* get the backing and support she needed?

No.

Damn it. Going to war wasn't nearly as easy as everyone seemed to think it would be.

4

Veronica *refused* to share any information with me on the way back to our accommodations out in the middle of the woods. She just blew me off, not even saying that she'd tell me later.

I was starting to get real pissed.

Our lodging turned out to be a tree house out back. Yeah, I'm not even kidding, but to be fair, this tree house was really freaking decked the deck out. This thing had electricity, WiFi, and plumbing. I kinda wanted to know how it all worked, but I really just wanted to revel in the awe of it without knowing.

So, to get settled in, I threw open our backpacks on the bed and jammed to some Caro Emeral as I found homes for everything. Yeah, I know. You'd think I was into something a bit more modern and the modern stuff is good, but my heart belongs to the 1940's.

Veronica was quiet as she helped, but she seemed content to let me boogie woogie my way through our non-conversation. She knew singing was my way of dealing with issues and the big issue right now was that I was pissed off with the woman I loved.

Someone flew onto our porch and shifted into a young woman who looked a lot like Paige, but with lightning dancing in her eyes. She turned at me as I took off my headphones, then nodded at Veronica. "Mom's calling a meeting. She wants to know if you're going to come."

Veronica blinked and then looked up at me. "You go."

"Uh, no." Because if there was any kind of meeting, I wasn't the person to join in. I represented no one. "Sorry, kid. I guess we ain't coming."

The girl shrugged. "Suit yourself. It's at the house if you wanna come later, I guess." She turned and flew away again in the shape of some sort of falcon.

I turned to Veronica to see if she was going to start talking, share some information with me.

Nope.

So, I put my headphones back on and let Caro's sultry voice and big band backup take me away.

Veronica stood up and took my headphones off, holding them in her hands. "Babe. You're mad at me."

Yeah, I was and if she wasn't going to share, I wasn't going to talk.

"I need to go search for Threknal."

"You mean that big bad guy you need my karmic witch power to bring in?" I didn't know what was going on here, but I knew in my gut that something *was* and that she wasn't being honest with me.

That little voice inside my head was letting me know something was wrong, and it'd never steered me wrong before.

"Yeah, babe. That. Just..." She took a strand of my hair and tucked it behind my shoulder. She leaned in to whisper something to me.

I pulled away because I didn't know if maybe she had some whisper power or some pheromone power or whatever.

All I knew was that I thought more clearly when I didn't let her get close. I took a step back.

Veronica closed her eyes and shook her head with a tight expression on her face. "Go to this meeting. Sit in for me. Take notes."

Take... notes. "I'm not really the secretary kind of gal, Vee." And she should know that.

She pulled a pained face, balling both hands into fists and walked away. "What do you want, Wy? What is this?"

I *loved* confrontation. *She* didn't. If I pushed too hard, she'd run. Before I was ready? "You're hiding something from me."

She closed her eyes and shook her head. "Baby, please. It's for your own good."

"So, you are!"

Opening her mouth, she gnashed her teeth on whatever she'd been about to say. "We had a plan."

"We? We who?"

She met my gaze and held it, walking toward me, her skirt dancing around her long legs. She took my face in both her hands.

I pulled away so that whatever magick she was about to throw on me had less of an effect.

"You are so much more important to me than you will ever know."

For the first time since I met that woman, I didn't fall into her eyes and melt. She was telling me something *more* and I didn't know what.

But that little voice in the back of my head whispered to me, telling me to trust her, not to push too hard, to just believe we were on the right path because we were.

What the hell was going on here?

She kissed me, gentle at first.

The fight I'd had dissolved under her touch. My body—

47

my whole damned soul craved that woman's touch too damned much. I deepened the kiss, reaching around her, bringing her closer to me. If I couldn't win my answers through conversation, I'd do it in bed.

She pulled away with a hiss and a woeful look. "*Chèrie*, you are too much for me."

Unlikely. But I still felt like myself. Well, mostly. If she'd just the whammy back on me, it hadn't taken full effect.

"Go to the meeting and listen. Really listen. What you report back and your thoughts on it will shape our choices."

That was weird because I'd never been on the inside of their power circle. Why now?

Her eyes searched mine. "You are our future. Do not ever forget yourself in what we do."

That pulled on something inside my soul, though I didn't know what. Like, it pulled from something behind that voice in my head telling me something was off and that everything was okay and that I needed to trust her and go along with what she was telling me.

"I love you," she whispered against my lips and then kissed me before she spun and shimmied down the rope ladder.

That woman... she could turn me upside down and hang me wet. And I didn't mean that in a kinky way, no sexual reference at all. It's just how my soul felt. Like a wet towel in a thunderstorm.

After I pulled myself together, I walked down the wooden stairs that wrapped around the trunk of the tree a little like what I imagined homes in elven cities to be like. Before, that thought had always been trapped in my head, where all the characters of *Lord of the Rings* resided, though, I'd taken more than a few liberties. They're in my head, so I can. Frodo's a lot stronger and Sam's a bit sexier, for one.

I won't go into the rest.

Walking through the forest toward the house, I focused on the sounds. Happiness. Families. Fights. Kids.

It sounded like... life.

I stopped as soon as I saw the house, the lights from inside shining bright in the fading light. What was I doing there? I was just one witch with a broom that was more exciting than I was. What did I have to offer this discussion?

Ears. For Veronica and Mama Gee.

Right. Well, then, I'd better get in there and listen.

The dining room table was surrounded by people, and some pretty powerful ones. I didn't know them all. Okay? These people weren't anywhere in *my* circles. But I could *feel* the power emanating from them.

I found the open liquor bottles on the kitchen island. There were a bunch. Also, there were coffee pods and boxes of tea set out on the counter between the sink and the stove. Basically, it was serve yourself whatever you wanted.

Well, I wanted a... huh. I'd have to actually sit through the entire meeting and not fall asleep? That sounded like a call for coffee.

With a shot of Baileys. I couldn't be *all* responsible.

Some guy with short black hair and blazing blue eyes gestured to the empty chair beside him and then promptly ignored me. That made me feel a *little* hurt until I saw the scarred woman beside him give me the I'll-eat-you-if-you-touch-him glare.

So, I reached out and touched his arm with a smile that screamed innocence.

She narrowed her eyes and growled.

He turned to me with a look in his eyes that asked me what I wanted.

"Have you seen my broom?" Because Whomper hadn't returned home yet and I didn't know if that meant he'd run away or was just lost.

The scarred woman leaned forward. "The kids have him upstairs."

Oh. "Am I allowed to go up there and get him?" Because I needed to know just how "open door" this house was.

Scar Face shook her head but didn't glare.

Beautiful Blue Eyes turned his attention back to Paige.

I didn't hate Scar Face. I didn't. But I also didn't answer to an obvious bitch move without one of my own because, come on. Bitch, please. Men are just men and not chew toys.

Unless they were, you know... toys.

I put that thought away as Paige—the *only* person I actually knew—took a sippy cup and banged it on the table.

People shut up pretty quick and turned to her.

"Walton did what we thought he would," she said. "He's going to push the Registration Act."

"And your secretarial position?" Beautiful Blue Eyes asked with a soft, Greek accent.

Sexy.

"Gone. We knew that already though because it's what he said on TV. He just made it official today." Paige shrugged. "I need to know if we still stand by the original idea."

What original idea?

A lot of the people around the L-shaped table nodded their agreement and very few seemed hesitant.

I raised my hand. "What plan are we talking about?"

Paige pushed a one-cheek breath through her lips and gestured to me. "Wynonna Hunt, karmic witch from New Orleans." She closed her eyes for a beat and then opened them again. "Civil war."

"Uh." They couldn't be serious.

"But our secession votes were decided as unconstitutional," one person said. She was blonde and had this kinda cat thing going on in the eyes that was super-hot. And scary. Which was probably why it was hot.

Paige nodded. "As we already knew they'd rule. So, it's not a surprise."

Cat Eyes gestured with her right hand and stretched her neck the other way. "The last time this topic came up, you said no."

No to war? I kinda had to side with Paige on that one.

"That was before." Paige shook her head, her expression almost haunted.

That right there hit me. You know, just, *je sais pa*. The karmic punch of her eyes told me what her lack of words didn't. She'd seen a lot trying to fight to stop this. She wasn't taking this lightly.

Okay. Well, I didn't know if I had the *full* support of Mama Gee's circle especially since I wasn't a part of it, but if I was taking information back to Veronica, I needed to start asking some questions. "All right, then, how's this gonna work?"

Paige took in a deep breath and settled into her kitchen chair. "Well, we can't be the one to strike this match first."

Oh, the rules of the playground. Who hit first?

"They already did," a woman with dark hair and smelled of wood said beside me.

"DoDO did," Paige said, raising a finger.

"With her approval."

I had to assume Woodsmoke—who was also more than a little sexy in a dominatrix kind of way—was talking about the ex-president.

"And they removed her from office for that," Paige said. "If we go to war now over that, we would be going to war over the wrong thing. She created a situation. They solved it by removing her from office."

"So?" the man beside her said in frustration. "People *died,* and she's just removed from office and we're okay?"

She scrubbed her forehead with her fingertips. "War is

going to happen. Yes. There'll be fighting and punching and you'll finally get to blow stuff up."

He winced, shaking his head at her. "I never actually blew —" He stopped himself, his green eyes looking away.

I almost wanted to know that story but shut up my inner voice to listen.

"The other part of this is going be making alliances." Paige leaned forward on the table, folding her hands. "We make the wrong choices, use the wrong reasons, and we're losing allies while they're gaining new ones."

Oh. That was one thing I hadn't thought of. I was a small fish in a big pond. I was *allowed* to not understand a lot of things and I was okay with that.

"What states do we have?" she asked.

"Oregon," Beautiful Blue Eyes said. "And Washington. I have spoken with our representatives. They have all declared their willingness, pending certain provisos."

"I'll need to know what those are."

"I will send them to Willo—"

Paige flinched.

"Ismail—" He paused and held up a hand in apology. "— by the end of the day."

So, Paige had lost someone. Interesting.

They continued shouting out names of states and the names of the people who were on board. Of course, not everyone was. But there had actually been a real vote—which had made the news for a day and then had been buried.

Along with those two? California, Idaho—though apparently just barely—Montana, both Dakotas, Nebraska, Wyoming, Florida, Vermont, Hawaii, Texas, Alaska, New Hampshire, and Florida.

I gotta say, I was a bit surprised to hear Alaska was on that list. Last I'd seen, they were proud, red, and ultra-patriotic. Like, they took *pride* in how *hard* it was to be a Constitution-following American in the bush.

Paige sat through this entire discussion and just accepted it for what it was. Though, Dexx was a lot less cool. He didn't say much, and when he did, it was super snarky and so pop culture, even I struggled to understand him. He obviously watched more movies than I did.

But I think the thing I took away from all this was that no one was *thrilled* to be going to civil war over this.

"We're going to need bases," Paige said next. "With wards and protections. Ideas? These are going to have to be in areas where we don't have to steal land, which could be an issue."

Some smokey-smelling man with amazing amber eyes stood up and launched into a litany of places we could hole up, places he and his kind owned. He, apparently, was a dragon.

And here I'd thought my walking broom was cool.

Listening, it'd almost escaped my attention that Louisiana was nowhere on that list of defecting states. Frankly, none of the southern states were and that seemed... well, I'd been surprised to hear Alaska wanted to break away though, they were so remote it wasn't super hard to *imagine* it. There wasn't a ton they *needed* from anyone else. Not really. But the southern states? They'd wanted to break away since 1861.

They talked about resources and how to relocate those who didn't want to be in the proposed new areas anymore, though, who did they think were just going to uproot themselves and move away? That hadn't been a thing for the most part during the first Civil War. Too many poor people didn't have that luxury. But these guys were just focused on the war.

"What about the people?" I asked over everyone as they talked about places to keep soldiers and ways to find supplies. "What about the people just trying to earn a wage? Go to hospitals? Get healthy? Go to school?"

"Everything would stay the same for them," Cat Eyes said in a miffed tone.

"But it won't." And I knew this because I liked watching the History Channel. "They'll put blockades up on any cities they deem sanctuary cities. They'll drive away business. They could cut off our communication, electricity?"

Paige smiled. "Those are good points and things we are already familiar with. We're going to need teams sharing what we've done here. We'll need new communication systems." She held up her phone. "I don't know how much longer these will last."

"And how will we talk to those outside your states?" Because that was me. I was outside those states. But my family? The one up in Alaska? They were going to stay in their state, though they'd probably be fine. I couldn't see the fight really heading in that direction. It was hard enough for outsiders just to *get* to Alaska. A war up there? My Alaskans would eat anyone for lunch. And then take their rifles and ammunition.

Paige met my gaze. "How do we get paranormals to safety?"

"You mean making them leave their homes and come here?"

Paige nodded.

That wasn't gonna... happen. "Would you move to New Orleans if I said the war was happening here?"

Raising her face to the ceiling, Paige looked away. "There's got to be a way to keep them safe."

Beautiful Blue Eyes shook his head. "If they choose to stay knowing how their government is going to treat them, there is nothing we can do. We can merely offer a better way."

"Hopefully," I snorted.

He gestured to me and nodded. "Hopefully a better way."

Paige rubbed her head and then ran through a list of assignments that were needed if they were going to proceed. Then she adjourned the meeting. "Wynonna," she called. "Could you stay?"

Ew. It felt like being called out by the teacher for being a jerk in class. But after everyone spilled out—almost everyone doing some small part to clean up before leaving which was a treat to watch—I kept my cool and my seat.

She joined me with a full queso jar full of red wine.

You know, I had to approve of the recycling. Salsa jars were just the right size and shape for drinking out of.

"I need the south," Paige said.

And how was I supposed to help with that?

She nodded like she understood my nonverbal, which she probably did.

I was a good communicator. Very few people ever asked what I'd said. They typically only asked if I'd *actually* said it.

"I've tried to get in to see them." She shook her head. "I need someone with connections. You know people. Mama Gee does, I hope. Veronica?"

I didn't know what I could accomplish. "I'll tell Vee and Mama, I guess?"

Paige nodded and leaned back in her chair, draping one arm over the table, the other over the back of her chair. "You should have seen him."

Uh, why was she confiding in me? "Who?"

"Walton." Paige frowned and licked her lips. "He was so damned cocky."

"Cocky enough to bring us to war over an ego?" I had to ask.

Shaking her head, she sipped her wine and then set the salsa jar down gently. "You know, the chief of staff mourns the thought that we couldn't find a peaceful solution, and I reminded him that if we'd tried harder with everyone else, we might have been able to do something with the paranormals."

By everyone else, I took that to mean queers and non-white people. Well, I mean, and others, but those were the two biggest groups making the news in the last few centuries.

"But Walton? He just seemed pleased." Paige shook her head as if shellshocked. "Just like... I don't know, like this was what he'd been working toward."

"Well, he is white and male and..." What was his religion? Well, he was in politics, so it was some type of Christianity whether he believed or not. He still enjoyed the power that came with his cross.

Paige pressed her bottom lip into her teeth with her finger. "I *want* to be more open. But how can I when he—" Paige met my gaze. "He *flaunted* his privilege in my face and basically told me that all of us just had to suck it up like the people who'd come before us."

Okay. Well, the karmic meter in me turned red. "And the spell I gave you?"

"I painted it everywhere," she said. "In the White House, the Eisenhower Building, everywhere I could think."

Wow. Okay. "A little karma goes a long ways."

Paige shook her head and clunked her glass against the table in frustration. "I'd been making such progress."

Yeah, well. I hadn't always been a successful witch. Back in the day, I'd fucked things up on the regular, which was one of the many reasons I'd left my kid in Alaska and headed as far from that poor thing as I could. Her and my aunt and my sister and...well, the rest of my family, my friends.

Fox.

Yeah. I'd thought I'd been making progress then too.

Right before it'd all blown up in my face. "You really think this is the best way forward?"

"Unless you think indentured servitude is the way to go."

I most certainly did not.

"Well, then." Paige stared into her jar. "You think you could get us in touch with the people needed for this?"

Hell no. That was what, senators and stuff? "I'll talk to Mama Gee. She might."

"It's all I can ask." Paige got to her feet. "Hey, babe. Ready for bed?"

I got up and looked behind me. I hadn't heard her man walk in. I raised my chin at Dexx in greeting. "Well, good night then."

"Yeah." Paige wrapped her arm around her man's waist and rested her head against his chest. "And keep bringing up those questions. Okay? We need them."

Right.

I still didn't think I should have been sitting in that meeting or discussion or whatever, but I was kinda glad I had been.

The world was in for a big shake-up and I needed to make sure some karmic protections were up to keep as many people safe as possible. Karma wasn't just a weapon. It could be a shelter as well. I just had to hope it wasn't too late to set that up.

5

When I made it back to the tree house, Veronica wasn't there. I wasn't worried. Yet. But I compiled my notes and sent them to Mama Gee in an email.

She called me in the weeeeeee hours of the next morning.

I'm not a morning girl unless you're talkin' one o'clock in the morning because that I can do. But waking up bright-eyed and coherent? That seriously wasn't my thing.

I don't even know what I told her. I mean, I hope I got the right information out there for her. Paige needed the southern states. We were going to war. Did I think we should? No because war was dumb. And it's hard. And it messes with karma.

I then rolled over after hanging up with her and went back to sleep until noon.

I woke up to Veronica handing me a steaming cup of coffee with a smile.

Like she was going to win me over just like that.

I got up, took the coffee, and then watched her move around the tree house. She didn't wear one of her normal skirts. This time, she wore pants. With pockets. That's the only reason she wore pants was if they had pockets. And she wore boots, which was strange for me to take in because she almost always wore sandals.

Which meant she was on business. Where she might be involved with the magick-throwing kind.

Great. Well, I could get in on some of that action. "What's on the agenda today?"

She turned her smile to me, but her attention was elsewhere. "Paige mentioned using your karma magick on her wards to protect the town."

When had that conversation happened? Probably in the morning hours, which meant Paige had to be one of those sick morning people, too. Gross. "Sure. But what's on your agenda?"

Stopping, she gave me her full and undivided attention. "I'm hunting Threknal."

"I'm going too." With pants, which I had packed. I don't always wear the short skirts that my lover loves. I wear jeans too. Yoga pants occasionally as well, especially if I'm going to eat a lot.

"No. You're not." Veronica gave me that look that said the conversation was over.

I don't know why she continued to try that because it *never* worked. But instead of fighting, like I usually did, I just kept getting dressed, stashing a few knives I'd magickally hidden and more than my share of charms. Yes, I was the reason we'd been so incredibly frisked by DoDO on the plane ride over. But how was I supposed to've known they'd have *magick* detectors?

I'm karma magick, which means in a battle, I can't throw the Hollywood visual effects around. Typically. So, I have to be smarter, go in prepared.

If we were going after a demon, I'd need my three karmic

blades—which were actually cooler than they sounded. They literally cut with karma. So, the crappier your karmic payback, the longer and sharper the blade, which also helped in getting them through TSA. As long as they weren't *reacting* or *interacting* with karma, they were just pieces of wood. I also put on all eight of my prepped spell rings. They were one-shots for the most part, though they *did* recharge after a bit.

"You're not coming with me."

I wasn't going to argue with her. I was just going with her.

"Wy."

So, she wasn't going to leave it alone. Fine. "You brought me along to handle Threknal, right?"

Veronica didn't respond. Probably because she couldn't and she knew it.

"Then, don't put me on the sidelines."

She took my arms and gave me a frank look that bordered on edginess. "I need you but not yet."

It didn't make sense. But she wasn't budging either. That was okay, though. She might not budge, but neither was I. I didn't know what was going on, but I was going to find out, one way or another.

Paige walked through the funerals, keeping her heart shrouded. Inside, she was howling. There were funerals being held in five other locations, but not nearly as many people had been lost in those cities as they had in Troutdale. The cemeteries were filled with people burying their dead. It wasn't just her small group. Everyone was spread thin trying to visit the members of those who needed to be put to rest.

She paid homage to Willow and the two other members of her staff who had died and were being buried so far from their homes. Walton had been serious. Troutdale was on lockdown. Door magick still worked, but she wasn't going to put it to the test just yet. She didn't want to give Walton and DoDO reason to trace door magick like Quinn and her people had.

But then, she milled around the other wakes, offering support as best she could. By the end of the day, her feet were sore, and she was ready to go home, get her feet out of those stupid pumps, and get something real done.

With her feet ensconced in fuzzy slippers and her legs encased in the only pair of yoga pants she owned, Paige sat at her desk and wrote out the names of the people she needed on her side of things.

General McCormick. Ruben. The Secretary of State, Salma Vargas. She also needed to get in touch with the congressmen and women who had gotten her voted into position in the first place. None had returned her call yet, which probably meant they knew her intentions and didn't care to entertain any ideas of a civil war.

Well, they'd tried peace. They'd put her in a position of power and that hadn't worked. What else could they do? Paige was at a loss. She'd thought that... reacting to how the government had treated paranormals, she'd be justified. But she wasn't. She knew—she *knew*—paranormals wouldn't get the same kind of treatment as minorities before them. She also knew that the minorities before them had been treated terribly, but things would still be worse off for them this time.

"Mom," Bobby said at her door.

She looked up in surprise. The office building wasn't a place for the kids, though no one had banished them. They'd still never really entered. "What's up, Bobbo?"

He fidgeted with his hands as he hesitantly stepped in. "I, um—" He stopped physically and verbally.

She knew better than to push. He'd grown a lot in the last few months and was still working on who he was going to become. Well, weren't they all? But him most of all, it seemed.

He met her gaze, his blue eyes taking on a slight golden sheen. "Whatever you're doing right now is bad."

Were they about to have a prophecy finally? Roxxie had thought that was the reason he'd grown older so fast, leaving Kammy—who'd been born on the same day—behind, but to date, they hadn't received a single prophecy.

He came to her desk and took her hand.

She was slammed with visions.

People being herded through a chain link gate with razor wire coiled above it. Temporary buildings stretched beyond the fence in what could only be seen as a concentration camp.

Leah being beaten, her lip bloodied, one eye swollen shut as she was tied to a chair.

Troutdale in rubble and seemingly abandoned.

A wall of cement and stone being erected around New York City.

Another concentration camp, but inside. She could see jagged mountains around her as she was led inside a dark room and pushed into a chair and strapped in. Cries of others in similar chairs hit her ears, filling her mind.

Bobby pulled away, blinking back tears.

Okay. What was she doing wrong, then? "What starts this?"

"Not acting," he whispered.

She met her son's eyes, biting back what she wanted to say, not even knowing what that was. "We are headed to war."

He shook his head. "No, we're not. Not yet. *This* is the path you're on."

"What—" What question should she ask her two-year-old teenager?

"They are going to deploy a toxin into the water that will… stop you from using your abilities. I think. But I don't know where they do this. Only that after they do it in one city and win, they do it everywhere and we fall."

That was good information and something she could act on. "I'll handle it. What kind of time frame do we have?"

He shook his head, his face filled with fear. "Not a lot? I don't know."

That wasn't helpful, but she understood it was the *only* information he had. "Science or magick?"

He thought about it for a moment, then blinked quickly and nodded. "Both. Mostly magick, though, I think."

Okay. Finally, she had a focus. She got up, walked around her desk and hugged her son. "Can you shake this off? Enjoy your day? Or do you need ice cream and Netflix?"

"I don't know." He stayed in her arms, shivering slightly.

"Try shaking it off." How was she supposed to tell her son how to cope with depression and shock? As his mother, she should be staying by him and helping him through it, not releasing him on his own to do it.

She wasn't that kind of mom. She'd never *been*, and it was high time she owned it instead of crying about it. She raised tough kids because of this, good, bad, or just ugly.

She pulled away, cupping his cheek. "If you can't, there's some Rocky Road in my freezer." Which wasn't her freezer. It was her corner of the second big chest freezer in the garage. "And we still have Netflix, I think. I recommend choosing something with lots of episodes that isn't depressing."

"Like *Supernatural?*"

So, that probably wasn't kid friendly, but it wasn't *not* kid friendly. "Yeah." She kissed the top of his head and sent him on his way.

Veronica was at the door, wearing pants and looking outfitted for witchy war with several pendants, pouches, and rings. "I have a request."

Paige gestured for the Voudon witch to take a chair as she reclaimed her own, watching her son disappear through the door. "What's up?"

"Wynonna." Veronica licked her lips, folding her hands in her lap. "I need to keep her busy while I track down Threknal."

Sirens wailed inside Paige's head. "Why?"

Veronica narrowed her dark eyes in thought, then bit her bottom lip with a wince. "We buried her memories," she said quickly.

They what? This wasn't okay. Alma had done that to her. Bussemi had done that to Dexx.

"It was Wy's idea. Valfire is... he is a threat. And the only real defense we have against him is Wy and Threknal. Wy with her karmic magick and Threknal because... well, he's powerful and he used to *be* a witch, which is why he's able to touch your magick. But it's also how we can use him."

That didn't tell Paige—who'd also had her memories blocked once—why Wy's memories were being blocked now.

Veronica lowered her eyelids and raised her chin. "She needs to love me in order to kill Valfire."

That didn't make sense. "She does, doesn't she? Love you?" If this was some mind game, manipulation thing, Paige wasn't going to back it.

"She does. Yes. But her heart was given to someone else. And after this, she will return to him and I want that for her. I do. But... her magick, karma, it's... it's fickle. It *can be* powerful. But it can also be... It can be useless if it isn't supported properly."

There was one thing Veronica had said before though. "Wy's aware of this."

"Well, yes. Not now. But she *is* the one who puts the memory blockers on. We've had to break them a few times. She just... she breaks through them. She's very smart, even able to outwit herself." The expression on Veronica's face said this frustrated her more than she wanted to admit.

Which didn't sit right with Paige. "Where do I fit this?" Because adding one more thing to her already overflowing to-do list wasn't on the table.

"I just need her... occupied." Veronica took in a deep breath. "Can she babysit?"

That shocked Paige more than a little. "She doesn't seem fond of kids."

"She isn't. She..." Veronica released a puffed-up breath and then took in a breath through her teeth. "She ran away from her daughter when she graduated high school. And, um, I don't—she's afraid of kids."

No, she wasn't. Paige understood that all too well. Wy was afraid of herself. Paige also realized there was a lot more to that story than a woman running away from her child. Teenager. Fear. Being a witch. Yeah, Paige would bet money—if that was even still a thing—that there was more to that story. "Okay. Could she look in on Bobby? He had a prophecy that really threw him."

"Yeah." Veronica beamed a failing smile and stood. "Thank you. This... I could use the distraction for a while, probably."

"Well, our kids will keep her occupied." Though out of trouble? Probably not.

Veronica left with a few more pleasantries, but then Paige was left to sit and ponder what her son had shown her. She ran through the visions, trying to figure out how to best to handle this.

She needed a scientist who also understood magick. And the only person that came to mind—outside Leslie who was still in a coma—was Brack Waugh, their *local* dragon. Paige didn't like his father, Ken. He just rubbed her the wrong way. But if anyone had the kinds of connections she needed, it would be a dragon.

Dexx stepped out of his office as voices rose. Again. "Knock the shit off!"

At least this time, Frey and Scout stopped their argument long enough to turn to him.

By now, everyone else was used to their squabbles, and were still working.

Frey clamped her lips shut and pointed at Scout. "I can't work with her.

Something flashed over Scout's face that could have been regret or guilt or, well, just knowing the end was near on her job there. But she closed her eyes and gnashed her teeth, biting off whatever she was about to say.

Dexx needed to find a solution to these two and fast. He couldn't keep Scout on just because Paige had felt it in her heart to hire the woman.

Though, her heart had been right about Rainbow.

But he wasn't going to admit that out loud. It still hurt not seeing her anymore.

But the contention between these two was big and it was destroying his team. "Scout," he said, walking toward her. "We're going to find a solution."

Frey frowned sharply and moved to stand in front of the harpy. "What do you mean?"

He didn't know. "There are other departments that could use her skills."

Frey bared her teeth and held out one of her hands. "We're just having a disagreement."

"You just said you couldn't work with her." But if she was defending the harpy then maybe things weren't as bad off as had seemed.

"We're both…" Frey struggled for a word and then glared as she finished. "Passionate."

Let them work it out, cub, Hattie said inside his head. *Sometimes kittens fight when working together.*

Well, that's going to get old fast. "Well, be passionate quietly." That could be taken all manner of ways. "And professionally." This wasn't getting any better. It was time to walk away.

Tuck came through the door and saved him. "We need to talk."

That saying always invoked panic. Dexx led the way to his office and sat as Tuck closed the door. Also not a good sign.

The sheriff sat down and hooked his hat on his propped-up foot. "We've got new marching orders."

"You'll have to be clearer than that, chief."

"Sheriff," Tuck said, his bushy grey eyebrows rising, "The president has ordered you and your team to stand down."

"Sorry, that's not going to happen."

"I agree." Tuck grabbed his raised knee and glared at the wall behind Dexx's head. "I don't answer to the president."

It still wasn't clear to Dexx just what Tuck's role was. "Who do you answer to? The governor?"

Tuck shook his head, his gaze unfocused. "He might be the only person who can arrest me, but I don't answer to him either."

Well, okay then. "What do we do, boss?"

Tuck ran his tongue along the front of his teeth and nodded, rising. "Proceed as normal but tread carefully." He glanced significantly out Dexx's windows at the bullpen. "Real carefully."

Dexx understood, but if they were headed to war, they

might not have to worry about that much longer anyway. "I'll do my best."

"Sure you will." Tuck rapped his knuckles on Dexx's desk. "Sorry again about Rainbow. She'll be missed."

She sure would be.

But what he *wouldn't* do was lose anyone else on his team.

6

I stared at my lover like she'd lost her damned mind. "You want me to what?"

I was surrounded by kids. Most of them looked like they were related except for the girl with the elf ears. She didn't.

And Veronica, the woman I loved above all others until this moment, stood over them, looking at me with a defiant challenge. "Babysitting."

I knew what was really going on here. She wanted me out of the way so she could track down this demon without me. Well, if she thought she was getting rid of me this easily, she had another thing coming. So, I pushed my upset to the back of my eyes and tipped my head in a nod. "Sure." I wasn't babysitting these kids. They were old enough to not need one.

Veronica looked toward the kids and then back at me. She opened her mouth to say something as the defiance in her expression slipped away to something closer to regret. She closed her all-too-kissable lips and turned away.

What was going on here? I released a semi-shaky breath

as emotions rumbled over me like a tiny tank. Love. Anger. Betrayal because she *knew* what this meant for me. Fear. More anger. Guilt.

The blonde girl with the blue eyes folded her arms over her blooming chest and glared at me.

The boy with the darkest hair turned away from the girl who was a spitting image of him, his eyes lighting with fire.

His spitting image gave me an ew-look, her eyes danced with blue electricity.

Okay. Well, these kids had super-powers. Great. "Look, you don't need a babysitter. I don't need to be babysitting you. We're good."

Blondie frowned at me. "Okay."

The boy who shared her coloring pushed her aside, his blue eyes serious. "No. She needs our help."

Blondie rolled her eyes. "No. We've gotta go do the…" She flicked her head to the side. "…thing."

That sounded like trouble. "Yeah. Why don't you guys go do *the thing*."

The blue-eyed boy touched his hand to mine.

My eyes didn't see what I was seeing anymore as the faces of the kids slid away. Instead, I saw a green dumpster beside a brick building. It moved as a man came out from behind it.

The visions shifted and Veronica was pinned in place against the wall, her hands clawing at something invisible, her sneakered feet trying to find purchase in the air. The man rested on the dumpster, smirking, his lips moving.

The boy took his hand away and he closed his eyes.

Blondie took his shoulders and hugged him close. "What did you see?"

The kids came into focus slowly. I mean, I saw Blondie take her brother's hand, but not in crystal clear picture. "What was that?"

"What did you see?"

"Look, Blondie," I said, rubbing my eyes. "Don't use that tone with me." I was still… taller than she was.

She shrugged and sighed at Fire Eyes. "At least it's not Zombie."

"I could get used to that name." But *did* I like that one? And why did I care? What had that vision been?

"Someone's in trouble," Vision Boy—or just Vision? Oracle?—said.

"Who?" Blondie asked with concern.

That vision'd come from *him*? "My girlfriend." And these kids *weren't* coming. "Zombie."

Her expression told me I was being immature. "My name's Leah."

"I don't care. I don't want your names and I don't want you anywhere near where I am."

Blondie—Zombie gave me a look that told me where I could go in no uncertain terms.

One of the other kids—the thinner of them—piped up. "I like this idea. We're taking on superhero names."

They could do whatever they wanted. Here. Away from me. I turned from them and stepped away.

Whomper got in my way and stopped me, along with a soft, small hand on my arm.

I looked down and found it was Oracle. He frowned up at me, his blue eyes telling me to listen.

I *was* listening. Veronica needed my help. I didn't know where I needed to go, but I'd figure out something. I was a witch. I had resources. I wasn't… all powerful or anything, but I'd figure it out. Besides, I had to put karmic protections up around the town anyway. I could kill two birds with one stone.

"I know where and when," Oracle said quietly, looking me right in the eye. "And I know that we can help you."

I'd stopped listening to the other kids. I closed my eyes

and took in a deep breath, trying to settle a calm over nerves I hadn't realized were this tight. Helping my lover wasn't the issue.

Bringing kids into trouble was.

The thin, hyper kid pushed Oracle out of the way, but gently. Sort of. "Okay. I'm Bard because I can do things with my voice."

"I don't care." I didn't want their names because that implied a connection to them I didn't want.

"Yeah. You do." He turned away and pointed to Zombie. "This is—"

Oh, for crying out loud. If he was going to shove himself on me, I'd be making up the names. "You do things with your voice?" I'd heard stories about bards in the bayou. "Like change people's minds and stuff?"

"Yeah." He frowned at me. "And explode things."

"Remix." I looked at Zombie. "You... do things with dead people?"

She nodded and then raised her chin. "I raise them."

Cool. "Necro. Fire-in-the-Eyes," I said, pointing to the boy twin. "Blaze. You?" I pointed to the girl twin. "Guessing lightning?"

She nodded. "Thunderbird."

Oh. Why would anyone think these kids needed a babysitter? "You got a choice. Storm or Boom."

She pulled back for a second then smirked. "Storm."

"You can't have that name," Remix said highly upset. "The X-men have it."

Storm narrowed her eyes as lightning danced dangerously in them. "Is it trademarked? Or...whatever?"

Probably. It wasn't like there'd be police running behind them enforcing that. "You're a kid. Who cares?"

Her eyes flared as she crossed her arms over her chest and pulled her shaking head back. "Well, fine, then. Still Storm."

Fine then. "You?" I pointed to the girl with the long wavy hair.

Her hands lit up with fire.

She was like a talking candle. "There are two of you?"

Blaze opened his mouth to say something.

I didn't need to know. "Pyro. You?" I pointed to a boy at the back.

"Bear."

Roger-roger. I didn't want to admit this, but I was having fun. "Kodiak. Ears." I pointed to the elf.

"I'm not being called that," she said clearly.

"Fine then." I smiled sweetly. "Peck."

She shrugged.

I had to giggle inside. Obviously, none of them had seen *Willow*. Well, I wasn't going to be the one to tell her. "If that's everyone?"

It was. For now.

Necro and Remix turned to Oracle, waiting.

"They're behind Lou's coffee shop," Oracle said.

Great. "Where's that?"

"Downtown," Necro said, reaching up to braid her straight blonde hair, tying it off with a rubber band on her wrist. She turned to Blaze. "I need a ride."

He grumbled but nodded. "I'm not being a horse again." Then he shifted into a kangaroo.

Wait. A kangaroo? A *flaming* kangaroo? Was this an anime? Had I taken a wrong turn into weirdo world?

"I'm not riding that." Necro made a circle gesture with one finger as if telling him to turn around.

Peck came over with a grin. "I could."

"It bounces," Necro said indignantly.

"So?"

They wandered off as Blaze shifted into a few other shapes before settling into a lion.

That was a new trick, being able to pick your own shape. What wonderful magick world had I stepped into?

Storm looked at me. "I've gotta carry Bobby and Mandy." She shook her head and shifted into an elephant, gesturing with her trunk toward Oracle.

Interesting. Could they all do that?

Kodiak took off his clothes and shifted into a bear.

Remix grabbed the clothes off the ground and tied them up around his arm, looping the shoestrings together before leaping onto Kodiak's back. "You can join us."

I shook my head, still not quite sure what I was seeing here—I mean, I *knew* what I was seeing. I was having a hard time believing I was going into danger with a bunch of kids.

Whomper flew over as if he was a good broom now and sidled up to me.

Flying by broom wasn't nearly as comfortable as you might think. It was literally riding on a stick. When I *knew* I'd be flying, I put a bicycle seat on him that made things a little better. As it stood, I only had the protections I'd put on him over the years to keep me from falling off.

I flew through the trees, just over their heads missing *most* of the branches. Whomper and I could have gone much faster, and I *tried* to get him to, but he had other plans. He was sticking by those kids.

You know. Which was cool.

Except that he was *my* broom!

When we got to the outskirts of town, I *thought* we'd all resume something a bit more normal.

Nope. Storm stayed an elephant. Blaze shifted from a lion to an elephant. He totally could have taken two people. Kodiak stayed a bear.

So, I continued to ride Whomper, though a little closer to Storm. She was the bigger of the two elephants. Was she bigger because she was older? More powerful?

Did it matter?

Storm led the way, skirting cars, and turned down the main street.

The people in town simply didn't react. Well, a couple of them waved.

One of the girls came over, stripped, and changed into a gorgeous black horse.

Because teenaged girls stripping in the middle of town was just a thing now. And no one reacted there either. So... maybe it wasn't weird?

Necro clambered off Blaze's back, gathered the clothes, and then leapt onto the horse's back.

Blaze shifted into a kangaroo with Peck still on his back.

The elf girl grinned wildly, then let out a whoop as the two of them took off.

There was no way they were getting into danger without me being there. I pushed Whomper forward.

We raced the kangaroo and his elven rider down the main drag neck and neck.

Until he dodged left and went down a side street I hadn't realized we'd be turning down.

I reigned Whomper in, but he went in for an overhead swooping maneuver, turning us upside down before righting again and then zoomed to follow in Blaze's dust.

There are many reasons I've put the riding protections I have on him. He's insane.

Before we turned the corner, I caught a glimpse of the sheriff talking to the kids we'd left behind.

They didn't seem to be in trouble, but I could hope the good sheriff would keep them entertained until I could take care of a demon.

Though, how I was going to do that, I didn't know. Karma magick was okay, but not super great in a fight.

Whomper came to a screaming stop at the mouth of an alley and tipped backward so I could dismount.

My body hurt. Riding by broomstick was *not* my preferred method of travel. "I'm riding the elephant next time," I told him.

He jiggled himself side-to-side as if he were giving me sass.

Blaze had already shifted back from his kangaroo form and stood before me fully clothed.

Peck had her hands on her knees, her face split in a huge grin. "That was amazing. We are doing that again."

He shrugged, pleased with himself. "Where're the others?"

"The sheriff got them. Maybe you could go check it out? See if they're safe?"

"They are." He turned and scoped out the alleyway. "We must've beat them."

Ugh. Kids. But by *them,* I assumed he was talking about Veronica and Threknal. "Maybe they'll get arrested." *I* was referring to the kids Blaze was refusing to save.

"For what?" Peck asked incredulously.

"Improper..." I didn't know. "...elephanting."

Peck gave me a look, her eyes flashing violet, that said that wasn't a thing.

Okay. Fine. I knew it wasn't a thing, but— "I'm not taking you guys into danger. There's a demon here."

"We know," Blaze said, holding a hand out and down as if telling me to calm down. He tipped his head to the side as he gnawed on his bottom lip. "I think I see something," he said in a hushed tone.

I'll tell the others, a young voice said inside my head.

Oh heck no. "What was that?"

"My little brother," Pyro said, slipping off Storm's back as she shifted from an elephant into a human girl. "Kammy."

"Don't need names." *Hey, Speakeasy,* I called out tele-pathically.

He giggled back.

"You are so good with the names," Remix said as he walked past me. "I'm a little jealous."

I was a little insane. *Speakeasy, can we all speak telepathically through you? Or do you only relay information?*

We can hear you, Remix said, staying by my side, craning his head in for a better view.

Great. Wait. Not great. I worked hard to project *only* what I wanted heard. I was a pretty loud internal speaker. *Let's go radio silent until we find this thing.*

Got it, Necro said, pulling back a little as her friend, a tall girl with long black hair got dressed. *What do we do?*

Doesn't your mom open a door, Pyro asked, as she tucked in close behind me, *and send demons back to, you know, Hell or whatever?*

Great idea, I said, *but we can't do that.*

Leah can. Pyro breathed down my neck, giving me the shivers.

I jerked away from her and glared. "No." Whoops. *Stop breathing on me.*

Pyro backed away, her hands in the air as if in surrender.

Storm crouched down, placing her fingertips on the ground. *Bobs—Oracle. Whatever. When does it happen?*

He's on his way, Oracle said. *He gets here before she does.*

And what does he want? With my girlfriend besides to kill her?

Oracle looked at me with haunted blue eyes. *She's going to trap him again and he doesn't want that.*

Right. Well, who would? *'Kay. I'm gonna go in there. Lay down some magick—* I didn't know what. *—and you're all going to stay here. Safe. Hidden.*

Storm surveyed the area, then gestured to her twin and flicked her head toward the garbage bin.

Are they using a secret channel?

They're twins, Speakeasy said.

Something didn't quite sit right with me. *Why aren't you here, Speakeasy?*

Because I'm two, he said with enough snark to light a match.

Oh.

Storm and Blaze led the way to the big garbage bin. *Here?* she asked.

Oracle nodded, hanging back, his blue eyes staying alert. *He comes from above.*

That wasn't something I'd seen. *He can fly?* That was worth noting.

The boy nodded again.

Okay. Well, if the demon—the *demon*—could *fly* then... what did they have? And if this demon could—I kept my inside voice low—touch Paige's magick, then what could I actually do to him?

None of the other kids reacted to that, so I felt pretty safe in the fact that Speakeasy hadn't heard my *quiet* mind voice.

I had a few traps that would slow him down and mess him up. Would it take immediate affect? Probably not, but it might be enough to hinder him. I pulled off one of my rings and took out a card from my back pocket.

What kind of witch are you? Remix asked, giving my ring a dubious look.

I gave him a half-cocked smile and knelt on the ground where I'd seen our demon attack my girl. *Karma, baby.*

He snorted, looking toward Kodiak as if I'd just gotten ten times cooler.

Which was a bad thing. I didn't *need* to be any cooler to

these kids. We needed to be very far apart from each other. As I was showing in this moment of poor judgement.

Storm looked at my ring and her eyes lit up, literally. She smiled and called little sparks of lightning to dance between her fingers.

What are you doing? I asked, not sure what her magick would do to mine.

She didn't answer but knelt beside me and zapped my spell-laden ring and card with her electricity.

Blaze added his fire, his hair engulfing in flames, giving him a very Hades look.

Well, great, I said to the mind meld. *There goes that*. I reached for another ring. *Leave this one—*

He's here, Oracle said, his tone filled with fear.

We didn't have time to react, but I wasn't going to just let this demon go free and attack my lover, either. So, I pulled off another ring, glared at the twins, and set it in place at the corner of the garbage dumpster I'd seen in the vision.

Then, it was time to hide.

The kids were doing this thing where they were standing around, searching for something—like a place to hide—and finding... nothing.

So, I ran past them, flagged down Whomper and dove behind some cars—because the alley emptied into a kind of parking lot—hoping none of them had a car alarm. I also called up a karma protection spell to help us find what we needed and just hoped they had clean karma so we weren't discovered.

The man I'd seen in the vision leapt off the roof of one of the buildings and landed lightly on his feet, his dark eyes narrowing as he looked around. He was tall, kinda beefy, had a man bun, and dressed like a vagabond, but the cool ones from the eighties when we thought that traveling the world as a bum was a romantic idea. Was that only me? Well, it was a great idea anyway.

He raised his nose to the air as if he could sense something wasn't right. Maybe he could smell us.

I farted, Kodiak said. *Sorry.*

Speakeasy, was he just reading my mind? I asked because that was very, very uncool.

You're a loud thinker, the bear boy replied with a salty tone.

Veronica came out of a door and stopped, crossing her arms over her chest. "You're getting sloppy, Threknal."

He spread his hands. "I couldn't *really* ignore this invitation."

Invitation?

"Do you really think I'm going willingly?"

Veronica's face pinched in a yeah-really expression as she tipped her head to the side.

"Yeah, no." Threknal reached out a hand, but he was too far away for him to touch her.

She went flying against the brick wall anyway.

I made a move to rise from my crouched position, to go and help her.

Several hands stopped me.

You set your trap, Storm said, her lightning-filled eyes meeting mine. *We're staying out of danger. Remember?*

You are. I'm helping her.

Whomper came in and whacked me in the head. Not enough to knock me out, but enough to hurt.

I glared at him and then turned my attention back to scene.

Threknal walked forward, studying Veronica where she was pinned to the wall. "What are you really trying to do here?"

Just another step forward. He was sooooo close to the dumpster and the trap.

Veronica kicked the wall, clawing at her throat with one hand, her other hand reaching into her pocket.

But before she could bring anything out, he touched the corner of the dumpster and electricity laced through him, catching his hair and clothes on fire. He jerked and quivered in place for a bit, his magick hold releasing Veronica.

Her feet found the ground, her eyes narrowed in confusion. But she pulled out a sigil stone and held it up to him.

With a roar, he disappeared into thin air.

We'd won and Veronica was safe.

But I didn't know that I wanted to fill her in on who'd helped her. I had questions that needed answers and I knew she wasn't going to give them to me.

7

Paige was assured by Brack Waugh that the poison situation was being handled by the finest scientists the paranormal world could manage. She didn't know this before, but they actually had their own laboratory devoted to finding cures to paranormal ailments, which was great. Bobby spent some time in the labs giving the lead scientist, Zoe something or other, the information she needed to keep the water safe.

Paige had then asked about water elementals and paranormals to patrol the waterways and to ensure that something like what Bobby saw didn't happen.

The situation was being handled and didn't need to be micromanaged, but it frightened Paige that something like water could be used against them.

The next three weeks were spent meeting with governors and trying to make alliances. She'd quickly discovered that just because a bunch of high-ranking paranormals had decided they wanted war, didn't mean that was necessarily going to just happen.

They couldn't afford to heed Walton's mandate that she

stop using door magick anymore. Bobby had said that *inaction* would be the end of their fight and she couldn't allow that. She just put up more protections around the doors to make sure they weren't discovered. And so far, things seemed to be working.

But for how long?

And... the match hadn't been struck. No one had been arrested yet. No one had been killed yet. The "language" was still being tweaked. The Registration Act had been voted down six times so far.

It felt like standing in the eye of a hurricane with this constant panic surging in her just waiting to be released. A part of her hoped that this meant they'd find a peaceful solution.

The other part of her knew that wasn't the case and this was just a lull before things got really bad.

But it was becoming increasingly apparent that what they needed more than anything was someone who could help them in matters of military strategy. She'd reached out to Merry Eastwood, who'd gotten Paige in contact with a number of ex-military people, but Paige, frankly, didn't feel comfortable with any of them.

She was starting to get a bit more comfortable with being the face of this movement, though, so that was helping. Sort of. She still woke, walked, and slept with a near-constant wave of panic driving her. There was so much hanging in the balance here. If she messed this up...

People could die, or live in concentration camps for the rest of their shortened lives or... worse. She didn't even know what "worse" could look like. A part of her wanted this *wait* to be over with already.

She knew she needed help though. She needed someone with the kinds of resources that would *actually* help them because this lull wouldn't last long. She wasn't going up against a demon or a demon army or... any of the other enemies she'd faced before.

Pulling herself out of the space of her own head, she focused on the people around her who were talking.

Ishmail met her gaze, saying nothing, his pen ready to take down whatever notes he needed.

She shook her head and gestured to the door with her chin. She needed to do this herself.

Without a word, he stood up and ushered the team out of her office, closing the door behind him.

This was a dumb idea. Paige knew that. Conferring with the enemy to save today? But she'd done that once before with Merry Eastwood. They'd saved Troutdale, saved the world, and she hadn't murdered anyone—at least none that Paige knew about. If Merry Eastwood could turn over a new leaf and help those around her, then... maybe Dawn Flynn could as well.

Sinking into her office chair, Paige took out her cell phone and dialed the number Dawn had given her.

Dawn picked up on the third ring. "Yes?"

"I need help."

Silence was the immediate reply. Then, Dawn sighed. "My bags are already packed."

Okay, so these kids weren't bad. If anything, I was probably a terrible influence over them. They were supposed to be in school and I did make sure to get them there every day.

But as each day wore on, I slowly started collecting those kids and more. I'm not kidding. I had a growing number of *children* joining me on my hunt for Threknal. That... wasn't disturbing in the least little bit.

Right.

They'd taken ownership of my broom, though, and that was more than a little frustrating. Granted, it was a little nice because it meant he was clobbering someone else for a change. There was a reason his name was Whomper and not something cute like Bristles.

But in the past three weeks, I'd made a few discoveries. I didn't know how or why, but Threknal was indeed in the Troutdale area.

And he seemed to be after Veronica, which meant he was distracted from his original intent, which was good. I hoped.

Veronica was being even more secretive than normal, but she was so preoccupied with her own search, that she didn't even pay attention to what I was doing.

Which was good because I'd gone snooping through her things. I'd been following her. The kids had been following her.

And we still knew nothing.

I waited for the kids in the woods outside the school. I'd gotten used to traveling by broom—after telling the kids that if they wanted in, I needed my broom back—and I'd managed to get my hands on one of the comfy bicycle seats. Not at a store, mind you, because they were all out of stock. Like, seriously. Troutdale *had* a Walmart. It was closed because there were no stock trucks coming in or out of the town.

Which was insane. I didn't know how the town was getting supplies and I kinda didn't need to know because, well, I had other things on my mind. But I was curious.

The kids started trickling in. I'd long since stopped getting names for everyone. I didn't even have code names for them all. Well, okay. I *had* code names, but some of them changed often, making things very confusing in my head. But there were just so many of them.

Necro and Dash—the horse. Her code name was short for Rainbow Dash, which was a play on My Little Ponies—

walked toward me, talking excitedly to one another. As soon as they saw me, they ran over and filled me in.

I got none of it. They were speaking words. I was sure of it. But there were so many incomplete sentences and they were talking on top of each other.

Necro held up her hand to stop them both and shook her head. Taking in a calming breath, she said, "We figured out why he's here."

"Oh." See, this was the other thing with these kids and one of the reasons I was going against my fear to work with them in spite of the fact that they were kids, and I was putting them in danger. They were resourceful. "What?"

She then went into a full story about how this person had talked to that person who tied the shoe of this person who loved this person by they weren't right for each other, so they talked to the wrong person who had the right answer—which was a complete and total surprise because she's *such* a jerk and nobody likes her—and how by working with this other person, they were able to combine the abilities of three kids and now— "We have a spy camera."

"Oh." Okay. Neat. "Did we pick up anything?"

Necro nodded, sidling up closer to me. "He's here for some stones."

Not what I'd thought, but okay. "What stones?"

"Hey, did you tell her?" Remix asked as he and Kodiak thundered onto the scene.

Kodiak shifted back into a human.

Remix shoved his clothes at him, giving Necro a look that told her to spill.

"Yes," she said impatiently. "I was just telling her about what we found."

"How we got there was so epic," he said, his hands balled into fists as he arched back in a howling-werewolf position.

"Okay, crazy pants," I said, not sure how to keep a lid on

these guys. Though, did I want to? They were kinda fun to hang out with. Which wasn't something I ever thought I'd hear myself say. "I need details. Without howling."

Necro waved Remix off as a few more kids ran to join them. "He was trying to dig them up."

"The stones?" Why? Were they like magick crystals? Power... cells? Okay. I had no idea.

"We know where one is," Dash said, her dark hair billowing around as she smiled. "We were thinking we could go check it out."

"Check what out?" a very adult-sounding voice demanded.

I spun around and saw a medium height woman with curly dark shoulder-length hair approach us with a look of mild exasperation on her face.

She met my gaze and tipped her head to the side. "Mrs. Blancher."

"Peggy," Necro leaned in and muttered. "She's super great."

I smiled. If kids weren't my specialty, women certainly weren't unless I was trying to turn them on. Mrs. Peggy Blancher didn't seem to be the kind of woman who would find my charms charming. "Mrs. Blancher. Wy Hunt. Can I call you Peggy?"

She offered her hand and narrowed her eyes through her smile. "Interesting name."

"Short for Wynonna," I said, drawing out the name with a wince as I took her hand.

She chuckled. "Gotcha. Yeah. Okay. What are you up to?"

I could try to lie my way out of this situation, which Remix was already getting ready to do, but I'd laid down a *lot* of karmic energy to keep us protected. So, unless I wanted everything to suddenly go sideways, I needed to be honest. "We're tracking a demon, but we're staying away from it." I said the last part fast as her mouth opened. "They're not going anywhere near it." Except for the one time. In the alley.

Mrs. Peggy Blancher got real serious and squared up, rising to her full height. "A demon?"

She needed to understand how serious I was about keeping the kids safe, so I let a little bit of the troubled teen who'd nearly gotten her daughter killed to trap another demon, a little bit of the woman who'd left her daughter behind to protect her shine through my eyes.

Mrs. Peggy Blancher swallowed and nodded, a confused frown furrowing her brows.

Blinking, I pushed that version of myself back into the recesses she belonged and popped my neck. "They discovered something."

"Well, I hope so. They've been using the science labs a lot."

The kids exploded with explanations.

She raised her hands, but only looked to me. "All I'm saying is that they're doing well in school and that's good. But maybe I should come along on this one."

That... sounded just fine.

Leslie searched through the red room, trying to find anything that could help her get out. Everything was bathed in ruby light and a screechy noise that deafened her. She fumbled through the desk, searching for anything. There were research notes, pens—worthless things.

What she needed was something to make the noise stop killing her brain.

She continued to search, her feet unsteady. The noise was affecting her ability to see straight. Eventually, she found a pair of noise canceling headphones and put those on.

Sweet blessed bliss. She leaned against the wall for a moment, just enjoying the moment.

But then it was time to get out of there.

She found doors a lot of them, but all the writing was backwards, like she was on the wrong side. Doors that should have led to the outside didn't. They just led into different rooms, or sometimes the same room.

Where was she?

It seemed like an odd mix between a prison and a medical facility. She recalled what Paige had told her about the prison she'd freed the paranormals from. This… could be something like that. Sure. Yeah.

But how had she gotten there?

She realized after some time, that wherever she was, it wasn't… real.

The doors that led to rooms or sometimes the same rooms.

The words that were backwards.

The journals and books that were backwards.

This was a dream of some sort. But it wasn't hers.

So, whose was it?

Instead of looking for doors to get out of there, she looked for another pair of headphones—because whoever was here with her would need them. That noise was still intense even with it being muffled. This time, as she searched, she looked for clues of the other person with her.

There were logos all over the place of a bird in a crescent moon. Maybe this wasn't a prison. Maybe this was some kind of headquarters or something.

But where was the person?

She found several pairs of earplugs and brought them all in a backpack she'd located, grabbing a few weapons along the way. There weren't guns, but she'd found scalpels, knives, a really big wrench. Those were all good enough for her.

The biggest issue she had, though, was that in this world, she had no magick.

And Robin was nowhere to be found inside her head. For the first time since she'd bonded with him, it was silent.

Well, not silent. The blaring noise deafening everything overrode that. Murphy's Law, probably.

She found a Sharpie and started marking the rooms and doors she uncovered with big x's. This area was a big circle with one door she couldn't get into.

At first, she didn't *see* the door.

Then, when she did, it didn't have a doorknob.

Now, it *had* a knob, but it was locked.

She tried everything she could to get that door to open. She tried hitting it, freezing it because she had bottled nitrogen at her disposal. She even tried blowing it up.

Through this, she discovered she couldn't be hurt there. She didn't bleed. She didn't get burned or frozen.

And neither could that door.

She banged on it in frustration, shouting and raging against it.

A loud click sounded over the alarm and the door opened.

Wow. That'd actually worked?

Grabbing her backpack, and holding a knife in her off hand, she opened the door and peered inside.

A woman with matted blonde hair sat curled up against the wall, tears streaking down her bloodied face.

Well, Leslie had found the person who owned the dream. Now, it was time to find a way out.

Dexx peered around the corner of the building, making sure to keep himself hidden. *You with me, fat cat?*

She didn't respond but gave him a gentle nudge.

The Red Star team was doing pretty good. It helped that crime was down in Troutdale, so they were doing other things like helping to organize supply runs and stuff.

That's what they were doing at the moment, though, Dexx had another mission.

While his team was busy doing their actual job, he'd been trying to track down Bussemi, using Ethel, though she'd been pulled in to help Barn with his coma patient studies. They were both important, but if they had any chance of winning this war, Dexx knew he had to get Bussemi off the board once and for all.

Do you see anything?

Hattie shifted his vision from normal to infrared and they saw a single heat signature.

Ethel had been able to hack into a single computer that was tied "loosely" to the DoDO mainframe, whatever that meant. But he had a location. Here. So, when they'd needed groceries, he'd offered up this city in the hopes of catching a door to see who was playing around. It seemed like someone was baiting a trap.

It was a very DoDO thing to do.

Creeping forward, Dexx used Hattie's hunter abilities to not make a sound, while he searched for cameras that might catch him. They'd used some sort of camera blocking device George and the boys and the garage had made, but that was over where they were getting supplies. That wasn't here. Here, he still had to be careful not to be caught.

"They're turned off," a familiar female voice said in a harsh whisper.

"Quinn?" Dexx was surprised and then chided himself for *being* shocked it was her. "What are you doing?"

"Were you followed?"

"No." After London, Dexx had gotten much better at making sure he *wasn't* followed. He surveyed the area. Just parked cars—empty parked cars for as far as his eyes could see. He stood up and walked around the car Quinn hid behind, shifting his vision back to plain-old human.

She stashed her laptop in her black backpack and stood. "Tell me you have a way out of here."

"Yeah." But what was going on here?

"That offer still good?"

Offer?

"To come back."

Oh. That offer. "Yeah." He didn't want to have that conversation with Frey and Scout though. The two were finally getting along. Kind of. He didn't want to throw Quinn Winters, siren-extraordinaire into that mix of dynamite.

"Good." She gestured for him to lead the way. "I have information, details, and a direct line to an inside guy. Let's go."

While this was what they needed, Dexx couldn't shake the feeling that there was something she wasn't telling him.

Something that could get them all killed. Or worse.

But for now, he'd take the win. "Follow me."

8

I t felt a little like a field trip, mostly because Peggy managed to grab a bus. The guys at the local garage had been working on ways to combine magick and tech, which was cool, so the buses were slowly being updated to no longer need gas. Which was good because the fuel stations were no longer getting restocked.

I, frankly, was freaking out about that fact more than a little because that was crazy and just didn't happen the U.S., but Peggy was quick to let me know that this was their third blockade and that they were well-versed in how to deal with this kind of stuff now.

The kids gave the driver directions to one of the vineyards in the area. Actually, it was kinda down the road from the Whiskey lands. I mean, kinda. Okay. By that, I mean, the Whiskeys lived in the vineyard and farm side of things, so, yeah. Anyway. I suck at directions that don't involve mountain peak names.

We all piled out of the bus and Peggy and I took lead.

"What are we looking for?"

Storm stepped up with a sketchbook. "This."

The picture she'd drawn was of an oval-ish stone sunk into the grass with a sigil carved into it.

Sigil work, huh? Great.

"Well, we could look for that," I said, initiating a sigil stone I'd made a couple of weeks ago, "but we should look for traps first." I gestured for the kids to get their sigil stones glowing too.

They were amulets, mostly. But I make them out of wood chips or stone chips or sometimes just polymer clay. It really was just whatever I could get my hands on. But as a karmic witch, I also worked with sigils because sigil magick is all about *intent,* as was karmic magick. So, the two worked great together.

The *intent* I'd given these amulets was to work with the individual's natural abilities so they could see when there were traps or danger. Remix was a bit of a problem because any kind of karmic spell I gave him tended to blow up. He was a good kid. He just liked bending the rules. A lot. So, he didn't have one.

Storm looked around and then gestured with her chin somewhere in front of us and to the right. "Energy field."

"Like a ward?" The one thing I'd discovered since being here was that Paige Whiskey reeeeeally loved her wards. She'd even had me add karmic magick to them. I told her it wasn't always a good idea, but she just said that it'd keep everyone honest and that was important too.

I mean, yeah. She wasn't wrong, exactly. But good people did bad things all the time. Just take Remix for example. He enjoyed pushing people's buttons for no real reason except to get a reaction. He kept things lively and entertaining. But... yeah. My magick was shaping him. Harshly. He'd received more than a few bruises for payment of his actions in the past three weeks.

Storm shook her head. "It's... I don't know. It feels like the area around a power place."

A power place? "Like a transformer?"

She shrugged.

"Like where electricity comes in for a house?" Because I needed an answer.

"Like the bigger ones. For a town." She glanced at Peggy and shook her head with a shrug. "It's just a lot of electricity."

Blaze walked in a slow circle but didn't venture too far away from us. He'd learned the hard way not to a week ago. His hands were low and out. Usually, when he did this, they were on fire, but they weren't that day. He shook his head. "It's hot right over there." He pointed in the same direction Storm had indicated.

Peggy looked at me and shook her head. "The kids are staying here."

"Agreed."

They didn't, but I let Peggy deal with that as I hopped the ditch and then walked through the rows of vines.

A blue butterfly landed on a full grape plant.

It was hard not to reach over and pluck a purple fruit, but I was already trespassing, and I wasn't going to add that to my list.

An orange butterfly landed next to the blue one.

Frowning, I stopped and looked around the ground, trying to find what Storm had drawn.

A clump of grass at the base of the grape vine hid a hand-sized stone that was buried deep in the ground.

Well, this couldn't be the work of Threknal because this thing looked like it had been buried ages ago. I pulled the grass away to reveal the sigil.

"Can I help you?" a man called out on his way up the row, coming from the opposite direction of the bus.

One of the butterflies rose and became larger until Storm stood where the butterfly had been. "Hey, Mr. Sloan."

"Rai," he said, coming to stand beside us. "Ember. What are you doing in my vineyard? You aren't eating anything, are you?"

"Karma won't let us," Ember said grouchily, finishing his transformation.

That's the code name they'd given me. "You can thank me later," I told him, then looked up at Mr. Sloan. "Is there anything you can tell me about this stone and if you have more of them?"

Mr. Sloan frowned. "Niles. They've just always been here. We've tried digging them out, but they're actually part of a much bigger rock."

"We?"

"My family. We've been here for over a hundred and sixty years."

Interesting. "How many do you have?"

"Eight." He turned and pointed to the east. "Six more of them are that way. There's another that way." He pointed to the west and kinda south.

I needed to trace this sigil to see what its intent was, but I didn't want to do that with everyone standing so close. Sometimes, doing that would set off charges that could be rather... explodey. "Are they all different?"

"Oh, yeah." He looked to the kids. "What are you guys into?"

"Research paper," Storm said. "Which we'll actually be writing," she said, the words directed at me.

"You better." Because her hand had been *on* her sigil amulet. "Is there any way we could see the others, Niles?"

"Oh, sure. I mean, you guys could come in. We've got drawings of them at the house."

"Can we bring the rest of the class?" Blaze asked

behind me.

"Rest of the class?" Niles asked surprised.

"We found out about these in class," Storm said with a smile that looked like it hadn't been practiced in a decade, "and we're all interested in them."

He snorted. "Well, then in that case, yes. Meet at the house. If you really are doing a research project on this, we—a lot of us who first settled here—have a lot of information. And once you get us talking about it, you might wish you hadn't."

I nodded to Storm and gestured with my eyes for her and Blaze to get back to the bus.

She nodded gravely and turned, taking her brother with her. "Did you want a ride, Mr. Sloan?"

"Oh, sure." He moved to walk around me.

"I'll be right there," I called after them.

After they were a good distance away, I steadied my nerves and ran my left forefinger along the line of the sigil.

The power was ancient but strong. The intent was hard to interpret, as if there was a language barrier or something, but I got the distinct impression that this stone was meant to *replenish*. But to replenish what? I didn't know.

But it looked like it wasn't a threat.

Could it be used to help us? Well, it was time to find out.

———

Paige left the house confused. The kids should have been back from school, but the house was empty. Of all the kids. Well, except for Kammy. Tru wasn't letting him out of his sight.

Which was understandable. As one of the few people in the Whiskey house without any sort of magickal abilities, it could be tough trying to protect your kids. And Kammy was the only little one left.

Hey, she thought, sending her voice to her nephew. *Are the kids safe?*

Yeah, Kammy said, but he didn't add to it.

Well, Paige had other things to worry about, so she let it go and headed to the business complex.

Ishmail met her at the front door with a latte in hand. "We have a new milk foaming machine. Naomi's going nuts with it."

"Did she get her family settled?" Paige had initiated the move of all the families of her staff to Troutdale or somewhere in the western states where they'd be more protected. She didn't want her staff to be in the line of fire and worried about their families. Not everyone had easy family dynamics. Most were divorced and there were battles over kids and dogs and an iguana and houses.

"She's fine." He gestured to the latte. "But really going through a lot of heavy whipping cream which is expensive. Anyway, President Dawn Flynn is waiting in your office."

"Why didn't you lead with that?"

"I needed to tell you about the frother." His expression said it was a mild emergency.

It really wasn't. "We're planning a war. Let her froth. Does Dawn have a—" Paige lifted her cup.

He nodded. "Of course. Everyone does. However, President Flynn also brought a lot of bags and her cat."

Paige was confused. "She's the *ex*-president."

He shook his head, walking around the table that had been moved into the middle of the path from the front door to the offices. "She will always be President Flynn or Madam President."

Okay. Good to know. But she was also planning on staying a while. That, too, was good to know. "Okay. Well, let's see if we can find her some lodging that won't insult an ex-president."

He nodded and disappeared.

The common area was nearly empty, but the office doors were open, showing people were working—or at least were on their computers. How much longer would they have internet or have the ability to transmit information from one device to another?

She had given Tru the directive to find a solution to that and he said he was working on it, but with Leslie in the hospital, he hadn't been ultra-focused.

Paige stepped into her office and smiled.

Dawn sat with her back to the door, but stood, setting her cup on the coffee table to turn and offer her hand. "Paige."

She took it, watching Dawn's blue eyes for any sign of what Paige could expect. "It's a pleasure to see you, Madame President."

Dawn took her hand back and waved off the title. "First names, please."

Paige nodded and took a seat in one of the dark leather couches. "What brings you?"

"You called me."

"You were ready to move in."

Dawn didn't react.

"You brought your cat."

Finally, Dawn licked her lips, clenching her fists momentarily before retrieving her drink. "Are you serious about going to war?"

Paige had thought she was, but if Bobby's visions were true, then... "Yes."

The breath Dawn took in straightened her spine and pushed her shoulders back. "Then, you need to move carefully and decisively."

99

"You're here to advise." Tentative relief swelled in Paige. "How can I trust you? You were the one who started this."

Dawn leaned back in her leather chair and sipped her coffee.

Paige took a moment to try hers. It tasted like candy. Damn. Was this good for her? She wasn't a shifter anymore, and she was nearing forty. She'd be gaining weight by *looking* at food again.

Setting her cup in her lap, Dawn met Paige's gaze. "I was wrong about how to approach this. I wasn't wrong in being upset about how my situation was handled. It needed to be dealt with in a court of law. But I went too far. I abused the power of my office."

Well, she wasn't wrong. "And I'm supposed to trust you? How?"

"Do. Don't." Dawn shrugged. "I have my own staff. Lawyers. People with the kinds of experience you don't have."

That got her attention. "Like who?"

"Ruben." Dawn held Paige's gaze and raised her chin. "Generals."

"Who would be willing to come to this side." Was that even possible? "If we lose, they lose everything."

"No. If we lose, we're all thrown in a prison no one talks about. And that's if we survive long enough to be arrested."

Paige swallowed, then took another sip of her coffee that tasted like a candy bar. "What do you recommend?"

"First," Dawn said, leaning forward, but keeping her mug, "the seceding states need to proclaim legally that they are sanctuary states for paranormals. That will give them the legal protections they need."

"To stand up to the federal government."

Dawn shook her head. "The federal government isn't all powerful. This was a country of states. If they do this, if they ratify legislature that supports their state constitutions protecting *all citizens* of their states, then Walton will have a harder time making a case against them."

This was the best information Paige'd heard so far. It pointed to a match she could use. "Okay."

"And you need to ratify a constitution of your seceded states."

How was Paige supposed to do that?

Dawn waved a hand as if to dismiss that question. "It can be done. The reason we're doing this is to get generals, units, ships especially, squadrons of planes from relocating when Walton orders it."

"What do you mean?" That sounded bad.

Dawn nodded as if acknowledging that it was bad. "Walton knows that when he gets the Registration Act passed, you're likely to declare war."

Would that be—"Would that be something we could declare war on?"

"Sure." Dawn shrugged. "Anyone can declare anything they like about anything they want. It depends on what they have for support. Now, you have the paranormal armies."

Paige wouldn't call them armies.

"And Walton is doing everything he can to make sure those armies don't get bigger."

"By locking us down."

Dawn nodded and held up her free hand. "If we can get a few generals, a few of Walton's armies, that would bring us to a greater advantage."

That sounded great.

"We're not just looking at the war front with Walton. When we go to war, we'll have to defend ourselves against other countries."

This was something Paige didn't want to hear.

"Any moment of weakness, they will invade. But even if

we can't get the generals to *join* us now, if our constitution is close enough to the one they swore to defend, we might get them to at the very least not obey Walton."

That was a thing they could do?

Dawn raised her eyebrows and took a drink. Licking her lips, she stared at her cup as she lowered it. "They swore to protect our country, not the office. So, yes. In theory, they could refuse to join either side."

That brought a whole new view of things.

"And one more thing."

Did Paige want to hear this one?

"You're going to need to get your shifter back. You need to be as strong as you can be. They will be coming after you with everything they have."

Paige met Dawn's gaze. "What do you need?"

Dexx led Quinn back to the Costco where the delivery truck they'd driven through the Blackman door was being loaded with supplies by forklift. "Why now? Why not then?"

Quinn kept up with him step for step. "Like I said. My cover was blown."

He didn't know if he trusted that for a can of beans. "Let's get you across and then we'll talk about how you can help us." If he allowed it at all because he was now starting to question everything.

They got to the back of the truck as the door was being pulled closed. "We're done," Scout told him, her eyes scanning the area. "We should get out of here."

Dexx nodded and looked at Derrick who stood at the nose of the truck in his trench coat, looking very Harry Dresden. "Door."

Derrick nodded and pointed at the driver. He nodded again, and then opened a large, black-ringed door.

The truck started up and rolled forward.

Dexx grabbed the handle on the back of the truck and hopped onto the bumper.

Quinn followed suit on the other side as Scout followed on foot.

The parking lot remained quiet. The people who had helped fill the truck simply went back to work. There were no other cars in the immediate area. No attacks.

Derrick walked after the truck and Scout and closed the door as they went through.

Dexx hopped down once they reached Troutdale, his feet hitting the main street asphalt. What *was* he going to do with Quinn?

A car screeched to a halt as it was going by and was hastily put in park. Lovejoy got out, looking between Dexx and Quinn. She pointed at Quinn, but directed her attention on Dexx with a look that told him to talk.

He shrugged. "She was the ping we got. Followed the lead. Led to her. She wants to come in."

Lovejoy bit her lip, clawed her hands, and then pointed to her car. "You," she said, gesturing to Quinn with her other hand, "get in. You," she said, gesturing to him, "get back to work. People are coming out of their comas. Hospital's in chaos."

He wanted to go with Lovejoy to hear what was going on with Quinn, but—

If Leslie was coming out of her coma, he needed to be there. So, he nodded, and shifted shape, reveling the feel of running down main street on four massive paws.

It was time to bring his entire pack back together.

9

Okay, so the stones weren't really getting me any closer to Threknal, but they were interesting. I hoped they weren't a complete waste of time.

They were, however, interesting and a great distraction and might be helpful on bigger things. What those were, I didn't know. But... bigger things.

Using the kids' spy cameras helped me keep a watchful eye on Veronica. The more time I spent away from her, the more clear-headed I became to the point where I started avoiding her all together. She didn't seem to even notice. She was so singularly focused on tracking down Threknal. Who was this woman? What secrets did she have and how was she tied to a demon like Valfire?

Which, aside from a really cool name, I still knew next to nothing about him.

I can't even tell you how tempting it was to go to Paige and ask her to summon him or some flunkies or something so we could discover more about him. I'd even gone to her office to ask her to do just that, but, crap, that woman was busy and was constantly surrounded by people. Seriously, if I was her, I'd be going bat sh— well, crazy already.

But the stones?

We'd caught Threknal trying to unearth them in several locations. Mr. Niles Sloan and his neighbors were continuing to flood us with information on these things. Locations. Documentation. Test results. They'd spent years studying these stones and had all kinds of crazy theories.

"I think it's aliens." Niles held up his hands as if to stall us, though no one rose quickly to tell him he was crazy. "I know what you're going to say."

He probably didn't.

A couple of the kids around the table of his cramped-with-all-these-kids kitchen wore varying expression that mirrored my inner commentary.

"It seems a bit far-fetched, but it makes sense. To me, if no one else."

And, you know, it kinda did. After all, these rocks were *massive*. Picture an iceberg, if you will. You know how we can only see the small top part, and how the massive part remains in the ocean? Well, these were a lot like that.

"These rocks are hard," Niles continued.

"Like granite?" Remix asked, leaning on Nile's kitchen table covered with piles of notes. He picked up a rock sample. "It could be, right?"

"Very close." Niles took the rock sample from Remix and leaned on his elbows, holding the rock up for everyone to see.

His table wasn't big enough for that. It was one of those round ones with the metal legs from, like, the seventies. You remember those? He even had a full set of four yellow, vinyl covered chairs, but they'd been pushed to the side to make room for as many of us as we could fit. "Granite and gabbro were created similarly. When the magma cooled slowly, they both became very hard. But granite has quartz, mica, and crystals. Gabbro has feldspar crystals in a dark grey matrix. Both are very dense and that means very hard."

"What's feldspar?" Peggy asked, biting down on her smile.

Niles looked up at her from his stooped position and smiled in a this-could-be-a-Hallmark-romance kind of way.

It was so cute. I wanted to snuggle in a blanky on my couch and eat ice cream while continuing to watch it.

"Rocks created by mineral deposits. But not just *any* kind of minerals. These are tectosilicate minerals, which are super cool."

"As rocks?" Pyro asked, her face contorting in a how-could-this-ever-be-cool look.

But I knew this one. "They're silicates."

"That's correct," Niles said, his tone giving me a verbal gold star.

"I use them in face creams." I glanced at Peggy and shook my head kind of apologizing. "I zap wrinkles."

She nodded as the corners of her mouth turned down.

"Ah, yes," Niles said, holding up a finger. "These are a bit different."

"I'd say. They'd make a heck of an exfoliant scrub." What I really wanted to was to know if his information dump had anything I could use.

He straightened, his smile saying he took my hint. "You might not like it on your face, but they hold a special place in the rock world." He winced and bounced his head from side to side as if to say it wasn't that *high* of a place in the rock world. "They're framework silicates. They have a three-dimensional framework of silicate tetrahedra and silica dioxide. Okay, so let's just put this in perspective, okay? There are companies out there making money by selling the idea that their products have silica dioxide properties."

I still wasn't catching on.

He licked his lips and nodded once as if cueing the fact he was finally getting to his point. "They repel water, so they don't corrode with wear and time. They're hard, so they're nearly unbreakable. And," he said with a smirky smile, sliding his gaze around the group and landing on Peggy, "they're self-healing."

Oh. Okay. So that was interesting. "Thanks for the science lesson, Professor Sloan." I actually meant that.

He gave me a two-fingered salute and bowed his head. "Now, the rocks themselves aren't as self-healing as it sounds. They have all those benefits and more when added to other things, which is the reason for the developing tech in *our* market." He pulled a pocket knife out and scratched the broken surface of his sample. "See? It's not healing itself. But —and here's why I'm going with the alien theory—the outside of the rock is a blend of zinc and feldspar." He scratched that surface.

And it started healing before our eyes.

"Someone *made* these rocks, these massive rocks, and made them to be nearly impenetrable and indestructible. Eons ago. Back when the earth was still being shaped."

Technically, the earth was *still* being shaped, but I got his reference. "How big is this thing?"

"Near as we can tell, these eight stones—" He set the sample down and rummaged through the stacks of paper that had started off organized and pulled out the map of the area, pointing at eight of the stones on the surrounding lands. "— are part of the same monolith."

Wait. "Isn't that like a structure or something? Like art?"

Peggy shook her head. "It's just a big rock. A *single* rock."

Niles nodded in agreement. "They can be entire mountains, but the key is that they're one rock."

"So, you're saying that these—" Fingers of a massive rock

hand. "—could be the size of a mountain buried in our backyards."

He nodded, pursing his lips as he studied the map.

"Surrounded in a protective coating to ensure they survived thousands of years."

"Millions, actually."

Okay. But why?

Niles looked up at me. "What do they mean? These symbols?"

I'd grown up hiding information like that. Okay, I mean, for the most part. When I'd been in high school, I'd had a group of magick-using buddies and we'd gone up against the magickal baddies of the Mat-Su valley, which, surprisingly, there were quite a few. But since I ran away like a scared girl with my tail tucked between my legs after nearly sacrificing my baby daughter to conquer a body-shredding demon, I'd kept a pretty tight lid on who I invited into my knowing circle and who got to know the real truth behind what I did.

"I've seen you studying them, trying to read them. You've visited each one and we—" He chuckled as he gestured to the kids. "—we have the ability to see what you're doing. You've been tracing them."

We were gonna have to have a conversation about cameras and privacy. "They're sigils," I said. "But they're ancient. Like really ancient. Some of the structures follow the rules I know. So, if this is aliens, maybe they're the ones who created the sigil rules we now follow, but what I know is the evolved version. I don't know. But they obviously changed or shifted."

"Like Telephone," Niles said.

I nodded.

Not all the kids were catching up, but they were staying relatively quiet. Even Remix.

Peggy wasn't going to let it slide, though. "It's a game we

used to play where we formed a circle and one person whispered something to the person next to them, and then the message was passed around the circle until it got back to the person who started it."

"Oh," Pyro said. "We call that Lies."

"No, we don't," Necro said, her face twisting. "We don't call it anything."

"Yeah," Remix said, thinking. "We do. So, you think—" he said, pointing at me, "—that a bunch of aliens made these and gave us instruction manuals."

That wasn't what I'd said, but... "Sure. Yeah. Okay. Well, this one is... like, filling the cup, I guess." I pointed at the marker in Nile's vineyard. I went down the line. "Kill them if they're trying to kill you. Break in case of emergency."

"I doubt it's break," Niles said, his eyes following my finger.

Now that I knew a little more about the rocks, I had to agree. "Then, use? I don't know."

"That's really close to home," Storm said, her eyes narrowed. She turned to Blaze. "I wonder if we have one too."

"You probably do." Niles grabbed a straight-edge —the spine of a notebook—and a pen and connected the dots. "I would say there are at least two on the Whiskey lands. And I would guess they're here and here."

Looking at it on the map actually brought things into a bit of clarity. They were not only connected, but they were semi-evenly spaced. "This can't be natural or random."

Niles and Peggy nodded.

I continued down the list with the understanding I now had. "The meanings are complicated and really deep. So, when I throw out the one- or two-word thing, just know there's a lot more to it. But, okay. So, this one?" I continued to point at each one as I ran down the line. "Calibrate for intent, influx regulator—kind of. Capacity indicator—which is low, by the way—transformer, and output regulator." I shrugged at everyone. Now that we were putting the pieces together, it sounded more like a machine. But for who and why?

"Government base," Remix said randomly, snapping his fingers and then shaking them.

We'd all been doing that a lot lately—just saying things out loud with no context because we were all just trying to figure out what was these things were and how to not let Threknal—or anyone, really—use them against us.

"Ley lines," Grumpy said. He was another bear shifter. I didn't call him Grumpy in reference to Snow White's dwarf. It was a reference to the Care Bears. I actually had a lot of references to Care Bears, Rainbow Bright, My Little Ponies, Smurfs, and Scooby Doo in their growing list of code names.

I... had... so... many... kids... to... keep... straight.

And I didn't *hate* it.

I looked over at Grumpy and thought with him, trying to figure out where that might end. "What do you know of ley lines?"

He shrugged. "Only that they're there and they're magickal and stuff."

Well, that was about what I knew about them, too. But I also knew there were maps of them. Not great ones, but still... you know, maps. So, I pulled up Google on my phone and asked for a map of the ley lines of Oregon.

There weren't a lot that I could actually pull up and *read*. We weren't a hot spot for ley line activity, go figure. Most of the ley line activity in this area seemed to come from Seattle. But we did have two lines running in our area.

And one of them ran right along our edge of connect-the-dot monolith finger points.

I looked around to everyone in the room—well, those I

could because a lot of people were crammed behind thick heads. "I think we found our connection."

But what did it all mean?

Paige's birthday passed without incident, or a lot of fanfare, something she took as a kindness. It was a low-key affair. They had cake, but Paige realized that she was starting to get reactions from food now. Her joints were swelling, and she was starting to get fatigued easily. Was she developing an allergic reaction to something?

Maybe Dawn was right. Maybe she should ask for Dexx's bite. But... a part of her didn't want to. Yes. She missed the strength that came with being a shifter witch, and she really enjoyed being able to shift into any animal she wanted, being able to hear anything she wanted, see better, especially in the dark.

But she was also afraid of how powerful she was getting.

So, she put that on the backburner as she, Dawn, and both their staffs minus Ruben, along with the local governors worked to draw up and ratify a constitution for the western states. They were calling themselves ParaWest.

All the while, the kids were eerily quiet. But they hadn't gotten into any trouble. So, Paige wasn't going to invest energy she didn't have into worrying.

Developing ParaWest felt like playing Risk as she and Dawn reviewed the resources of each state, their incoming and outgoing revenue streams, their military bases, and the merits for going after each state.

Walton had indeed begun withdrawing the troops, but it was a lot harder than issuing an order and getting it fulfilled right away. Troops were able to deploy back to the east coast, but to actually withdraw them? That took time, resources, and money Walton was running out of.

"The thing working in our favor," Dawn said, staring at their map in what they were now calling the war room, "is that he's deploying a lot of his troops to the south." She looked over at Paige significantly. "You can thank Generals McCormick and Saul for that."

General Saul was who Paige had called General Female before because she hadn't had any other name to call her by. "Why?"

"Because," Dawn said, rising and heading over to the coffee station to pour herself yet another cup, "the south is following our lead. They're recalling their Senate and House members, and drawing up their own constitution, which was technically written already. It just needs a few updates."

That was great news because that meant that *if* Walton truly did take this to war, ParaWest might have a higher chance of winning. "How close are we with our constitution updates?"

"They're being finalized as we speak."

Which was a little terrifying. But step one was telling President Walton of their united intent to make their states places of sanctuary and refuge for paranormals—well, anyone who needed it, really. He still could pull back, stop this before it got started. Paige had her doubts, but it could. "We have our contingencies in place?"

Ishmail nodded. "We do. We're still working on our communication network, but it *is* up and running. We have the ability to tap into it using these." He held up what looked like a pair of headphones. They slid onto the back of the head and sat just in front of the ears. "But this is only one proto-type. We're working on phones, computers, you name it. We're also implementing renewable energy grids, and we're growing the team to convert cars to use magetech."

It wasn't actually technology that only the mages of DoDO could use. It was actually magick technology anyone could use.

"Protections are in place," Lovejoy said, from her chair near the corner, "around all our door witches who will be targeted and along our current borders."

Paige understood that Lovejoy was referring to the border they now had between ParaWest and the rest of the United States.

"We should be able to keep up with shipments," Lovejoy continued, "and we might even improve shipping times."

If Phoebe wanted to, she could go into business on that alone.

What they were saying, though, was that they'd thought of everything they could. It was going to take a long time to get what they were initiating to everyone. They solidly had Montana, Idaho, Washington, Oregon, north and south California—because that'd been a fight—Nevada, Utah, Arizona, New Mexico, Colorado, Wyoming, and North and South Dakota. Paige wanted Kansans, Oklahoma, and Nebraska, but Dawn didn't agree they were worth the fight, and they'd refused to join. Paige wanted to take Walton's food supply out. Alaska and Hawaii were both on the fence, not sure if they wanted to even play, but they might not need either state.

What Paige needed was a general or ten who could tell her which strategy would work best.

If the south also split, though, maybe Walton would see that standing his ground in this way was a bad idea and might back off.

Paige nodded to Ishmail. "Let's make this happen."

When Walton heard their declaration of paranormal sanctuary, his actions would decide whether or not they ratified the ParaWest constitution and declared their intent to break away from the States.

Paige already knew what Walton would say, though. They just didn't know *how* he'd say it. Or when he'd respond.

Paige hoped for more time but knew in her heart their hourglass was emptying all too quickly.

Leslie sat up in bed and wished like crap she hadn't. The extreme noise from the red world was back, screaming at her but in a different way.

With that noise came colors and light that attacked her almost as much as the sound. Something freezing cold moved in her veins from a pinprick of pain in her forearm. She reached down and yanked it out.

People dressed in blue ran into the room, talking to her, but she couldn't hear or understand anything they said. The noise was overwhelming everything.

One took lead, a woman with short dark hair. She talked through a smile, but Leslie could hear none of that.

You found me, a woman's voice said.

The words didn't match the lead nurse's lips, though.

Leslie looked around the room and found the blonde-headed woman with the bloodied face. That was the same woman from the dream world, which meant...

She probably wasn't real. Well, real, yes. Physical? No.

Who are you? Leslie asked, projecting her mind.

Kelly. The blonde woman stepped forward, her feet bare, and looked at the nurses, careful to step out of their way.

A light was shone in Leslie's eyes.

She batted it away. *Kelly, I need you to turn off this noise.*

Kelly side-stepped the lead nurse. *It's not me.*

The lead nurse shoved her face in Leslie's to get her attention and said something else.

The noise was too loud though. Leslie mimed that her ears weren't working, but someone grabbed her arm with a gloved hand.

Leslie reacted, slapping him away forcefully.

The man fell into the machine behind him.

More people grabbed her, pushing her to the bed.

She fought instinctively, still not quite sure what the heck was even going on. Where the crap was Robin? Why had he chosen *now* to be silent?

Something sharp was inserted into her arm and the world went fuzzy.

The lead nurse patted Leslie's shoulder and mouthed, "It's okay. Rest now."

Leslie slid into darkness.

But the noise followed her.

10

D exx woke up with the strangest feeling in the part of his soul where his connection to the pack was located. Panic.

He sat up in bed, jostling Paige, but she grabbed at the covers sealing herself away from cold air.

Hattie, that can't be good.

It is a pack member. The griffin.

Leslie? She's in a coma.

Her ancient stirs.

"Fuck. Pea, get up, we need to get to the hospital *right now*. I got the coffee." He flew through the room, throwing clothes on and possibly mixing socks.

The coffee machine was half-way through the cycle when Paige thumped down the stairs, tying her hair back. She grabbed the cup and slid another one under the drip.

Dexx pointed to the garage and Paige silently turned and made her way to her car. She had enough brain activity to sit in the passenger seat.

By the time they reached the hospital, Paige had both eyes open and synapses were firing.

They stood at the nurse's desk waiting for approval to visit Leslie when his alpha sense tugged at him again. Dexx turned away from the less than helpful nurse to Leslie's room.

"Sir, you have to wait," the nurse commanded. "You need an escort to go in there."

Dexx was already moving, and the nurse was almost yelling for Dexx to stop.

Paige offered apologies for his juvenile tendencies but hurried after him.

Dexx hit the door almost at a run, slamming it open just as Leslie bolted in bed with a scream that no human could make, her arms flung out to her sides.

A sphere of blue force burst out from her blasting everything away.

Dexx and Paige were blown out of the door and skidded into the hall, crashing into the nurse's desk.

Ouch. Dexx had to think of something. Fast. *Get to Robin. Can you talk with him?*

I can talk but he may not listen.

Do what you can. Damn, he's strong. Dexx picked his head up and Paige already had her witch hands out and reaching for Leslie. They were tipped in green life magick and calming energies.

"Good call." He stood and pushed out with his alpha will.

Leslie took in another breath and was ready to explode it out. Robin must be furious.

Orange crackles of light played over her skin and hospital gown.

Leslie wasn't Leslie behind the eyes of an enraged griffin.

Oh, crap. Dexx pushed harder as she began her scream. The blue shock wave shot from her again, but this time Paige had a ward in place just as it would have incinerated Dexx and part of the walls.

Robin and Leslie resisted the push, both of them too strong to be easily quelled.

With the defensive attack held for a moment, Paige reformed the ward and funneled the energy out and away from the hospital and danger.

Confusion lit Leslie's face for an instant.

That was the opening Dexx needed. He pushed hard. First was to stop the attack. Next was to communicate that they were all right.

Robin and Leslie went for round three, and... they deflated. She fell back against the hospital bed, spent.

Paige knelt in the hall, having used a lot of her power just to contain the one attack.

Dexx made it to the bed and took Leslie's hand. "Hey, it's me. Calm yourself. You're in the hospital. It's okay. You hear me?"

Leslie rocked her head back and forth. "Not okay. Robin is out of control."

"Saw that."

"It's Kelly."

Paige frowned as she came to the other side of Leslie's bed. "Who?"

Leslie closed her eyes. "The ghost who attacked me."

Paige met Dexx's gaze across the bed. "What can you tell us?"

Dexx focused his alpha will on Leslie, trying to give her an anchor she could use to come back and maintain control.

"Kelly was a para?" Leslie's voice went up in a question, though she didn't seem be asking one. "I have the layout of the place she was held in. I can see the logo. It's a bird with a crescent moon."

Paige frowned.

Dexx didn't know what that was about. "You need to get Kelly to move on." It was his job to get his pack under

118

control and safe. And Robin and Leslie, two powerhouses, being out of control when they were going to war was not good. For any of them.

Leslie nodded, biting her lips and looking at him. "Will you stay with me?"

"Of course." There might be other things he would need to do soon, but he could tell when he was needed somewhere. He met Paige's gaze. "See what you can find out about that logo?"

She nodded and pressed a kiss onto her sister's cheek. "Help her move on and then come home. 'Kay. Shit's crazy without you."

Leslie gave a pained chuckle. "Love you." Her head fell back and a sigh escaped her lips.

"Love you back." Paige touched Dexx's shoulder on her way by and gave it a squeeze. "Love you too."

"Yeah, yeah." He gave her a peck of a kiss and then focused on Leslie. "I don't know what to do here, so you lead."

He'd be her anchor. He was her alpha and it was high time he started filling that role to its fullest.

Quinn looked around the office complex after being cleared and searched and screened. That whole process had taken a couple of days, which she had to approve of. It had also given her a lot of time to stew, to allow her mind to wander and for her emotions to build.

She was anxious and nervous and a lot could go wrong.

Like the office Lovejoy was leading her through. This wasn't what Quinn'd expected. For Paige to step up her game like this? To accept the office of leadership to this degree? This reminded her of a government office, not like a para

119

leader's. Had they made a mistake in supporting Paige in taking the office of secretary? Had that stint tainted the leader she'd become? Or had to become?

The people Quinn worked for had very careful plans for Paige and they didn't involve her bringing the corporate status quo to the para life.

Quinn followed Lovejoy through the main lobby and down the hall on the right, past several offices with people busily working.

Lovejoy hadn't said a single word the entire drive from downtown and Quinn was okay with that. She was still trying to get herself settled from the hell storm she'd just escaped, and she didn't know if she'd be able to completely control her voice. If she slipped now? With this person? While she was trying to build trust?

Quinn was the inside woman because she could work her way in. That would be harder here. Paige was the type of person who invoked genuineness of character and that's what she brought to her like a magnet. If Quinn showed she was manipulating how people felt or thought—no matter her intentions—she'd be thrown out.

Her mission was too important to screw up. More than just her life was on the line.

Finally, Lovejoy led them to an office, stood by the door until Quinn entered, and then closed it behind her before settling behind a rather beat-up desk. "Don't siren me."

Quinn kept her lips clamped shut and nodded, her emotions boiling just under the surface. She had to keep those away from her vocal cords.

"Why now?"

"Cover's blown," Quinn said carefully.

The look on Lovejoy's face said she understood that. "How bad?"

The welt of guilt and remembrance of fear made talking

nearly impossible. "In order to escape DoDO, I had to fake my death. I also had to…" Her eyes dropped for a moment. "I had to leave my partner unprotected and alone. I abandoned her."

Lovejoy nodded. "Sorry to hear that. Leaving someone behind is difficult."

Quinn nodded, not even allowing herself to clear her throat. More than difficult. The person she'd left behind had become *more* that a partner.

Studying Quinn with her amber eyes, Lovejoy took a moment before talking. "Do you have information that can help us?"

That was an emotionally safer answer. "Yes."

"Good. And you're willing to?"

"Yes." Quinn was loyal to a group of people who had taken her in, and they were hedging their bets on Paige. So, yes. Lovejoy had her loyalty. For the time being.

Lovejoy studied Quinn for a long moment and then sat back, steepling her fingers. "I had a siren on my team before. We have a room you scream into. That should help."

That was interesting, though Quinn wasn't going to let her guard down. She couldn't risk it.

"But then we're going to review what information you have," Lovejoy said firmly, leaning forward. "And if the information isn't valuable, I'm getting rid of you. We can't afford surprises like you."

They couldn't afford to send Quinn away, but it would be up to her to find a way to get Paige and her team to trust her while protecting the identity of those she served.

Paige stepped into the office and then stopped, staring at Quinn in surprise. "Uh, hey."

Quinn's job wasn't to get close to Paige, but just to stay close enough, to guide, share information, get her to go in the direction they needed. She raised her chin in greeting, fighting to get her emotions under control.

"She's been through a harrowing ordeal," Lovejoy told Paige. "She's a siren. Highly emotional. Could be volatile. It's best she not speak right now."

"Okay." Paige frowned then shook her head as she stepped into the room. "Look, Leslie came out of her coma with some information. She was attacked by a ghost by the name of Kelly and she saw a logo. A bird and a crescent moon?"

Quinn was here for *that*. "I know that logo," she said quietly. "I have information on a drug they are working on."

Paige closed her eyes for a minute and then turned to Quinn. "To mute paranormal powers?"

Quinn frowned. "How do you know that?"

Paige shook her head and turned to Lovejoy. "Get what information you can. If that—" she said, pointing at Quinn, "—is connected to the ghost attack on the town, then we need to take down the facility."

Lovejoy nodded, her lips tight. "Will do, ma'am."

Paige's expression said she wasn't sure she liked that term, but she backed out of the room. She gave Quinn a tight wave. "Glad you're not dead." And then she closed the door behind her.

Lovejoy turned a tight smile to Quinn. "I suggest you go scream so we can get to work. I need to take down that facility with minimal force."

Quinn didn't know how they were going to do that with minimal force, but if she could that and protect her partner, she'd give it her best shot.

Me chasing Veronica like this wasn't how I'd planned this

little vacation. Okay. So, it wasn't a vacation and I'd kinda known that going in, but... growing up like I did, I'd listened to the ramblings of the patriots around me. Alaskans are *very* patriotic. That should have prepared me for this "war" we were headed into. It should have. And it should have prepared me for following my lover into it. I should have.

It didn't.

Wondering where we were headed as a nation was so second-seat to how I worried over Veronica. Not because I thought she was more important than coming battles that would probably be nothing more than post wars on social media—who could get the most likes and shares. That was so above me.

It was the fact that at least *this* was something I could do something about. The kids and I had told Tru and the energy guys about the stones, thinking they could use the power grid or whatever the stones even were to help with their mage tech or whatever. I'd even put myself on the list to get a new phone because chances were good that they wouldn't work much longer. It was already getting harder and harder to get signal. Why? I didn't know. I just knew that coverage was getting really shoddy.

But Veronica.

I didn't understand what I was feeling about her.

I missed the way she held me at the end of a long day.

I missed the way she smelled after she performed magick.

I missed the way she moved the air as she walked.

I missed the little things she did for me when she was around.

I missed doing little things for her, knowing they'd make her day just a little brighter.

We were growing apart and my soul ached for it.

And felt relieved at the same time. That didn't make any sense. Right? We should be working *together* tracking down this demon, but the closer I got to her, to helping her, the harder she drove me away.

The kids had actually talked me into a game after dishes. I sat at the large dining room table by myself—though I wasn't the only one there. Paige and her husband—or non-husband. I didn't understand how a ceremony changed that—sat at one end with Tru.

I liked that guy. He reminded me a little like Wash from *Firefly*, but Tru was a lot more serious, like Wash would be if he was leading a part of a war or something. And Tru kinda was, I guess. You know, in that running the family kind of way. He was the unsung hero of the Whiskey family, the one no one really talked about, never really got a spotlight shown on him. That's how he got things handled. I could see that looking from the outside. Did anyone else?

Leslie had made it home and they were having a hard time getting her to take it easy. I didn't know what was going on, but I was staying out of that fight. Tru finally got up and escorted Leslie up to their room.

Paige glanced at me and then said something to Dexx, making a move to get up.

And come to me, which wasn't what I wanted. It was one thing to hang out with the kids, but hanging out with that woman? She was *intense*.

Okay. I realize the complete one-eighty I've made on the kid front.

That didn't stop me from getting up.

She held out her hand to stop me and pulled out a chair to sit opposite me, setting her coffee cup down.

I swear that woman always had a cup of coffee in her hand.

"Leslie's being a bit of a handful," Paige said, grimacing with her lips and shaking her head.

I didn't know what to say. I didn't know her sister and I

was crap with siblings anyway. I'd abandoned mine when I'd left my daughter over a decade ago. So, I grunted at her.

Paige glanced over at the kids and then ducked her gaze to the table. "Veronica said you weren't good with them, but you're..." She shrugged.

Well, the good news was Paige wasn't great with small talk either. So, this was going to go well. "Yeah, well, they're not terrible."

"I doubt your daughter was either."

I swallowed the knot of guilt and... some dark emotion I couldn't even name down.

Paige bit her lips and looked at something over my shoulder. "Failed mothers don't get to... talk about it. You know?"

Everything in my head stopped. I was so shocked with where she was taking this. Normally, when people found out about my mother status, I was greeted with insta-judgement. But that wasn't in Paige's eyes. Understanding was.

That twisted my chest churning a storm of emotions threatening to rise. I didn't know *why*. I'd *made* my peace with what I'd done long ago.

"We're not allowed a voice because we did something unforgiveable." She stared into her cup for a long moment.

I let her as the memories rolled inside my head of what I'd done.

"I didn't fight hard enough," Paige said quietly. "Or... I fought wrong? I wasn't enough?" She licked her lips. "I got a second chance and I..." A frown flickered between her eyebrows as she glanced at her kids fighting with smiles in the kitchen. "I'm not sure I'm doing much better now."

I didn't think she was fishing for compliments, so I didn't offer one. "What happened to you isn't the same as what I did."

She nodded and turned her attention back to the table. "Did you ever have someone you could talk to?"

"Sure." And I had. I'd talked to Aunt Gerty who'd been outraged and... well, her reaction had been the reason I'd run.

"I mean someone who didn't judge you."

A stillness hit me. The weight of my actions were heavy because I knew the weight of the judgement of everyone around me. If they knew what I'd done, they wouldn't be all smiles and acceptance. "No."

Paige pressed her fingers around her cup, then shrugged and met my gaze.

"I don't need it."

She didn't say anything.

This was dumb. "We're here to fight a war. To stop a demon."

She nodded. "But every single moment isn't that battle. We—" She stopped herself and bit the inside of her cheek. "We fight for those we love even if they're not with us, even if they're not talking to us. We still fight for *them*."

I leaned back in my chair and let my head fall back, not wanting to put a voice to the ache I ignored knowing that the people I loved most in this world wanted nothing to do with me. To them, I was nothing and no one. For reasons. Sure. Yeah. Absolutely. I wasn't going to give myself some sob story about how I wasn't deserving of that role. I'd fully earned it.

That didn't change the fact it still hurt.

"Who are you fighting for?"

I watched the kids bicker and fling water at each other. "My sister. My daughter. My aunt."

"Tell me about them."

No one had asked about them. Not even Veronica. I didn't even know what to say about any of them. I'd barely talked to any of them in years. "Gertie does what she can to keep me abreast of what they're all up to. The shop is doing good."

"Shop?"

Why was Paige acting interested? But it didn't seem to matter. The words were pouring out of my mouth like some dam had been broken. "Her occult shop. In Palmer, Alaska of all the places. You have never seen a place a witch didn't belong as much as Palmer. Great place. Really pretty. Gorgeous, really. Rugged. Strong. Crazy hard to survive. But open and inviting? Not even a little. But Gertie made it. She sold candles and hope. When the community failed people—which did a lot because if you couldn't handle it on your own, you were showing weakness—she'd be there, offering what she could. Might only be a bag of herbs, but it was there. She didn't care what people though of her. She just..." Persevered.

I always thought I was like her, being the rebel, doing as I pleased.

"There were things there that... I don't know. Just magick. Lots of magick. It's like a magnet. The whole valley. It's like, I don't know, like... like the people there are so blind, darkness and danger and magick can just hide in plain sight. And so creatures just go there and wreak all kinds of havoc. Gertie did what she could. Alone. But she was good."

Paige sipped her coffee and didn't offer anything.

Which was good because I didn't know... I don't know. Like, I didn't know if I'd stop talking if she interrupted or if I just wanted to babble. Why now?

Because we were going to battle a demon and I didn't know if I'd get a chance to say good-bye to them. Or because we were headed toward war with the government and I might be imprisoned and Gertie or my sister would never know how much I loved them. Or my... daughter would never know... I was still connected to her. Somehow. I still felt for her. I still wanted to be a part of her life. I couldn't call it love. Love implied knowing the person I cared for and I didn't.

That didn't mean I didn't want to.

I didn't have the right to want that though.

"Things started attacking the high school, so I decided to do something about it, follow in Aunt Gertie's footsteps. It didn't—um—" I scratched my head. "It worked. I had a few friends. We created a magickal fight club. But karma has consequences." I knew I wasn't making any sense. "Fox, my boyfriend, did something and I lashed out. I had sex with someone else and wound up getting pregnant."

Paige frowned in confusion but didn't voice her question.

"I'm pan," I said, knowing what she was confused about. Cis people were so bound up in the black and white rules of their sexual engagement. "Anyway, I was trying to get Fox back. And... I did something I shouldn't have. It created a karmic back blow I couldn't control. And a monster—a karmic monster was born. And..." The horror of the aftermath flooded my memories. The blood. The chaos.

Paige raised her chin, her expression lacking any judgement at all.

"After Charlie was born, I tried to contain that monster. Several different ways, but each time, it escaped and was more horrible than the last. Each murder was on me."

Paige met my gaze, warm with brutal understanding.

I latched onto it like a lifeline. "I offered Char as a sacrifice to lure it into a cave and then trapped it."

"Knowing you could save her or prepared to sacrifice her?"

At the time, I'd been so sure, but there'd been a moment —*just* a moment, where I'd been forced to be honest with myself. "I don't know."

Paige raked her top lip with her bottom teeth. "I think you do. Those of us who have failed were faced with situations bigger than us. We carry the burden of that so that others—people who haven't faced what have—can feel better about doing *their* best in the face of *their* adversity."

The truth of those words rang in my ears like a bell that silenced everything else.

"The real test of courage will be facing her again."

"Charlie?"

Paige nodded.

I knew her words to be truth, but I wasn't ready. Not yet.

"You've shown you're good with kids."

I snorted. "No." But I didn't want to admit to this woman that I'd thrown her kids at a demon on my first day watching them. Self-perseverance kept my mouth shut.

Paige frowned into her cup. "You can get a second chance if you want. You just have to take it."

I shook my head. I'd been gone too long. I wasn't even a person in their lives anymore.

"I didn't say it'd be easy. I said you could do it if you wanted."

Well, it certainly wouldn't be a cake-walk. That was for sure.

Her left eye twitched. She took in a deep breath and popped her neck. "Veronica put a blocker on your memories. She said you're aware of it and that you helped put that blocker there."

The shock that ran through me was like a brick of ice. "What?"

She bit her lip. "You're going after Veronica. You're so focused on that, you're willing to put your fear of kids aside, which is big. You've got a lot of reason to fear them. I see that now. I still think you can overcome it, but you're willing to go *that far* to uncover the truth, I can't—" Her hand balled into a fist and she released it again as she bared her teeth. "You will get my kids harmed and I won't allow that."

The reason for this entire conversation hit me like a bucket of water. "I will—" Stop seeing the kids who were actually helping me?

She slashed her hand in frustration. "No. Get the memory blockers off. Go into this knowingly. The kids? They're—" She chewed on her words for a moment. "They're capable of taking care of themselves and they're happy to help you. Fiercely protective of it, actually. So, all I ask—"

Her tone said it was a demand.

"—is that you figure out the real danger you're putting my kids into. All of them. And yourself. Then, when you leave, put the blockers on again if you need to." She stood with a little force, her chair squealing as it shifted back. She stopped and turned back to the table to meet my gaze. "You're fighting for her, for Charlie. Be worthy to claim her as your daughter."

The sting of her words hit me as I sat in the wake of her sudden silence.

It was time to find my lover and get some answers. Charlie would just have to wait.

11

I stayed to play games with the kids because I'd already said I was going to. Hey, they were still people, so... yeah. I wasn't just going to bail because I was feeling all stewy.

Necro frowned at me over her UNO hand. "What's wrong?" she asked quietly.

I shook my head and focused on my cards. We were playing zeros and sevens with draw-till-you-play rules which meant this game was likely *never* going to end. I was waiting for Veronica to come home. I'd stationed Whomper to let me know when that happened.

Speakeasy slapped down a yellow one on top of a green six.

"Hey," I said and thought the color yellow at him.

He was two or so? I didn't know. Also, I didn't really care. He was toddler-terrorist age. That's all I really knew. But the kid was smart. He knew his colors and he was learning to recognize the patterns on the cards.

"He's getting tired," Pyro said and pulled at a yellow card he had lying on the table in front of him.

He slapped her away and grabbed his yellow one with a frustrated sigh. *You're paying attention.*

I didn't understand how that kid could be so small, have a speaking vocabulary that consisted mostly of grunts and poorly formed sentences, but could talk like a person mentally. It didn't make sense. Nor did I like the fact that all of his adults were like, "Yeah. Well, that's just Kammy." Like, no. There had to be a reason.

But, you know, they had two teens who had been newborns a few months ago, so yeah, maybe they were a bit overwhelmed. It felt as though the gods were being a little lazy though. But, hey, maybe it was like Australia. They just got bored and started throwing things at Paige for the heck of it. Or Leslie. Speakeasy belonged to him.

Dang it. I couldn't focus on UNO.

I was really trying *not* to run through all the things I wanted to say to Veronica. I was currently pretending a conversation where I let her have it with both barrels. The churning anger and hurt in me felt vindicated by that scenario, but I doubted I'd actually get anything out of her if I came at her that way.

Necro sighed, played a green seven on her turn and gave me her hand.

Which was a lot of cards. She had a unique ability to take a hand with two cards and turn it into twenty in a heartbeat.

I gave her my two with a look of aggravation. I didn't *actually* think I'd go out. I didn't think any of us would win that evening, but I was getting overly antsy to talk to Veronica.

"Girlfriend?" Necro asked, her blue eyes pinched and her question ending in almost a squeak.

That basically said she had no experience with this kind of stuff and wasn't sure what she could even offer. Which was cool. It wasn't like I was going to unload on her anyway, you know. So, I shrugged and waited for Oracle to play a blue seven and take Necro's newly obtained cards.

The good news was that if they could just keep playing sevens, I could, in theory, get my hand back. I *had* a seven.

She sighed and glanced at Peck as she said something about being annoyed.

That was the other thing about it being so noisy. I couldn't *actually* hear all the things everyone said.

However, she didn't play a seven. Or a yellow. Crap.

I knew that yelling at Veronica wasn't going to work. She did not react well to confrontation. But I didn't really have it in me to be nice or to go into the coming conversation with an overabundance of patience. That wasn't something I had on a good day. "Dang it, Peck," I growled as I fished out a blue two. "I was going to get my hand back."

"Peck?" Dexx asked as he walked past us. He stopped and gave the elf a long, pained look.

I looked up at him and shrugged deeply because *he'd* obviously watched *Willow*.

He rolled his eyes and continued walking toward the sink. "We've got a date to fix this."

Peck didn't have a clue as to what he was even talking about. Her violet eyes were drawn to the adult's game on the other end of the "L."

They were playing some weird card game with munchkins or something? There was screaming involved and monsters and I didn't know what else. They'd invited me, but it'd seemed complicated. With my inability to focus, UNO really was the best I could do.

After Remix and Blaze played several reverses on each other, Necro yawned and scratched her neck, leaving a red mark. "You should go."

Her tone wasn't grumpy in a get-out-of-here kind of

voice. It was peppy like she was trying to be an adult and offer sage advice.

"She's not home yet," I said low enough for her to hear over Blaze and Storm yelling at each other.

Speakeasy slapped the table and gave them an exaggerated would-you-hurry-up look, slapping his other hand to his face and letting it slide down like goo.

The twins ignored him.

Necro let her head fall into her hand as she watched the almost literal fireworks until Pyro finally got the chance to play. "You don't gotta be here."

But being there was nicer than being in an empty treehouse waiting for my Juliet to call up to me. "I'm already pissed."

Necro flattened her lips and nodded as she played on top of Speakeasy's four. "Yeah?"

These kids made it hard for me to remember that I was scared of children. *They* were like people. Smaller, dumber, less-experienced... people.

Maybe Charlie was too. Crap. "Vee's been lying to me."

Necro scratched her head but didn't talk as the play went around the table.

"How do I react to that?"

"You've been going through it." She gestured with her cards, showcasing a nearly red hand.

"I didn't realize you were the telepath."

She rolled her eyes and jutted her head forward in a weird posture that reminded me of a vulture, then brought her head back to her hand. "I live around people. You have that same angry, counting-cards-while-pretending-to-bury-bodies look on your face."

That was a thing a teen girl paid attention to? "Well, it's not going to work."

"Sitting here won't either."

"She's still not home."

Necro looked around, her lips tight again. "And you're not here."

As nice as it was to be in a house that wasn't lonely, the girl was right. With or without Whomper, I needed to go to our treehouse, and I needed to have it out with Veronica. I released a tight sigh and stood, handing my cards over to Blaze who seemed to love a good challenge. "Thanks." I paused as something pushed out of my mouth with a force almost of its own. "Lee."

She gave a sideways smile that said she'd noticed the name drop and liked it, but she didn't look up at me as I left.

Which was good. It kept things from getting awkward.

I took my time walking from the house to the treehouse in the woods out back. The sun had set hours ago. My feet made pleasant swishing sounds in the leaves as I pulled out my flashlight I'd learned to carry with me since our phones might not always work anymore, and lit my way to the back.

What was I going to say to Veronica? How would I get her to realize I needed to know? Or that whatever was going on had to stop?

But the thing that really irked me was that I was somehow behind this? I somehow knew about this and was okay with the mind-blockers? Why would I do that? I knew me. I knew that knowing that would drive me nuts. I knew that I would pick at things that didn't make sense until …

Until I confronted her and they were removed.

How many times had we danced this dance?

That comment actually made me feel better. The nerves running through my system subsided and left only a dull ache as if knowing what was to come.

By the time I made it to the tree house, I was feeling a bit like my old self again. I mean, at least I wasn't coming out of my skin or anything.

I found Whomper tied up in the corner, a red scarf or something wrapped around his handle, tying him to the bedpost.

Veronica paused at the closet, a sad look in her eyes, her hands filled with her clothes as she moved to fill her bag. She went to the bed and set the clothes down, then ran a hand over her thick hair. "Hey."

Just hey. Nothing more.

What... Like, what was I supposed to say to that?

Veronica let her hands fall to her thighs and she sat down on the bed, biting her lips, her eyebrows raised as if in question.

Was she asking me if I realized my memories were being blocked? I didn't know, so I just nodded and shoved my fingers in my pockets.

She looked away with an expression that said, "Well, shit." But the way she said it which I couldn't repeat as I'm pretty certain it wasn't even in English.

I didn't know what else to say, so I went to Whomper and freed my broom.

And waited.

Whomper twisted between me and Veronica and then launched himself off the balcony and flew away, probably to go find the kids.

"Well - *sac a maam*." She sighed heavily and then gestured to me. "*Gris-gris*."

A flood of information overwhelmed me. Of arriving in New Orleans after coming back from Germany. Of meeting her on the streets and immediately getting into an argument because her karma was off the charts. Of her getting in a dust up with a demon. Of me saving her for who knew what reason. Of her telling me of the demon deal she had with Valfire. Of the fact he owned her soul and the souls of the other witches in Mama Gee's circle, and how he was going to turn them all into demons on their deaths.

And then of the conversation with her and Mama Gee as they tried to get me to agree to help them destroy Valfire. And to capture Threknal.

And how I had to tell them that my real power came from karma, not me. About how I wouldn't be any good to them as this person.

And then remembering what I'd done with Charlie, how by sacrificing her and then protecting her, I'd been able to use karma to protect her and catch my demon, stopping the blood-letting in Palmer.

I'd been the one to come up with the plan to trick me into loving her. I was the reason for the memory wipes. I was the reason for us running the shop—and I remembered why Lillianne kept glaring at me. It'd been my idea to take her shop from her and to run it with Veronica because... it'd always been the thing I'd wanted to do. I longed to return home and help Aunt Gertie run hers.

Veronica hung her head in defeat.

I also knew why. We only had one more memory blocker left. "Well, I can help with Threknal now."

She nodded, gripping the bed and looking away.

She loved me. She truly loved me. She had to in order for our ruse to work.

But because of the ruse, the karmic witch in me couldn't trust the love we had.

She gave me a sad smile and stood, gathering her clothes and putting them in the bag. "I've got another place I can sleep."

I didn't move to stop her. We'd done this three times before. We'd already tried fighting this, tried making it work for real, tried... everything. Until the memory blockers came back, we weren't great together and we certainly weren't girl-friends.

She left, gripping my shoulder with her lithe fingers. "We'll make it work."

She wasn't talking about us.

She was talking about destroying Valfire.

And that just set the karmic witch in me off even more.

12

P aige turned to the war council and listened. They had their Declaration of Sanctuary, making the ParaWest states safe for any who felt that the United States wasn't treating them fairly. Originally, it'd started off as paranormals, and there were quite a few who stuck with the idea that only paranormals should be included in their declaration.

But the conversation she'd had with President Walton had stuck with her. He'd *wanted* her to follow the same path as the people before her were *still fighting* for equal rights, equal pay, and fair treatment. He'd *wanted* her to back down because his society had already successfully repressed those before her.

She realized that the *reason* they hadn't gone to war was because *they* didn't have armies. They didn't have *enough* people willing to take up arms to defend them. Paranormals did, but mostly because they already came with claws and teeth. Their loved ones had been forced to accept them for who they were, or they were left behind no questions asked.

Not everyone was that lucky.

What Paige had to determine was the timing of it.

She had an ace up her sleeve she hadn't told anyone else about. She still wasn't certain it would happen, that the generals would show up. She hoped they would, but she couldn't start a war on hope.

Everyone else in the room was fighting over the best way to proceed, in getting people out of the unsafe states past the sanctuary boundary. There were a lot of moving pieces, parts that had to be thought out and then rethought out.

She wasn't certain they were getting all the kinks worked out of their plans, but she was tired of planning. There was only so much any of them could do. They needed to act.

Dawn stepped through the door to the war room and General Tall and General Female followed.

A hush fell over the room.

"Ladies and gentlemen," President Flynn said, straightening her shoulders and clenching her fists at her sides, "Generals McCormick and Saul are here to provide advice for the near future."

Paige couldn't ignore the wave of relief that washed over her just seeing them. "Are you with us?"

General Saul glanced up at General McCormick who dwarfed her slightly.

He shook his head and took in a deep breath that raised his wide and beefy shoulders. "I need to see just how serious you are."

"Are you on our side?" Dexx asked, puffing up a little.

Paige didn't need her alpha man turning this general away when they needed him.

General McCormick raised a hand, his expression tight and grim. "I serve the people of the United States."

"Which ones?" Dexx asked, his own green eyes narrowing as he rose to his feet.

General McCormick turned on Dexx, not backing down, but not being an alpha about it either. "All of them."

This was one reason they needed generals. Alphas were great leaders of their packs, but generals had to be able to lead everyone, no matter their attitude-size. Paige had a lot of people with big attitudes. "Let's bring them up to speed."

With a little hesitation, the people in the room shared where they were and what they were doing. It was repeat information for Paige, but hearing it again made her feel better, like double and triple checking a list before heading into Black Friday shopping.

By the time everyone was done, General Saul folded her arms over her chest and looked at Paige out of the corner of her eye. "What are you waiting for?"

General McCormick raised his chin and lowered an eyebrow so low, his eyelid lowered. "Are you waiting for a gilded invitation?"

Maybe, but when he said it like that... "He can still provide a solution."

General McCormick shook his head. "That's not likely. But if you're waiting for President Walton to do something that will incite you into war, you'll be waiting a long time. Other presidents might have been goaded into that kind of action, but he won't be."

Dawn flinched slightly at the verbal slap in the face, but otherwise didn't react.

"He's not going to make this easy on you. He's going to use the law and precedent to guide him."

Paige pressed her fingertips to her forehead, pushing back her growing headache. "So, you're telling me to go to war."

"You have justifiable reason," General Saul said, shaking her head as if not believing she was saying her words out loud. "You've got proof he's not treating his citizens equally. And you're offering sanctuary to all those who need equal rights and don't have them." She released a long breath, closing her eyes.

"We have our declaration ready to be submitted."

General McCormick's beefy shoulders moved minutely as he glared at their whiteboard. "Then be ready for his immediate response. He won't allow states under his federal rule to provide sanctuary his laws purposefully oppose."

Paige swallowed. She'd needed to hear that from someone who actually knew what they were doing. "Are you with us?"

He thought about that for a long moment, then shook his head. "I'm not against you, but I serve the United States." He looked down at General Saul.

She looked around the room for a long moment without answering.

The leaders in this room seemed to understand the weight of what was going on inside her head. They kept their mouths shut but were unafraid to meet her gaze.

Finally, she met Paige's gaze. "You need someone who understands militaries and strategies."

Did she ever. "Yes."

General Saul squeezed her arms over her chest and studied the board. "You have armed militias."

Paige'd had to do some research into how the United States had started. She was pretty certain that she'd slept through those classes when she was a kid. So, she understood that militias were regular citizens willing to stand up and fight. That was definitely something she had. "Yes." What she didn't have were fighter jets and bombs and she was afraid of Walton using those on her forces.

"Significant enough, do you think, that you could withstand a ground attack?"

They *had* withstood one in the elven city and then again in Lawrence. And they'd done that woefully unprepared. "Yes."

General Saul gave her a dead-eyed look. "Against an air strike?"

Paige shook her head. "But I'm sure we could... figure something out." And they had been working on it. With their shields and the flying paranormals. Also, there were dryad classes who could control vines or something and pull planes and helicopters to the ground. They still didn't have an answer to an actual bomb.

But they had the ability to respond in force with their magick. Paige could use door magick, get to a specific location, and release a magick kind of bomb that would do effectively the same amount of damage.

The female general blinked and then flicked an eyebrow up, glancing at General McCormick. "I'm staying."

Paige didn't want her to overthink her decision. "We can have your family moved here within the hour."

General Saul nodded. "This isn't going to be easy."

"We never thought it would be. We simply believe equality is something worth *fighting* for."

The female general released a long, hard breath. "Same. Same. We have a lot to discuss. If you will excuse us."

Paige and the rest remained quiet as the two generals left. As soon as the doors were closed, she turned to Ishmail. "When her family is secured, send President Walton our Declaration of Sanctuary."

He nodded and left the room as everyone else exploded, each moving forward with their part of the plan.

If this didn't go well, if they lost this war, things would be bad.

But not fighting would be just as bad. That's how she knew what they were doing was right.

Sitting in that war council made me feel weird. Not gonna lie. Here, I was just some karmic witch from the bush and all these people were so much bigger than me. I sat next to the alpha of North America. That woman had power just radiating off her.

Also, she really smelled like a cat.

And she kept talking to something near me and asked me if "it belonged" to me. I had no idea what she was talking about because Whomper was properly ensconced with the kids tracking down the other stones and the symbols on them, and keeping an eye on Threknal, making sure he didn't get too close to... well, anything important. They hadn't given the cameras over to Lovejoy because they *knew* she'd take them away from the kids and this was seriously too much fun for them.

But being on that council, understanding what we were doing by sending that declaration, I fully understood that my anger over Veronica—and myself—and my obsession with figuring out what she was doing wasn't helping anyone. So, I decided to put on my big girl panties and get the heck over it.

Of course, saying that inside my head and making the actions necessary to actually *do* that? Yeah. Not... really the same. But I gave it a solid effort.

I stayed behind as everyone trickled out. Not because I was special or anything, but I hadn't had an opportunity to tell Paige about the stones yet. That they were tied into the ley lines *had* to be important. The alternate energy guys hadn't been able to do anything with it yet, but maybe Paige could. Having magickal energy when going to war? Yeah. That was like saying we had nukes.

She finished speaking with someone who smelled like dirt and turned to me with a smile. "Wy."

I waved and stepped up. "We found something you might be interested in."

As I filled her in on the massive stone buried beneath the town and the stone fingers rising up from it, the symbols, the protections, and the ties to the ley lines, her dark eyes narrowed further, but her interest blossomed. "So, what do you think?"

The doubt warring inside me had nothing to do with whether I was right or wrong, but how we could use it. "Ley line magick."

Her dark gaze landed on mine. "DoDO uses that."

I nodded. I hadn't *known* that before I'd arrived here. The only thing I really knew was that some witches could *feel* the ley line energies, would gravitate to the nodes, and would tap into the powers there. Was it ley line? I'd thought so before, but after talking to Paige, I had to guess the answer was no. So, the ley lines must power other things as well.

Like the world around them. If these— "If these are the powerlines of the earth, if they're veins or whatever for other things...like, uh, I don't know, plants or—" I literally had no idea how other witches worked magick when they didn't have karma to pull from. "Yeah, uh, whatever, they're here for a reason. Can we tap into these somehow?"

Paige's gaze was still on me, but it wasn't focused. "I'll look into it."

"Okay." Great. The woman who had everything else to do was going to look into this one too. "The kids and I are going to continue our research to see what else we can come up with."

"That sounds good." She shook her head, dropping her gaze and flicking it back up again. "Anything... else?"

Nope. Not that I wanted to talk about. "I have my memories back." Why was I telling her this? "We're tracking down a pretty nasty demon who collects witch souls. We're trying to find a way to end him."

145

"Who is it? I'm the demon summoner. I might be able to help."

She could. "We came up with this plan before we knew you, so, yeah. Sure. The demon with her soul is Valfire." It couldn't hurt, could it?

"The kids are safe?"

They sure were. "Staying super focused on these stones."

"Well, that might be for the best. Are you going to help Veronica on her search?"

"Not until you give me information." I was still angry. I didn't know how I could be suckered into helping like this. I remembered all the times I'd be angry with her and then she'd get close and talk to me and then I'd suddenly *not* be angry with her. Was she manipulating me?

"I'll let you know what I find." She turned away in a clear dismissal.

I left and checked my phone. It was November fourteenth already. How had it—

I stopped in my tracks in the middle of the lounge of Paige's office building and stared at that date.

The fourteenth of November.

My sister's birthday.

Shit.

"Hey," Naomi said with a smile and a cup. "Latte?"

She was *still* on about the milk frother, though the craze over it had died down a bit. I took it with a smile of thanks and ducked out the front door, queuing up Evie's contact. When I was in the driveway and headed toward the entrance away from the house, I veered toward the surrounding woods and hit the call button.

She didn't answer and sent a message instead saying she was busy.

Of course she was. She was Evie freaking Hunt. She was a

busy, successful lawyer. She had a life and she probably had a ton of people wishing her a happy birthday.

I was getting ready to stash my phone in my back pocket when a video call chime came through.

Frowning, I looked to discover it was Evie calling me on Google Duo. I answered and turned on my video, waiting for the connection to sync. I wasn't sure I'd have enough bars out here to keep a good video connection, especially now with everything going on, but it seemed stable enough. "Hey, Ev."

She raised her head and gave me a look that said she wasn't sure why I'd called, her side-ways lip-crinkle raising her thick-rimmed glasses. Her dark hair was piled up neatly at the back of her head. "Hey."

Just get it over with. "I just called to wish you a happy birthday."

She nodded. "Okay."

"And, uh, to say sorry. I forgot to get you anything." There was a war going on.

"Everything's crazy right now. I get it."

Her tone said she did. "Yeah. Okay. Good. Uh, how are things?"

She narrowed her blue eyes and bit down on her overly full bottom lip. "What do you want, Wy?"

I didn't know. "To wish you a happy birthday."

"Okay. Got that. You don't need to hold on for anything else."

I *really* didn't have a good relationship with my sister. We were basically strangers, and it was totally my fault. I considered hanging up, but I realized I didn't *want* to. "How are things up there?"

"They're fine, Wynonna," she said, her tone ringing with frustration.

"Look, I get that you're pissed at me."

"Pissed?"

"And I'm not saying it's not due. Like, I get it. Seriously, I do. But with everything going on, I just…" Had a hole in my heart where my sister belonged. "I miss you."

"Really?" She looked at something beyond the screen and shook her head. "What part? What part about me do you miss? Because I was a kid when you left."

She wasn't telling me anything I didn't already know. "How's the Butte?" I knew that'd be a good conversation changer. It worked nearly every time.

"It's a hill," she said derisively. "Look, I've gotta go. There's—"

"Are you guys safe?" I blurted out. "Do you guys need—" Me? "—anything?"

Evie's expression folded in disbelief. "You really think we need you now after everything?"

Yes. "No."

"We made it this far without you. Just keep running, Wynonna. We're fine on our own."

"Is that Wy?" Aunt Gertie's voice called.

Evie rolled her eyes and jutted out her jaw before plastering on a smile and calling out, "Yeah. Did you want to talk to her?"

Something else was said, and then Evie got up, taking the phone with her.

"Ev," I called. "Just promise me that if anything goes down up there, you'll call me."

"Probably not," Evie said, glancing down at me from where she held me in her hand. She walked along the hallway that overlooked the kitchen and descended the stairs. "We're okay on our own."

"Hey, baby," a woman said and then the underside of boobs in a blue shirt filled the screen and I heard a kiss. "You okay?"

The picture jiggled in a way that could have made a person with a queasier stomach churn. And then a face filled the screen of a woman about Evie's age. She had the broad nose and pronounced cheek bones, skin tone, and dark eyes of someone with Indian descent. She beamed a smile into the phone. "Wynonna," she said in a tone that said she was actually happy to see me, "I've heard so much about you."

If she was calling me by my full name, I doubted it was good. "Oh. Thanks."

She chuckled and took the phone, holding it about chin level as she took the two steps into the living room. "I'm Bella, Evie's fiancé."

Oh. Well, just how out of the loop was I? "Congratulations."

She gave me a dimpled smile. "Thank you." She stopped next to the sofa I couldn't see but could tell judging by the exposed wooden beams of the white ceiling I could see. "When are you coming up?"

"Well, with everything going on right now? I don't know."

"Yeah. Flights have been canceled everywhere."

"I happen to know someone with door magick."

"Really," she said, her eyes expressive. "Then you *have* to come up here."

Oh. Really? "I will."

"Great. We'll be here and so excited to see you. Hey, here's Gert. You look great."

"Yeah," I said as the picture whizzed by and I was handed off. "You, too."

Aunt Gertie's aged yet gorgeous face filled the screen. She bit her bottom thin lip and tipped her head to the side. "Hey, you."

I couldn't help it. I melted a little. That woman was the

only mother I'd ever known, and I missed the crap out of her. "Hey, back."

"I love you."

My heart swelled with emotion. "I love you more," I said around tears.

"Things bad?"

I shook my head. "No. I was fine until I heard your voice." I closed my eyes to keep the tears in. They served no purpose.

"I miss you too."

I missed how she just *got* me. I opened my eyes and sniffled, shoving the tears aside. "I just wanted to see how things were going."

"They're fine here. For now. But..." Gertie looked toward the fireplace that sat in the corner—the only way I knew that was because that'd been the front room I'd grown up in. I could practically see it in my head. "Things are getting scary."

"Yeah. I know. I'm in Troutdale with Paige Whiskey now and it's... everything's so real here."

"You're with—" She stopped herself and shook her head. "Well, then." She closed her blue eyes for a moment and opened them. "Are you being safe?"

I nodded. "I should go. I just..." I couldn't finish that sentence.

"I know, boo," she said with a sad sigh. "It's been quiet up here. Still. It might be safe."

She was talking about the monster I'd unleashed, not the coming war. "Maybe." I still didn't quite know what'd I'd unleashed. "But she's not."

Gertie bit her lips and then rolled them out as she thought about that. "She wasn't. Things've changed now. You've changed."

I had. But was it enough? "What I did can't be forgiven."

"Then don't ask for forgiveness."

I didn't know if I could do that. "I love you."

"I love you more," she said, kissing her fingertips and pressing them to the screen.

"I don't know how," I said as emotion forced its way into my throat and then I ended the phone call before either of us could say good-bye.

I clutched the phone to my chest, hugging her image and keeping it fresh for as long as I could.

After all this, I needed to go home. With or without Veronica.

13

The next day, Paige caught Dexx in the kitchen on his way out to work. She wasn't sure what he was doing all day, but she did know he was busy. "How's Leslie?"

He shrugged. "That griffin is a problem."

That wasn't exactly what Paige wanted to hear.

"She's a medium. Sometimes, you guys need her to do ghosty things and if they're going to use ghosts to attack us, we need her in our arsenal. But all we got is a witch who knows *how* to talk to ghosts and can't because her animal spirit is a damned scardy cat?" He rolled his eyes, expelling a long breath.

They had to have a better answer to the ghost attack. There had to be other mediums out there. Other... death talkers? Reapers? She'd mention it to Lovejoy and see what she could do, though, knowing her and General Saul, they were already working on something. "How's she doing otherwise?"

"Fine." He rubbed his head. "She's very Leslie."

Which said a lot. "I need your opinion."

He returned to methodically reaching into various cabinets, pulling out what he needed for a drink and breakfast. His drink comprised of juice which he was drinking from a travel mug, and breakfast was five oranges and a bowl of a sugary cereal with more sugar added to it. "What's up?"

How did that man keep his able-bodied figure? His shifter. "I want the bite." She pulled back, surprised she'd blurted that out loud because that was absolutely *not* what she'd been *about* to say.

He paused in pouring his milk and looked at her. "As in *the* bite?" He made a non-sexy sexy face. "Or a bite... bite?" His brow furrowed as he bared his teeth.

That man. "I want my shifter back."

"And the power that comes with it, I suppose."

Yeah. Maybe. "I don't know." Having that much power still kind of scared her. She was... powerful enough as it was but planning a *war* and *not* being at full power felt like preparing for a hurricane by going to the beach with an umbrella.

He set the milk jug on the counter and turned to her, leaning on one hand. "You're sure? What if I'm not?"

Why was he hesitating now? "I thought you were okay with this."

He shrugged. "And I thought you weren't. So, I've been thinking about it and the more I think about it the more concerned I get."

Well, that was seriously unhelpful. "We're going to war."

"Right." He bugged his eyes out, an opened-mouth serious expression on his lips. "And you're the one who keeps going on about balance. I don't know. I listen."

Did he though?

"What's to say you being..." He gestured to her with his free hand and resituated against the counter, crossing his arms over his chest. "You know. Maybe you're the reason we're going to war." His green eyes lit with a light of dawning realization as his face folded in horror. He looked at her. "Nuh-uh. Right?"

Maybe. The laws of balance said that when one thing got too big, something equal and opposite rose to balance it. "We should think about it more."

He shook his head and pushed off the counter, unfurling his arms. "Babe, you want the bite, I'll bite you."

No. He was right. She reached up and pecked a kiss on his cheek. "Love you."

"I know." He kissed her back and pulled away with a frown.

Paige didn't give him a chance to talk more about it. She made the rounds, kissing all of her kids for the day, which took about thirty minutes. They were still going to school, but transportation was a lot different now. Most of their kids just shifted and carried those who couldn't. However, who knew where they slept each night because it wasn't in the same spot every time.

She finally made it to the front door and was greeted by her big brother who wore his now normal trench coat and rings. "You do realize where we're going, right?"

He shrugged. "If Harry can make this cool, so can I."

She appreciated a good Harry Dresden reference like anyone else. Was he based on a real character? Would she ever know? Anyway. "I can get us there."

"I can get us back," Derek said with a grimace. "I hate this idea."

She didn't particularly like it either, but Dawn wasn't kidding when she'd said they needed armies. Parawest didn't have airplanes or missiles or ships—why would they need ships? Paige didn't know.

But they did have access to demons.

So, she reached within her, to the heart of her magick,

and letting her own energy radiate through her, down her arms, powering her hands and then extending out in a shadow-form. Teal magick laced through the inky black hands of her magick as she wove and then opened a ragged door, thinking of their location.

As the demon summoner, she had a connection to Hell few others had. It'd been seared into her bones until Cawli had sacrificed himself to save her. Her gut twisted at that, but she pushed that aside and moved forward, fighting the connection to Hell. After they'd defeated Sven and revealed themselves to the world, they'd only just barely managed to keep Earth, Hell, and Heaven connected. The gates themselves had been distanced, making it harder for demons to show up unexpectantly. It had affected angels a little differently, making them weaker.

When Paige sent demon souls back to hell, she opened a door and shoved them through, not really caring what happened to them.

But this was different. The portal she created had to be stable enough for two very physical forms to step through.

And what would happen when their physical bodies landed on the other side? Hell was a mystical place.

Or was it? The Vaada Bhoomi, the land of the spirit animals, wasn't as mystical as it was purported to be. Dexx and Rainbow had *been* over there for weeks with a very physical and real Hattie.

Paige had to admit that there was a lot she didn't understand about the universe.

Without a demon to send back, she didn't exactly have a location in mind when she opened the portal, so she wasn't sure where she was even going. But she had her intent. She wanted to talk to someone about gathering armies she could use to protect the people of ParaWest. After that, she just had to hope for the best.

So, she did what she could, calling on the beacon of Hell. Her gate rippled around the edges and wavered as if they were looking at a vertical pool of jet-black water. When the darkness faded away, a lush, green hillside beckoned.

Derek glanced at her out of the corner of his eye. "That's... Hell?"

She had no idea what she was looking at. "*The Bible* is a story?" She had no idea.

"It's not the only one that refers to Hell as fire and brimstone."

True. "Maybe they have a fiery desert area. I don't know." Also, how did the authors of *The Bible* even know what it was like? She gestured for him to lead the way through the door she'd made and then stepped through herself.

It felt like they'd stepped into the *Lord of the Rings,* which, she guessed meant it felt like stepping onto New Zealand. There were some sharp mountains to their left, rolling hills to their right. The tall grass was mostly green, though was tipped with yellow. There were a few flowers she didn't recognize, a few colors she couldn't place a name to. Something buzzed around her ear and she swatted it at.

The thing caught hold of her finger and stuck.

She had a moment of panic that only tiny bugs can give a person and then she calmed herself. She was on a different... planet? Dimension? She didn't know how Hell even worked. She scanned the sky for the sun, but there was a fine sheen of clouds in the relatively bright sky.

The thing on her finger squeezed.

She looked down, ready to squash the bug.

Only to find that it was a tiny demon-type creature about the size of a rather large horse fly. It had wings but was otherwise humanoid, though its hands and feet had grippers like a fly.

Dust rose on the horizon to her right and came toward them.

"Paige," Derrick said cautiously, stepping forward.

She didn't want to crush the bug demon just in case it was a terrible idea, but she also didn't want to wear it anymore. She brought her hand to eye-level and flicked the bug demon.

It went flying off and twisted around looking like a demented, angry pixie.

Wait. Paige looked around again, but this time tried to put her finger on what was familiar. This place *felt* familiar, like she'd been here before. But maybe not because it reminded her of landscapes she'd seen in movies.

This reminded her vaguely of Underhill.

Was this... where elves lived too? Was that... possible? After all, the myths said that elves lived below earth and that Hell resided in the bowels of earth.

Yeah. It was possible.

Derek flicked his trench coat and ran a hand along his longish, curly blonde hair. "Trouble do you think?"

"Probably." But she wasn't going to get herself too excited. "If it's more than we can handle, open a gate and get us home."

She didn't see him nod but was greeted with silence.

The bug demon darted away as the dust cloud made it to them.

The dust, it turned, out was a cloud of some sort and three demons stepped out as if it was a carriage. One had hooved feet and horns, but the other two were simply humanoid with grey skin and pointed ears.

The horned one raised his bearded chin. "Speak, demon summoner. Why do you invade our lands?"

Funny. Demons were the ones who invaded Earth all the

time, and *they* were angry humans had finally paid them back. "I need to speak to a leader. I have a proposition."

The horned demon narrowed his horizontally slitted amber gaze. "I am Ez'gizol, shepherd of these lands."

Uh. Okay. "Do you have a demon king?"

Ez'gizol gave her a frank look. "I will relay your message."

This was the best time to ask because she didn't know if she'd get a better one. "Is it really Lucifer?"

Ez'gizol narrowed his eyes. "Do you have a message?"

There was so much about Hell she didn't know. "We're headed to war in the United States."

"I am aware." Ez'gizol folded his long-fingered hands in front of him and gave a wide-legged stance.

Really. With the gates being further away from Earth, it seemed like it'd be pretty hard to be able to keep tabs on what humans were doing. "I want to know if you'd be willing to ally with us."

"Ally?" His tone made her feel stupid for asking. "With you?"

"Yes." She wasn't being stupid. She was being realistic. They needed an upper hand. She *couldn't* get airplanes or ships or armies with machine guns. But she could get something that might be better.

"What method of payment do you think would suffice?"

Paige had no idea what to even offer. "What do you want?"

He blinked in surprise.

If the description of this place was wrong— She also remembered when she'd stranded several DoDO agents in this realm and how they'd been returned *with* their souls. Okay, so if they had all of that wrong about demons, chances were good that Paige had no idea what they'd even want. "We're not resource rich, but..." She shrugged. "Let me know what you want and what you could offer and I will discuss it with my people."

"You are not their leader?"

"I am, but it's not a dictatorship. It's a democracy." Without any official democratic voting power, though they were working on that. "Give me your terms when you can, and I will determine if it's something we can agree to."

"And our messenger will not be attacked when he arrives?"

Paige shook her head and remembered the other reason she was there. But that brought up another interesting issue. "Can you get demons through after what we did with the gates?"

He studied her for a long moment. "What you did offered us protection."

Wait. "What?"

He pursed his purple-tinged lips and looked away. "Does this look anything like the Hell of your stories?"

It didn't.

He nodded. "We are at war with the creatures you call angels. They use your world to gain access to ours. With the gates distanced as you did, you kept the angels further removed."

"So…" They were grateful for what she'd done? Couldn't get through as effectively? What was the deal with all the demon possessions then? Things weren't entirely adding up.

"We owe you a grave debt."

"Okay." She could work with that, but… "I have questions."

"I'm sure you do." He shook his head and licked his lips with a violet tongue. "I am not at liberty to give you any more information than that."

"And if we become allies?" *If* that was a good idea.

"I believe you will find that our world is much more complicated than you were led to believe."

"In what way?" Though she had a feeling. They'd been led to believe Hell was a storage bin for souls for a hoarder who wanted to keep all the people who'd done bad things. She realized that part of that had to do with the *Bible* which was used to instruct children on how to be good, and like all good fairytales, there had to be boogeymen. She also understood that this particular fairytale was used to also gain excessive power across entire nations, so that boogeyman had to be massive. It had to be more than a witch with a wart and a single tower.

A nation of demons hoarding millions of souls was something men seeking power over the living millions could use as an incentive to manipulate people to a single banner.

Ez'gizol gestured his hand long-fingered hand to the landscape. "This is an entire world."

Which only added to the pieces she was putting together. These demons could have different species—like the bug—and different countries, governments, rulers, leaders, religions. Which meant she needed to learn who she was making bargains with. "Is Lucifer even a thing down here?"

"Of course."

Well, at least there was that. Was he as big of a deal down — No. She couldn't claim this was "down" anywhere. They weren't in the bowels of their earth. This place had a sun even though she couldn't see it. Maybe there was more information she could glean while she was here. After all, Ez'gozol "owed" her for what she'd done to move the gates between their two worlds. "What do you know of a demon named Valfire?"

Ez'gizol's expression clouded and he growled, looking away in a clear refusal to say anything else.

Paige had no idea what that meant. What kind of politics

were they even stepping into? Nothing in *The Bible* had prepared her for this. "Okay. What about Threknal?"

Ez'gizol twisted his upper lip and spat.

"Good to know. Thanks." She looked at Derek and gestured to him to open a door. "It's okay to leave?"

The horned demon bowed his head. "You were well-met, Summoner Whiskey."

She clasped her hands in front of her and bowed her head, mimicking him the best she could. "As were you, Demon Ez'gizol."

Amusement softened his lips.

But before he could say anything, Paige turned and left. Asking the demons for help had seemed like a good idea at the time when she'd thought she understood what their realm was about. But now?

She hoped she wasn't heaping more trouble on them than they could afford.

I stared at Paige like she'd lost her mind later that afternoon. "You want me to what?"

"Go to Alaska and talk to the people there, see if they could be talked into joining us." Paige sank into her leather chair as if she'd had a harrowing day already. "Because they haven't committed after we issued our Declaration of Sanctuary."

Her tone said there was more to it than that. "You need the State of Alaska and you think sending me up there is going to bring them in?"

She shrugged and closed her eyes.

"We don't all know one another. It's a really big place, you know."

"I'm aware, Wy." Paige opened her eyes and leaned

forward, folding her hands on top of her empty desk. "But I also know it's a *small world* up there. Lots of land? Sure. Lots of people? According the to the census, no."

A large portion of the people there hadn't filled out the census because prying eyes didn't need to know their business.

"Look," Paige said, opening one hand, "there's a bunch of shifters up there. I know that. The wood witches are up there. I know that, too. I also know the people I need are the people who were born there and won't talk to someone like me."

An outsider. Well, she certainly understood the Alaskan mentality. "Okay, but what do you want me to do?"

"Talk to people." She shrugged. "See what you hear. See what people are saying or thinking."

"Go to Freddy's and listen to what they're saying in the cereal aisle?"

Paige shook her head. "If that's a thing, sure."

Well, it kinda was. People gathered at church or Fred Meyers to gossip when big things happened. But I *could*, in theory, talk to Gertie and see what she might be able to scramble together. I didn't know hardly anyone. But Aunt Gertie had been an Alaskan witch since she was born. "When do you want me to leave?"

"Leah said she wanted to take you and she's ready after school."

Things happened so fast around Paige. "When are we leaving?"

Paige gave me a look that asked how she was supposed to know. "Ask Lee." And then she gave me that look that said I was dismissed.

It didn't take me long to find Leah—Necro. She came bouncing down the stairs from the bedroom level, a backpack thrown over her shoulder, her blonde hair done up in a braid. "You ready?"

"I just got the orders. Just need to grab my stuff."

Necro shrugged and pulled the corners of her mouth down and finished hopping down the stairs. "I'm gonna grab something to eat. Meet me here when you're done?"

"How long are we going?"

Necro led the way to the kitchen. "Until you're done, I guess. But I have a math final on Friday, so maybe before then."

I had three days, then. Great.

I made quick work of going to my treehouse and gathering a quick bag and my broom. I stopped myself as I wrote a note to Veronica, letting her know where I was. I didn't owe her information. I didn't understand the affect she had on me, but until I got to the bottom of that, I needed to keep my distance from her. That included not telling her where I was. Instead, I grabbed the winter-est gear I had, which wasn't a lot. I'd come up from New Orleans before it'd gotten cold, so I hadn't thought to bring snow gear, which I would need in Alaska.

Necro had finished washing her plate and fork by the time I made it through the back door. "You're bringing your cat?" she asked in surprise.

"Why does everyone keep mentioning a cat?" Was I going insane?

Necro's blue eyes went wide and she held up her hands in defense as she moved to retrieve her backpack. "I need a location."

I gave her the address to the house I'd grown up in and she cut open a black-rimmed door that stabilized and popped, the solid lines outlining my Aunt Gertie's front yard.

Necro glared at me. "You didn't tell me it was *snowing*."

I didn't think I'd *had* to. "Destination Alaska, dude. It's November."

The girl nodded as if that didn't mean anything.

Lower Forty-Eighters, man. Rolling my eyes, I stepped into the brisk November, Alaska air.

And really wished I'd packed a coat, even though I didn't even *own* one anymore. It wasn't cold by local standards, but it'd been over a decade since I'd experienced this level of cold.

The front lawn spilled into the massive parking lot in front of the house. The shop was directly in front of me, the two-story house to my left. A full forest of birch blocked the mountain view to my right. The smell of horses and sweet air filled my nostrils, making me completely forget about being cold.

For about three seconds.

I made my way to the front door and knocked before opening it and stepping into the arctic entry.

Necro followed and closed the door behind me.

"Shoes," I said, bending over to ditch my bag and boots. Then, I straightened and opened the inner door, walking into a haven of warmth, walking under Aunt Gertie's homemade broom and into the kitchen.

Aunt Gertie popped her head out of the plant room to my right, making her way into the living room and toward me. "Wynonna. I didn't actually expect you here."

"I know. Hey. I hope it's okay I—"

Gertie waved me off and walked stiffly up the two curved steps to give me a hug. "Been too long, girl."

"I know." Her arms felt so good. I pulled away. "Paige Whiskey sent me."

"Uh-huh." Gertie eyed Necro.

She extended her hand. "Leah Whiskey."

"Ah." Gertie took the girl's hand. "Gertrude Hunt. So, why are you here?"

I took in a deep breath and released it through one cheek, trying to figure out how to phrase this. "She needs people—namely the magickal people of Alaska."

Gertie grunted as if she wasn't surprised and pushed past me to get to the kitchen. "I reckon it's time, then, I guess."

"To what?" What did she know that I didn't?

"To call those fucking witches, that's what."

"Huh?"

Gertie put the kettle on the stove and lit the burner. "You'll see. Well, get a cup. You're in for a long day."

14

Bella came through the sliding glass door into the living room from the backdoor, stomping her feet to kick off the snow. "The chickens are in," she called. "Three eggs. Those ladies need to up their game if they're gonna pay rent this month."

I took a step back so I could see through the door separating the kitchen and living room. "Hey," I said with a wave.

"Holy—" A grin lit her face, making the end of her nose curve down. She paused for, like, half a second and then launched herself at me with long-strides, crossing the wide room in three and a half steps and clearing both the stairs in one small leap. She then wrapped me in long arms, pulling me close to a long and well-curvy body.

She was... comfortable in a my-soul-and-her-soul-could-share-the-same-space kinda way.

She pulled back, cupping my face with both her hands and looking down at me. The woman was tall. "I'm so glad to meet you finally and see your face in real space."

I chuckled mostly because this level of touch with my

sister's fiancè made me feel slightly uncomfortable. "I'm glad to meet you, too."

She crinkled one eye and gave me a tightly wound sideways smile as she moved to the sink, pulling her eggs out of her pockets. "We got a double-yolker."

Oh. Exciting. I thought. I didn't speak chicken. "That's good, right?"

She twisted around and grinned at me. "We've got six of them now. Angel food cake is happening." She nodded once with an oh-yeah-baby look on her face. "Tonight."

"Sweet." I chuckled but stayed out of the kitchen. It was small on a good day. It was u-shaped, but the right-hand leg of the u was under the stairs that led up to the bedrooms, and a small kitchen island filled the space in the middle, making things tight. This wasn't the Whiskey kitchen, that was for sure.

"Probably not," Gertie said at the stove. "We're gonna need compromise cookies."

Bella pulled a face, then turned a brighter smile to me. "How long you staying?"

Gertie pulled down another cup and set it on the counter next to the sink, tightlipped.

"Just long enough to…" Bring world peace? I had no idea, so I shrugged.

Bella's eyes widened and she nodded.

"Is it always this cold in Alaska?" Necro asked.

This house was super warm, just the way Gertie liked it. If I was acclimated, I'd take off my jacket, but I'd spent the better part of a decade in much warmer climates. "We've got Santa's Workshop up here. Reindeer. Real reindeer."

Bella squinched her eyes in amusement. "I think we even have some in the freezer. We could pull some for dinner."

"We will not," Gertie said, slapping the other woman on the arm.

Bella laughed and went to the counter under the stairs to rummage through tea boxes. "Come look what we got and take your pick," she said to Necro and I, gesturing with her head.

I nodded at her but didn't move immediately to step inside. Too many people. Tiny, little space. "So..." I hadn't *actually* thought we'd be able to do anything while we were there. I thought we'd show up, I'd talk awkwardly to some people, we'd pretend like me being back actually meant something, and we'd leave. "How long's this going to take?"

Gertie made a tsking noise and shrugged with one shoulder. "Dave's already on his way in and Billie's bringing Bertie."

Oh, Bertie and Gertie. This'd be great.

"But a few can't fly in because they've shut down even the planes into the villages."

"No, they didn't." Without planes, some of those villages were cut off. "Why would they do that?"

Gertie waved her hand. "Risks or some such. Anyway. We've been getting good at Zoom meetings, but Holly doesn't get great reception in Barrow."

Nothing super great happened in Barrow. It was as far north—almost—as it could get. Not really. But it was the town everyone talked about going dark through the winter.

Because that was a fun story. Every single year.

"Utqiagvik," Bella said.

"Bless you." I'd grown up around here, so I knew it was probably some native word, but I had no idea what it was or what it was in reference to.

"It's been Barrow since I was a kid," Gertie grumbled. "It's gonna take me a minute to remember the name change." The kettle whistled.

When did towns just change names? "Anyway," I said, getting back to the subject. "Can't get in or out?"

168

Gertie nodded, setting the kettle on the wood cutting board and waving for Necro to join her while also flicking her hand toward the tea.

"You really think we can…" I didn't even know what. "Paige just needs allies."

"Of course she does," Gertie said, taking her steaming mug and walking toward the small dinner table along the artic entry wall. "She's not dumb."

I shook my head, not sure how to respond to that. "Necro, you think you could retrieve a few people?"

"That depends," she said dumping a packet of hot cocoa mix in her mug and waiting for her turn at the kettle. "How many coats are you giving me?"

"How'd you bring that girl up here without a coat?"

"How was I supposed to know she didn't understand what 'we're going to Alaska' meant?" I also happened to know it didn't matter because if there was something that could be said for Alaskans, it was that we knew how to come prepared for those who weren't.

Gertie gave me a dirty look as she left her cup on the table and disappeared into the artic entry, leaving the door open and letting all the cold air to waft through under her broom. "Let me see what I can find."

After a few minutes of banter and drink preparation, Necro was ready to battle snow, wearing some of my old snow pants—that hadn't been thrown out—the largest coat we had—that also hadn't been thrown out since Gertie'd been a kid—gloves, boots, hats, and everything else she could want.

Looking like the kid from that Christmas move with the BB gun, Necro huffed, her arms not quite at her sides. "Where am I going?"

Gertie looked at me with a look that said she didn't know what to do next and shook her head.

"The girl's got skills. Just tell her where to go. Address. Landmarks. The color of the house. Sometimes, the name of the person you're sending her to. She's... real good."

With a shrug, Gertie tipped her head to the side and gave the girl the first address then went back to sipping her tea at the kitchen table as Leah disappeared through her doorway. "How long will this take?"

"Depends on the person she's collecting."

The air popped again and Leah stumbled through with a dazed and wild look on her face. She took a step backward as she turned to face the door she'd opened.

A short woman with Galadriel-type hair stepped through, looking every bit as regal as a witch could. "She was expected," the woman said.

"Holly," Gertie said, quirking her lips. "She needs to get the others. I hope you didn't scare her into staying."

"No, I'm good." Necro spun back to Gertie and then to me, her blue eyes wide.

What'd happened out there?

"I'm good. Next?"

Over the course of the next two hours, Necro shuttled three more witches to the house, including Dave who'd been driving down from Fairbanks. His truck was parked in the parking lot beside the house. Just so you know, Fairbanks is a good six hours from our house. On good roads, which, these weren't. She'd somehow found him, flagged him down, and then opened a door for his truck to drive through.

Which... now that I think about it, isn't that big a thing. They'd had to have been doing something like this for a while in Troutdale just for supplies.

Anyway, with the witches assembled, it was time to talk. I wasn't sure what I was supposed to say, but they were all looking at me.

Gertie hadn't been sitting around idly. She'd had me and

Bella cleaning the living room and the plant room for our guests, making a circle of chairs with tables beside each one. The plant room was actually the coldest room in the entire house, but it was two-stories with windows dominating most of the walls. They were all east-facing windows, making it the dumbest plant room in Alaska, but...

The plants didn't seem to care.

She still had the plant stand I'd built her in woodshop, though, good luck seeing it. A huge monstera philodendron filled one corner in a massive pot, the leaves as big as my head. Bigger. If we had to ever sell the house, that plant was staying.

Along with the massive palm tree in the other corner.

Or the vines and vines and vines draped from the plant stand that filled the entire east wall and crept along the string lights that lowered the ceiling and filled the room with a fairy feeling.

It was the coolest—pardon the pun—room I'd ever seen.

Gertie'd also been busy baking her compromise cookies among other things. She knew everyone's likes, dislikes, and allergies and baked accordingly.

There was also a cake in the oven. "Is that for us, too?" I asked, as the pleasant whiff of chocolate hit my nose.

She gave me a stop-being-dumb look. "It's goofy cake. For your sister's birthday."

Bella beamed at her and closed the glass doors closing us into the plant room. "I'll keep an eye on it."

Gertie waved her off and then turned to the circle of witches. And Dave.

I just had to say that because it makes me chuckle. I know I'm a bad, bad witch and a terrible person. Witches come in all shapes and sizes.

And Daves.

"The white witch has reached out to us."

White witch? Look, I realized it'd been a while since I'd moved away from Alaska, but I hadn't realized we'd grown *that* racist.

She gave me a look that said she saw all of that. "She's a ley-witch of healing." Gertie shook her head like I was an idiot.

A ley-witch, huh? Then, maybe those stones we'd found *would* help.

"What does she want exactly?" Dave asked, his socked feet flat on the floor. "We have duties *here* we can't abandon for a war that doesn't affect us."

"Doesn't affect us?" I asked. Okay. So, maybe I *had* forgotten just how remote things were up here. It really did feel like nothing could touch us up here and, you know, typically it didn't. Good and bad. We were the forgotten child in the frozen north. "They're arresting people for being... us."

"There," Dave said emphasizing his word with his hand as if he was soft-karate-chopping the air. "Not here."

"How long do you think it'll take until they come here?" I hadn't *actually* seen a lot of action, but I'd looked people in the eyes who had and that was enough. If *they* thought this was worth the cause when they *understood* what going to war *meant* for the safety of their *kids*, then I couldn't just poopoo this and push it under a rug. "Weeks? Months? Walton's gonna push that act—"

"We're not registering," Bertie said from her wheelchair. "They can't come take our guns. They can't come take our lands. And they ain't gonna find us if we don't want 'em to."

All true and valid points.

"They're the federal government, Ms. Black," Necro said, her voice small. She'd been offered a chair in the circle but had looked like she'd hoped the chair would swallow her. Now, she unfolded from it and sat up straight. "You haven't had them attack you." The girl met Bertie Black's dark eyes from across the circle. "I have."

That killed a lot of the chatter and the posturing.

A haunted look filled Necro's eyes as she looked down. She adjusted her back and perched on the edge of her seat. "I thought I was helping my mom..." She shook her head and shrugged. "...bring kids? To safety? I didn't—" She licked her lips and then bit them.

We waited, glancing at each other, not quite knowing what to expect, but knowing we needed to hear it.

"The elven city? They showed up with guns and were shooting... everyone. The elves were defending with *branches* and *plants*." Necro's voice cracked a little. "My mom was the only thing that kept them safe. Well, many of them. There were—I was walking on dead people. There were so many. And I thought that was bad. Like, really bad. Then, we got word about Lawrence. Mom told me to stay behind, but I went anyway. She needed door magick and I have that. So, I went. And..." Her blue eyes darted back and forth as they filled with tears. "I thought they'd be safe there. We invade other lands, you know. I don't know why, but we do and that's a thing, but *we're* safe. Our people are safe. But..." She shook her head.

I sat back in my chair, seeing a girl where a nickname had once sat. This kid had experience under her belt and that was something I could relate to.

"Then Denver happened. They set off a bomb. *They* set off a bomb. Not terrorists. *They* did. The prison? I saw so much bad stuff there. People collected for trying to leave, for trying to find some place safe."

I watched the faces of those around the circle. This was what they'd needed to hear. I didn't know what they could offer. They were just six witches, but covens could be mighty and that was something I understood.

"But when they attacked our house?" Necro—Leah clenched her jaw. "We nearly died. They killed hundreds of people and attacked us with *ghosts*." Snot bubbled out of her nose and Dave handed her a napkin. She took it and wiped her nose. "And you want to sit here and tell me that you think you're safe because you're up here? You're *not*. We were under wards, probably the best in the world and my brothers and sisters and I nearly died. I—" She closed her eyes and bowed her head before whispering, "We're not safe. None of us."

Gertie took in a deep breath and met Bertie's gaze.

Bertie raised a dark eyebrow and tipped her head to the side. "It's time, then."

"Indeed," Gertie replied.

"May the gods help us."

Dinner was a loud and noisy affair that involved bringing out all the folding tables and chairs so everyone could eat together. Evie joined us, as did Charlie.

I wasn't ready to see that kid.

I see you judging me, but unless you've ever actually had to leave your kid behind to save her life from you, then...

I was a wreck. I wanted to talk to her—but why? To what end? Because she'd come out of my body? She owed me conversation? She didn't.

And what rights did I have on her life? None. We had no bond. Zero. Zilch. Nada.

But from the snippets of conversation I'd been able to hear, she seemed like a pretty cool person and I wanted to get to know that, whether I had a right to get to know her or not.

If she was some stranger? I'd have had no problem just going up to her and talking to her. Okay. I'd have no problem talking to her as long as I was properly armed with a karmic charm I could throw at her if she decided to become uber childlike, you know? I was *working* on my fear of children.

But I was staring at the root cause of that not-so-irrational fear.

And... I was... frozen with it.

Evie just kept glaring even though Bella was being as nice as anyone could be. I didn't know if she was just oblivious to the crap between us, if she didn't know that I was Charlie's crap mother, or if she was doing this on purpose to get us all through dinner with guests.

Afterward, Leah was busy taking everyone home with her door magick.

Evie pinned me in the kitchen with my hands in the sudsy after goofy cake and birthday cards. "When are you leaving?"

I didn't know. My heart quivered and whispered, *Not soon enough,* but I forced my mouth to be cool as a cucumber. "As soon as I have something I can take to Paige."

Evie leaned against the dishwasher—which wasn't working? I'd have to look into that because I could fix things. Not great and not all the time, but I could probably fix this one—and folded her arms over her chest. She'd ditched her business jacket and boots but was still wearing her business skirt and blouse.

That outfit in Alaska? Didn't make much sense, but that woman was born and bred in this weather so if she was comfortable in it, who was I to judge?

"I want you gone before you break her heart."

"I didn't break her heart the first time." I nearly dropped the heavy plate I was washing but managed to catch it before it broke. It just kinda clunked in the stainless-steel tub. "She doesn't even remember me."

"Well, let's leave it that way."

I wasn't going to defend myself. I'd made a crap decision a long time ago. "'Kay. I'll do my best."

Her face folded in consternation. "What are you doing

176

here, Wy?" She unfurled her arms and advanced on me. "Why are you even here?"

What the hell? "You just told me to leave." I put another stack of dishes into the water. We went through a lot when we had people over. Good gods.

"I didn't *mean* it."

Didn't *mean* it? "How the hell was I supposed to know that?"

Her mouth opened and stuck there, mid-forming a word. She closed her eyes but not her mouth and shook her head. "What do you want, Wy?" She sighed and opened her eyes. "Why are you here?"

I glanced over at her and my heart tugged in my chest at what I saw.

An invitation.

Fuck. That hurt. It's not—if you've never made a massively humongous mistake, you'll never understand. I'd spent fourteen years getting comfortable with the fact that I was out with my family, that the woman who'd raised me didn't want me in her house, that my baby sister was glad I was gone. Hell, I hadn't even been told she'd been engaged. Strangers probably knew more about her life than I did.

Seeing that invitation—that pleading look in her blue eyes twisted the knife of guilt in my gut. I couldn't lie to her and I couldn't be flippant with her either. "I don't know," I whispered. My hands stopped moving in the dish water and I turned back to the window over the sink, looking into the witch's shack—grandpa's old office that was falling apart and now *looked* like a witch's shack.

She stood in front the rinse sink, her shoulder nearly touching mine. "Did you even miss us?"

Her voice was so quiet. I put a blanket on the terror running through me. "Yeah."

"You never call."

"I don't have the right."

"Don't have the—" She bowed her head and looked at me with a look that said she didn't understand.

"Ev." I didn't want to admit what I'd done. Just speaking of that monster could invoke him. I didn't know. All I knew was that I'd managed to trap it and that the valley was safe. As long as I stayed away. It was connected to me. Somehow. That's all I *knew*. I didn't want to summon it. I didn't want to awaken it. "I left to protect you. Both of you. Char most of all."

Her brow furrowed as she breathed through her nose.

"But I still left. Okay? That's not something I can ever undo. I'm not asking for forgiveness. I can't. What I did was unforgivable."

"You left your kid."

"Yeah. I know." But only after I'd nearly sacrificed her to save a town.

"When you were a *teen*. That's understandable."

I shook my head.

She straightened. "Wy."

I didn't know if she was saying my name or asking a question. I turned to her, dripping soapy water onto my socked feet. "Please believe me when I say that I did the right thing by leaving."

She nodded, studying me, her eyes narrowed, her lips pinched, struggling to understand, to figure out what to do next.

"But I'm still doing the right thing in staying away."

"No," she whispered, her right eye closing as her lips crumpled. "You're not."

"My karma won't allow—"

"Fuck your karma!"

With her raised tone, someone was going to notice we

were fighting. Would they interfere? "Ev, it ain't—isn't... fuck. Baby girl—"

"You don't get to 'baby girl' me, Wy." She pulled a wooden spoon out of the rinse water and slammed it down on the island with a loud crack. "You don't get to hide in your *karma* magick either. That ship has fucking sailed."

Oh-ho. She wanted to go there, did she? "You want to know what happens when I ignore karma, Ev? Bad things."

"Oh, for fuck's sake." She spun away.

Leah and Charlie crept up the stairs.

Leah's eyes were wide, and her lips were clamped shut as she held out her hands to me and shook her head as if to silently plead for me not to bring her into it.

I wasn't planning on it, but Evie had no idea what it meant to be clobbered with karma, to have it constantly guiding me, dictating what I could or could not do. "Let me tell you what happens when *I* do something that gives a karmic blow-back."

Evie rolled her eyes and yanked the towel off the cabinet door it'd been draped over. "I fucking know how karma works."

Everyone always fucking thought they fucking knew how fucking karma fucking worked. But *no one* understood. "I walk in karma every day. Every single action I take is bathed in it. I can't step out of line or it slaps me back into place. Three-fold."

She opened her mouth, grabbing the plate I'd nearly killed.

I slashed my hand, splattering her with what little water remained on my hand. "Shut up, Evie, and listen." I swallowed hard and rolled my eyes closed. Maybe it was time she understood what'd happened. "When I was in high school, I was dating a guy."

"Yeah. I know." She dried the plate and set it on the counter, ignoring it.

"Yeah, well, Charlie wasn't his."

"Yeah. I know." The look on her face told me to get to the point.

"I—" Fuck. "Did something. We were fighting some bad guy, a sorcerer or something—"

"A bunch of high schoolers were fighting a sorcerer." Her tone dripped with derision.

I let the truth fill my face as I gave her a rather deadpan look.

She gave a dry chuckle and shook her head. "Yeah. Okay. Sure. Why not. So, you and Scooby Doo were fighting ghosts in the van."

She could laugh it off all she liked. "I did a spell. It was supposed to protect everyone, but..." Intent in magick was everything, but when you were a karmic witch, you had no wiggle room. "I lied about what I was doing and why."

She narrowed her eyes and leaned forward. "What?"

"Instead of wanting to protect everyone so they'd be safe, I did it to make Fox like me again, to see me again. He was really mad about Charlie. Understandably. But he didn't even see me anymore. And I wanted him to just... look at me again."

A frown flickered across Evie's brow. "So? Witches do stuff like that all the time."

Yeah. They did. So did *everyone else* on the flipping planet. "I'm karma. What happens to people karmically when they lie?"

She shrugged but a light went on like someone was running up the dimmer dial. "You get slapped."

"Oh, I was slapped." The images hit me as I took in a deep breath and swallowed. "Remember Mrs. Ansley?"

She shook her head.

"She was your tea–"

"Oh my god." Evie's eyes lit with horror and she put a hand over her mouth. "She was murdered. I remember that…" She frowned. "…now."

"Her heart was ripped out of her chest and eaten." I pressed my mostly dry fingertips to my forehead. "She had a boyfriend she'd cheated on and was trying get back together with him."

Evie went still as she connected dots. She shook her head and then shook it again. "No."

It had taken me years to make the connection after I'd left. "And Jess?" I raked my top lip.

Evie's gaze settled on me. "No."

I nodded. "Same thing. She was cheating on her boyfriend. Her heart was ripped out and eaten."

"Wy."

I didn't know what she was saying. Was she asking me a question? Telling me to stop? "Angela Caterson was when I realized what was going on."

Evie breathed, her shoulders rigid. "Charlie's babysitter."

"Yeah."

She met my gaze. "Your karma did that?"

Yes. "Worse. It created a demon."

"And that's why you left."

Mostly. "Yes." She didn't need to know that I'd lured that demon to a cave, using my daughter as the sacrifice. She didn't need to know that I hadn't known for sure if I could kill or conquer that thing, if my daughter would be safe. She didn't need to know that Charlie had nearly died that day, how close she'd come, how barely I'd managed to save her.

"There's more to it," Evie said quietly.

I nodded and dropped my gaze. "I don't *deserve* to be here, Ev."

"You were a *kid*."

I had been, but that wasn't an *excuse* I could use with karma. "When I fuck up, those around me pay the price. That demon—my karma in literal form—was trying to get to you and Char to get at me."

Evie didn't answer for a long moment. She picked up her towel and then reached in the sink and got another plate, setting it in the dishwasher.

I didn't know if she was drying them or putting them in the dishwasher to dry because she was doing both, but when your brain is working its way through stuff, procedure doesn't always follow rules. Sometimes, she dried a dish or even put it away wet. Sometimes, it went in the dishwasher dry. Sometimes wet.

My sister wasn't really in the kitchen with me.

But we managed to get the dishes done. We even cleaned a few we didn't have to, like the kettle. I took the wrought iron racks off the stovetop and wiped that down, the hood, the counters. She rearranged the coffee and the tea under the stairs.

We worked together, putting the kitchen back to rights, working in silence.

But pretty soon, we were done. The kitchen just wasn't dirty enough for a long heart-hurt scrubbing. I mean, we could've started on the fridge, but I'd have to be hurting real damn hard to clean a fridge.

Evie folded the kitchen towel and hung it up. "You're older now."

Was it enough? "I am."

"Wiser."

I snorted.

"Stronger."

"True."

She met my gaze. "You *could* stay."

I didn't know if I wanted to. "I don't know how."

She blinked and her head jerked as if she couldn't believe what she'd heard.

"I haven't settled in one spot…" I took a breath, trying it again. "I'm not the kind of person people keep, Ev."

"Maybe you're trying to be kept by the wrong people."

She didn't understand. "I'm a hard person to be around. Being karma? All the hours of a day, all the days of the week, all the weeks of the—"

She cut me off with a slash of her hand. "Seriously."

She needed to understand *why* making me stay would be a bad idea. "I burn people out. The… I'm a hard person to stand beside."

She took in my appearance.

I might not be wearing my fishnets, but I still rocked some pretty awesome style with my sassy shirt, and I had a chain clipped from the top of my ear to my earlobe.

She met the challenge of my gaze. "I could."

"For how long? Knowing that every single decision you make could have dire karmic consequences."

She rolled her eyes and opened her mouth.

"You're a lawyer, right?"

Her widened eyes said, "Yeah, duh," without her having to say anything.

"And you care about your clients."

She winced. "Most of them?"

"Well, say you've got a client you care about and she's going to get hammered in court because the person you're going up against is slimier than you are. He's dirtier than you. He's more willing to get his hands filthy and break a few laws. Let's say you already know he's a law breaker, but you just don't have the evidence to prove it. So, let's say, to save your client, you plant evidence or tamper with something."

Something shifted across her face. "I wouldn't—"

But as a karmic witch, I *knew* different. I could *taste* it on

183

the air around her like she was bacon cooking in garlic butter.

She went completely still. "What would happen?"

I shook my head. "Who knows? Karma's unpredictable. It depends on your intent, on your honesty." I shrugged. "A bunch of different things."

"I could ruin her life, though, if you're here."

I nodded slowly. "I'm not a person people keep. For a reason."

Evie took in a deep breath and exhaled, turning to leave. With one hand on the handrail and one foot on the step, she looked at me and raised her chin. "I think you're full of shit, Wy. And it's time for you to come home."

I watched her walk up the stairs, letting a wild storm of emotions blow through me and settle.

Aunt Gertie pulled herself up the two steps that led from the living room, her dark eyebrows raised as she shuffled past the kitchen and down the hall that led to the garage and the spare bedroom. "She's not wrong, you know."

"Neither am I." I frowned, wondering where she was going.

"Nope." She gestured down the hall. "Can't do the stairs anymore. Your room's still made up. Whomper's already there. Next time you bring a cat, though, warn us. Charlie's allergic."

"I didn't bring a cat." What was with everyone?

She raised her eyebrows again and pulled her head back in a I'm-not-saying-anything-else kind of way and kept shuffling down the hall.

Well, for better or for worse, I was home.

But was I staying? *Could* I stay?

Paige needed my help—though, how? I didn't know. But I could help her just as well from here as I could down there.

But I'd told Veronica I'd help her with Valfire. I might not fully understand why I'd agreed to that, but I'd committed willingly. I'd see it through.

After that was done, I'd see about coming back. Until then?

Well, there was no sense getting comfortable when I was just going to leave again, was there?

Not really.

Paige stared at the paper in her hand and read the words again.

I, President Walton, do hereby declare your Declaration of Sanctuary to be unconstitutional. Any actions you may take to enforce said declaration will be seen as an act of war and any enforcing parties will be treated as war combatants.

It went on for two more pages.

She set it down on the desk and leaned back in her chair, looking first to Ishmail, then to Lovejoy and Dexx. "We have our war."

Dexx nodded. "About time. I don't like waiting."

"I don't like war."

He gave Paige a look that said he didn't either. "I'd rather be fighting than twiddling my thumbs."

True. They'd already gone through the battle plans, though. They'd quadruple checked all their checklists as best they could.

"Let's get started," Paige said. "We know what to do."

Lovejoy got up and left the room.

General Saul set down her cup and followed without saying a word.

"I bet she's wishing she'd stayed away now," Dexx said.

Ishmail chucked his chin at Paige. "What's my priority?"

"Now that things are about to move, we need to make

sure that people are safe. If they need to leave, we need to get them out and to safety."

"Everything's in place."

"Good. I need you to watch it and ensure it runs smoothly. We're not having what happened... gods. Last month?"

He shook his head, but held up a hand saying it didn't matter.

Time flew when it was standing still and they were busting their butts to get everything done they could. But he was right. That detail *didn't* matter. "We'll fight the war. You make sure people can get to safety."

"On it." He got up and left.

Dexx waited until the door closed and then came around the desk. "You think we got a shot?"

"Nope." But she had to. She couldn't just lead her people to slaughter. "We'll be fine."

He ran his fingers down her arm and lifted her out of the chair. "Of course we will."

The kiss they shared though was filled with hopeful desperation. Neither of them was an idiot. There were no guarantees that any of them would make it out of this alive.

Paige just hoped that what they were doing—what *she* was doing was really the right thing. Because from this moment forward, there was no going back, no do-overs, no second chances.

Just death and punishment.

And extreme prejudice.

They couldn't afford to lose.

16

"Hey," a familiar voice said, sending shivers of pleasure down my spine.

I slammed the refrigerator door shut and spun toward the artic entry door in surprise, my heart tripping over itself. "Fox."

He'd filled out since I'd seen him last. He'd always been tall, but now I'd have to stand on my tiptoes just to give him a kiss, which I wanted to desperately. But I'd left *because* of him, because I'd been so crazy in love with him I'd done stupid things that had gotten four people brutally murdered and had nearly cost my daughter's life, a daughter who should have been his instead was some dumb jock's.

He looked at me like I was sunshine on a rainy day, his brown eyes melting my bones, his light brown skin finding the pale winter light coming through the south-facing window and highlighting a smattering of freckles I'd always found super attractive. His head was shaved, which was new, and I liked it. It highlighted his face.

And he knew how to wear that well. He seriously had a great smile.

"I have a girlfriend," I blurted out. Who was I telling? Me or him?

The light on his face dimmed a bit, but he nodded. "Okay." He shrugged. "It's still good to see you."

Same. Same, same, same, saaaaame. But I seriously needed to pull myself out of whatever this was. "What are you doing..." That sounded rude. "...here?"

His grin widened as he came up to the kitchen island and leaned against it. "Gertie said the witches were convening. I got an invite."

"Oh?" Seriously? I mean, he'd been a part of our high school magickal defense squad, but he hadn't been really all that powerful.

The tight-lipped look he gave me said he heard my internal commentary, even though I doubted he could. Though, after meeting the Whiskey kids, I had to ask. *Can you hear me?*

Silence.

Oh, sweet relief. "So, you're a witch."

"I'm what they're calling a warrior witch." He shook his head and flicked his hand. "They really like to classify their sects. I don't care."

"So..." I had no idea what a *warrior witch* did. "You perform spells?"

"Sure." He turned and propped a hip against the island, folding his arms over his chest.

Those arms were... beefcakes and his red flannel shirt stretched to accommodate his muscles.

He licked his lips and ducked his head as he smiled. "Wy."

"Yeah?" Dear, blessed gods. "Oh, yeah. Gert's in the other room." I had no idea where she was, but I was pretty sure it wasn't outside because a cold front had moved in the night before and had dropped the temperature about fifty degrees, putting us double digits in the negative.

He flicked a come-hither smile at me and moved to enter the living room. "It's good see you, Wy."

"Yeah." Yeah? *Yeah?* That's the best I could come up with? Sweet baby Jesus. What a screwball.

But if Gertie was convening witches, then we needed information. "Necro," I shouted into the galley, knowing my voice would carry into the rooms upstairs.

No answer.

"Leah!"

Her head popped out of Charlie's room, her eyes wide. "Uh, yeah?"

"I need to get a message to your mom. You up for that?"

"Warmer weather?" Leah scrambled to her feet and out the door. "Yeah." She ran down the flight of stairs and nearly crashed into the artic door at the bottom.

"Smooth."

She gave me a look that told me to bite her...politely as she smoothed her second hoodie. "What's the message?"

"We're assembling the witches. What do I tell them?"

Leah bobbed her head front and back and side-to-side, then opened a door right there in the kitchen and stepped through.

Fox leaned back so his upper body appeared in the doorway that led to the living room, his dark eyes round. "That's a neat trick."

I shrugged and helped Gertie get the living room set up.

We needed a bigger room, apparently, because when the witches assembled, they really assembled. This wasn't just the leaders of the different covens. This was going to be all of them and we'd need the entire living room—which was big anyway—and the plant room. So, the furniture was pushed to the side or taken outdoors and covered. The sky was clear, which was why it was so cold out, so there wasn't a threat of snow, and it was too cold to really frost. So, things were safe. We only covered them in case we didn't feel like taking it all back in after everyone left.

A magickal door opened in Gertie's kitchen. I was getting used to the sound of it now. Well, it wasn't even really a sound. It was more a pressure change, like we were driving down the mountain too fast. My ears needed to pop.

Leah led Paige and a man in a trench coat through the door and down the two steps into the living room. She waved at me.

I made quick work of the introductions.

Gertie nodded. "I'm glad you came. Leah, be a dear and retrieve everyone for me, please."

The girl sighed but went and got her shoes and did as Gertie requested.

I wasn't really a part of the dream team of leadership on this, so I didn't really feel the need to be a part of every group discussion. Karmic magick wasn't always great in a battle. It could work for both sides because people would do whatever they needed to in the face of war. Lie, cheat, steal, murder. If it meant keeping those who meant the world to them safe? They'd do just about anything.

That was something I knew all too well.

But if I was needed, I'd step up. I'd just be as fucking careful about it as I could be.

Paige wasn't certain what she was walking into, but her morning hadn't started off well. She needed to keep Alaska from leaving ParaWest.

Because as of that morning, they'd lost Colorado, South California, Arizona, New Mexico, and South Dakota who had all taken Walton's declaration, tucked their tails, and had stood down.

Dawn was upset about southern California. Something about San Diego being important because of ships. Paige didn't understand how ships out on the ocean were going to help them when their fights were predominately going to be on land, but that's what Dawn was working to fix at the moment, bringing them back onboard with ParaWest.

Their war wasn't starting off super great. Paige needed a win. Or at the very least, not another loss. Alaska would be an easy one to lose, with as remote as it was. But with door magick, hopefully, they'd see that they weren't as cut off as they thought.

The house was warm and open. The fireplace in the corner was bubbling out some nice heat and snacks were plentiful. Gertrude Hunt reminded Paige a little of Alma with her feeding-the-soul routine. Were there spells baked into these too?

Probably not since these crackers had come out of a box.

"So," Gertie said after everyone had arrived and were sitting.

She'd promised to introduce as they went to keep things simpler, which was good because there were a *lot* of them and only one of her. She'd left Ishmail behind because his current job was more critical than helping Paige remember names.

Gertie drew herself up, placing both her hands on the arms of her camping chair. "What's the word?"

"We've declared our states to be sanctuary states."

Gertie and a few others nodded.

"What did he have to say about that?" the black man asked.

"Fox," Gertie said as way of an introduction. "Warrior witch."

Paige made a mental note and met the man's eyes. "He said don't. Basically."

"So, he declared war?" the man with the long silver hair said.

"Dave," Gertie said with a grunt. "Grey witch."

Paige didn't know what a grey witch was. "He said that if we act to protect our citizens, we're committing acts of war."

The grey witch grunted.

"Holly," said a woman with a long white braid. "Cosmic. What do you want from us? How do you see us helping?"

Paige looked around the room and saw a people who struggled just to survive. They all wore very worn clothing. The furniture in this room was all second-hand and mismatched. A lot of the decorations and even their clothes looked homemade. She'd done her demographics research too. This area wasn't rich. There were some who were better off than others, sure. But the crime rate was up—thefts and drugs, not murder. Jobs were low and the cost of living was high. People here fought hard to scrape by. "What do *you* want?"

"No," a woman in super-goth make-up said, her nose ring catching the light. "Maya, dark. And we're not entering into any kind of negotiating like that. You find something we want and then you dangle it in front of us like a carrot. No."

Paige sighed. "Okay. Then, let me be honest. I came here with the intention of asking for help. We're going to war. Walton's got guns."

A few of the people in the room snorted.

"He's got ammunition."

That garnered more than a few eye rolls.

Paige didn't know what that meant. That news might not concern them, but it scared the shit out of her. "I've got shifters and witches. He's got hundreds of thousands of soldiers. We have thousands."

"So, you need us to go fight and die in your war," Maya said.

As much as Paige *wanted* to say that wasn't the truth of it, it was. "Yes. But then I saw what you're facing and I can't…" She released a short sigh. "…ask that of you. But maybe if you just stay out of the war. Don't side with Walton. Don't side with us."

Gertie slid a glare from Paige to the old witch wearing a bright orange and dark red parka. "Now you're trying to tell us we're not good enough to fight in your war."

Was there anything she could say right in this situation? "You're remote. What are the chances you'll even be called on?"

Gertie harumphed. "Oh, our service members have already been called, but we've kept them here. For now."

Just how much say did these witches have over the way things were run? "You did?"

"The governor's my son-in-law," the woman in green said.

"Oh. Well, I know what I can offer." Maybe Paige should start there. "We have door magick. You struggle to get supplies."

"How many lives is that going to cost us?" Maya asked disgruntled.

"My broom isn't talkin'," Gertie said, her tone surly.

Paige knew what that meant. Gertie was telling Maya to settle down because the broom protecting the house hadn't gone off telling her there was an imminent threat. Thank goodness for the small things. "I need to know that if you're not going to join us, you won't join him."

"Join them," Maya said in a grouch. "We are—"

"Stop," Leah said, rising to her feet.

"Bean," Paige said in a cautionary tone, not wanting to slap her daughter down, but this wasn't the time or place for a teenaged angst-filled tantrum. "This isn't your circle, and you don't have a voice."

Gertie waved her off. "That girl's got more of a voice in this council than you do." She gestured to Leah to continue.

Paige gave her daughter a look that said, "Tread carefully, daughter. We don't want to make enemies."

Leah nodded and clenched her hands, getting a hold of her emotions. "You guys really think he's just going to let you stay living up here all by yourselves?"

Gertie sat back in her blue chair with a creak of weather-proofed material on metal, a look of deep thought on her face.

Maya shrugged. "There's no reason he'd come out here."

"He's *serious*," Leah said, turning to the dark witch. "Does he know there are magick users up here?"

"Yes," Paige said, wanting to see where Leah was going with this. "DoDO knows, so we have to assume Walton does too."

Billie Black shook her head as if wishing it wasn't so.

Leah gestured to Billie. "The only reason he hasn't made it up here yet is because he's been busy elsewhere and you can thank my mom for that. You're safe because of her. But what happens when things get too crazy? When he needs something and he can't get it?"

"When he needs an easy win," Paige added, seeing possibly where Leah was going.

She shrugged. "I guess that. Just because you're up here doesn't mean he's forgotten about you. You're on his plan. So, the only real question you have to ask yourself is what's yours?"

Paige raised her eyebrows as her daughter sat down. That kid'd grown up a lot since Texas.

Gertie sighed heavily. "You're offering supplies."

Paige shook her head. "Supply routes and delivery capabilities. I'll speak with Phoebe—she's the Blackman coven leader—and see if she can supply you with a couple of her witches."

"And what if we want Leah?" Gertie asked quietly.

Paige's breath caught in her throat. "As a hostage?"

Gertie shook her head, her mouth pulling down. "The girl's proven herself. She might not know how to dress for the cold, but she's got mettle and up here, that's not nothing."

This wasn't going to work out for Paige. "She's got school."

"We've got schools. We might even have better programs than you."

Paige doubted that. Her immediate answer was no because Leah was her *daughter* and not some bargaining chip. Her next immediate answer was yes because she needed Alaska not to quit. She met Leah's scared yet resolute blue eyes from across the room. "The decision will be hers." Paige's heart twisted but she knew this was the only right decision she had. "And she'll decide that in a week. When she comes back."

"But my math final."

"We'll find a way for you to take it." Paige swallowed hard and met Gertie's eyes, forcing a bit of her alpha-without-a-shifter-spirit will to the forefront. She wasn't certain it would even work without Cawli. "If she decides no, your decision can't be contingent."

Gertie nodded and pushed out her lips, dropping her gaze for a moment. "Anything else you can add while you're here?"

Paige had a lot of information, but not the kind she could share with partners who hadn't committed just yet. "It can wait."

"I'll see you out."

Paige didn't like leaving Leah there, but a thread of pride wormed its way into her as she stopped and gave Leah a parting hug and a kiss on her forehead. "You did good, Lee-bean," she whispered.

"I'm going to mess this up," Leah whispered back.

Paige threw her head back and chuckled quietly, then cupped her daughter's face in both of her hands. "That *is* how we learn." She kissed Leah's forehead again and walked out before she could cry. She didn't have time for that. And Leah hadn't made a decision yet, either.

But her heart already knew what Leah would choose. She'd decide to do what was right, what was needed.

And Paige needed to find a way to be okay with that.

Leah watched her mom leave surprised she wasn't feeling as much fear as she thought she would. Maybe this'd be okay. It should be. Right? She was surrounded by adults. Wy was cool. For an adult. She felt safe with Gertie.

Until she called the meeting to order again after reclaiming her seat. "We need to discuss the real issue here. Leah, you're being given a voice in this circle."

She took her seat and closed her mouth.

"But you need to remember how much you don't know yet. Okay? Wy, you're assigned to keep her safe and out of trouble until—"

Wy interrupted with a sound.

Gertie held up a hand to stop her, her expression telling Wy to shut it. "And you will keep her safe until she gets back home. Do you understand me?"

"Yes, ma'am," Wy muttered and sprawled out in her chair, her socked feet wide, her legs spread, her face defiant.

For all that, Leah felt safer already. "What's the real issue?"

Gertie looked around the room, her lips quirked to the side. She tipped her head to the side and began. "The Fucking Witches here in Alaska are protecting something pretty big."

"What do you mean?" Wy asked, sitting up.

"Why do you keep calling them by cuss words?" Leah asked because she *needed* to know.

"It's who we are," Gertie said.

Fox shrugged, his hands wide.

Dave shooed her concern away.

Oh, geez. Well... "So, what do the..." But she'd gotten in trouble each time she'd cursed in front of adults before. "...fucking..." Leah glanced around the room to see if anyone was going to yell at her. They didn't. "...witches protect?"

"A cage," Holly said derisively, shaking her head, her nearly white hair catching in the soft glow of the string lights along the ceiling.

"What?" Wy asked, giving her aunt her undivided attention.

Leah knew that look. It was the one that said she'd been in trouble for something that hadn't been her fault.

Gertie shook her head and held up a hand. "We have gods contained here." She looked around. "It's time everyone here knows. There's a reason we are a scattered coven of different witch types. The protections on the lands forms a seven-pointed star."

Oh. Leah'd just learned about this one. "The Elvan Star?" She didn't understand why everyone used the five-pointed star instead of the seven. With five points, you got the four elements and self. But with the seven-pointed star, you also got above and below which, in her mind, made the binding a bit more three-dimensional. So... better. More escape... proofy. That couldn't be a word.

"Green, cosmic, grey, divine, dark, wood, and warrior have been our point guardians, but it can be interchanged. We have in this room karma, white, elemental, death, and dimensional. That last one—" Gertie shook her head. "I didn't even know that was a thing. There are others out there. I'm sure of it. But right now, with the people in this room alone, we can make sure these protections remain secure."

That changed things. "If you have to stay here to keep this... prison safe—"

Fox shook his head. "That's true, but what you said is also true. What happens when the president turns his attention north? Huh? What then? What happens when no one's around to keep the doors shut? These gods get loose? Again?"

"What does it take?" Wy asked, staring at Fox as if she didn't know him.

This had to be a shocking conversation for her too. That made Leah feel not as overwhelmed.

"Power. Energy." He lifted a shoulder in a shrug. "Can't do all the things you sometimes need to."

"We need to consider this," Holly said. "We *do* need supplies."

"Damn straight we do," Maya said.

"But we can't let our wards get free," Gertie said into the quiet. "So, whatever we decide, that's our focus. We can't contain them if we're in jail, dead, or worse. Let's think on that."

The front door slammed open and someone raced in, out of breath and letting in a cold draft. It was a man, kinda short and slim. "Fox," he said, out of breath. "We've got the last one."

Fox glanced at Gertie and then let his eyes settle on Wynonna. "Let's go."

"What's going on?" Wy asked, getting to her feet.

Fox sighed and went to retrieve his shoes. "You'll see. Gert."

She raised a hand and then gestured to Leah. "Where you go, she goes."

Wy rolled her eyes and then looked at Leah with a what-are-you-waiting-for expression. "Come on."

17

P aige led the way to her office when they returned. She didn't want to think too hard about how she'd just left her not-even-an-adult-and-still-needing-to-pass-math daughter in another state to help her forge alliances. That felt a little too dynasty. Not the television show because she might have watched one or two episodes as a kid, but as in rulers who had kingdoms.

That didn't sit too well with her.

Dexx was waiting for her. "How's Leah?"

"Staying for a bit."

A frown furrowed his brow. "Are we okay with it?"

"Yes." But she shook her head. "What's the word on Colorado?"

He held up a finger and perched on the arm of the leather sofa. "Southern California is back thanks to Dawn. Don't know *how* she managed it. I'm sure words were exchanged. Also, maybe some money. I don't know. But we got the port back."

Paige still didn't know how or why they needed that.

"And we've got ships. So, there's that."

Wait. "What?"

He nodded, his semi-dark eyebrows high. "With soldiers —sailors, I guess, and weapons."

"But how does that help us?"

"Trust me. General Saul was very happy to hear this."

"Okay." Well, if she was happy, then Paige would just have to be content with having ships she had no idea how to use. "I think we might still have Alaska."

"Good? Were they really going to leave?"

"I don't think we ever *really* had them. I think they wanted to withdraw from big government, but they don't actually want to join the war."

"Yeah because so many people actually want to."

He had a point. "What about Colorado?"

He shook his head. "Dawn's focused next on South Dakota."

"Why?" There were resources there, sure, but... why?

Dexx shrugged. "Unknown, but she knows how to tread these waters better than me."

This coming from a guy who didn't trust Dawn or what she represented. "What's with the change?"

He stretched his neck out and then took in a deep breath. "This is just big, and we can't afford to screw it up. Which reminds me, I'm going out."

"On mission?"

He nodded. "Ishmail has a group of people coming in. I figured the pack and I could go make sure they make it in safely."

"Sounds good." Paige just hoped they could save as many people as possible, though there were going to be many who refused to leave or thought they couldn't for one reason or another. "Where are they going?"

"Some ranch in northern California?" He shook his head and got to his feet, coming to her and running his hands down her arms until he caught her hands. "It's safe. That's all I really know. Warded. Guarded. Set up for people. Whole deal. Naomi's done a great job there."

They still needed someone to help make sure this generation of kids didn't fall out of school or drop out of life skills. But that would be a discussion for later. In the meantime, she'd just keep her eyes peeled for someone who could help in that arena. "Be safe."

"You, too." He pecked three kisses on her lips and left.

Paige knew that Dawn didn't care as much about recapturing Colorado, but Paige wasn't ready to give that state up. It was resource rich in a lot of ways, including people. Even though Nederland had picked up and relocated, she knew there had to be several other paranormals in the area. It was a big state and with the big influx of people wanting legal marijuana sooner, the chances were good that there'd be people who needed to be fought for.

Not just paranormals, though. She had to remember that paranormals started this, but others had been fighting this fight far longer.

She picked up the new magetech phone Tru had delivered earlier that day and dialed Merry.

Her projected face hovered over the screen. She turned and saw Paige, and her expression soured. "What?"

If this was any other person, Paige might ask if she'd interrupted something, but with Merry the answer was always yes. But had Paige done good by interrupting? Probably. After this war, Paige was going to have to do something about Merry, like put her back in jail.

War first. Justice later.

"I need to find a way to talk to the people in real power in Colorado."

Merry shook her head with a frown that showed off more

wrinkles than the woman probably wanted to admit to. "Like who?"

"I don't know. Like... like the fucking witches of Alaska."

Merry's eyes narrowed. "How do you know about them?"

Paige didn't want to answer that. She sat on a circle of highly influential—wait.

She had seriously called the wrong person. "Never mind."

Merry's mouth opened, but Paige ended the call. Instead, she focused on the person she needed to talk to and dialed his number.

The dragon who owned the house with the monster chairs, Ken Waugh. His head swam above the phone and he gave her a polite smile. "Ms. Whiskey."

"Mr. Waugh." Paige didn't want to waste his time. "I need to talk to the people in power in Colorado."

His polite smile turned up a notch as he raised his chin and appraised her. "I think I can make that happen." He studied her and then nodded. "I'll be in touch." His face disappeared.

Paige checked Colorado off her list. All she had to do was figure out what they needed.

Probably supplies.

Phoebe was going to be ParaWest's greatest bargaining chip. Paige just had to make sure she didn't abuse that power.

They'd be sunk if the Blackman's left.

I followed Fox through the door Leah'd cut open. "What are we doing here?"

He glanced back at me, but when the magick door was closed, he turned his attention to Leah. "You should probably stay here."

Leah shook her head, silently letting him know she wasn't a baby.

But I nodded mine and gave her a look that said that we both agreed that the whole situation sucked but that she should do as he said.

She rolled her eyes and hung back.

He led the way through the tiny, yet cramped kitchen that looked like it belonged to a hoarder. More than that, it looked like it belonged to a poor hoarder because nothing was new, everything had crusts of caked on, baked on grease and who knew what else, and the wood paneling was warped on three of the walls. There were entire holes on the fourth.

I stepped into a long, skinny living room that was too full with a single couch, an overstuffed recliner and piles and piles of newspapers and magazines. Some of them were stacked all the way to the ceiling and I was fairly certain that was the only thing holding it up. There were holes in the ceiling filled with aged spray foam. "Is this place going to fall down on top of us?" I asked quietly. I knew better than to insult the home someone had fought so hard to maintain. You know, by collecting all the Gardner's Monthly magazines to hold the roof up with.

He gave me a look that said he didn't know and that he understood my meaning all at the same time, but kept walking, leading me down a narrow hallway. We passed the Pepto-Bismol pink bathroom, the washer and dryer that actually had a manual washer on top of it. And finally, we stopped at the bedroom.

I smelled it before we stepped through, though. Blood and lots of it. I braced myself for whatever I might see, pushing my emotions and my reactions down.

Fox stepped to the side, his hand to his nose.

Letting me get the full view.

A woman was sprawled on the bed, bathed in blood. A gaping hole remained where her heart should have been.

Fear churned inside me. It was back. I'd shown up and *brought* it back. I should have stayed away. My family —Charlie—

"This is the third body," Fox said.

Oh, dear gods no. There were *more*? I hadn't been back that long.

"One a week."

Wait. I pushed the fear down and swallowed. So, not me. But whatever this thing was...

No. It was connected to me. This was *my* karma demon. I *knew* that.

So, what had I done three weeks ago that would have unleashed this thing?

I'd been at the Whiskey house in Oregon. We'd been doing research on stones that were connected to ley-line magick. Was this—

"This guy comes back every year. Same thing. He comes. He kills three people, and then he disappears again."

Every year? I let those words sink in.

"This started our senior year."

"I know." But I'd trapped it—*the killer*—in a cave. The people of the area should have been safe. How'd the thing get out? "Three? And then it disappears?" But that... didn't make sense.

Fox nodded. "I'm hoping it gives me something more to trace. We've come really close a couple of times."

"Right." But if it was three, and this was the last one, then it was in hiding already. I knew where the cave was. I didn't want to get up there in the snow, but I had access to snow machines, so that wasn't really the issue. Worst case, I would come out about this time next year and I'd find a way to put this demon down for good.

"Can you see anything?"

Right. He needed my magick. And I needed to know how my karma demon had escaped. I looked with my witch eyes and saw a *lot* of karmic magick. But that's something I would expect from a karma demon. "Are we looking for anything in particular?"

"A trail."

I didn't *need* a trail. I knew right where this thing was headed. There was karma slime all over the walls. It reminded me a little of *Ghost Busters*.

It led out the window.

But that's where the blood trail went too.

"So, you're a cop?" I asked, walking around the room, careful not to touch anything.

He shook his head. "I failed out as a rookie."

I winced.

He waved me off. "I thought I could do the magick stuff and be a cop at the same time. Didn't work. But they understood what I was doing, so I work with them. Just as a civilian and I'm not *exactly* attached to the police department just in case something goes bad and they get sued."

I nodded. I'd never heard of anything like that, but then I met Dexx who ran the Red Star Department. So, anything was possible, I guessed.

"This has been a special case for me." His voice lowered.

I could feel his eyes on me. I wasn't ready for him or what he needed. And he *needed* something from me. An apology for one. But I was still wrapped up in Veronica and until I sorted that whole mess out, I couldn't seriously consider anything with Fox.

"Is this the reason you left?"

My words formed the word no, but then I remembered what lying to him the last time had done. It'd created a monster who was still killing people fourteen years later. I scratched an itch on my cheek and tried to get a read on the karmic energy. "Yes."

This karma was different than what I'd trapped all those years ago. It was mustier, darker, earthier, if that was even a thing. If I didn't know better, I'd have said this was someone else entirely.

But I did know differently. This was a karma demon. *My* karma demon. And it'd somehow broken free and killed again.

But why? And why did it leave again? *Was* it still in the cave?

"Because it scared you? Because you couldn't kill it? We were kids. We—"

"I created this," I blurted out. "I thought it was contained. That's why I stayed away so long. I thought that by *staying* away, you'd all be safe."

He stood at the edge of the blood stain on the grey carpet and studied me. "*You* created…" He pointed at the woman on the bed. "…this."

"Karma's a bitch." But in this case, karma was a six-foot man of flaming anger who ripped hearts out of people's chests.

"Can you track this thing?" Fox asked.

She fought to tell him no. "Yeah."

"Okay, then, let's go."

She shook her head. "I'm going alone."

"Like hell you are."

There wasn't anything else I could get out of that room except sick. The smell was getting to me. The room was cold as if the heating didn't work in there, and it likely didn't. Heating bedrooms was silly when you could just sleep under blankets.

I left the room, brushing past Fox on my way out. The hall seemed to constrict, but my stomach started to heave as

I passed the bathroom. I ducked in and closed the thin door. This was a mobile home, something you didn't see a lot of up there. Homemade homes built out of scraps and held together with spray foam, sure. Mobile homes? Not as much.

I lost whatever I'd eaten and flushed, sitting on the edge of the bathtub, soaking in the cool air of the non-heated room. How was I going to fight this thing off? Fighting karma with karma? That seemed like a mildly bad idea.

But so did ignoring it. That was a recipe for a karmic disaster.

Leah was still in the kitchen when I finally came out. "What—"

"We gotta get back to Gert's."

"Uh, okay."

"What are you doing?" Fox demanded, grabbing my arm and spinning me around.

I fucking didn't know. "I'm taking Leah back to the house where she'll be safe. Then I'm borrowing Gert's truck, loading up my snow machine, and tracking this thing down."

"What thing?" Leah asked hesitantly.

Fox snorted. "Good luck. I *broke* your sled two years ago hunting caribou."

Seriously? "You didn't."

"Oh, I did. I was planning on feeling bad about it, too, but now?" He made a nah face and shook head. "So, next plan."

"I'll take one of the other machines."

"No. They're *all* broke."

"All of them?" That didn't sound right. "Gert's too good a mechanic for that."

"I don't know if you noticed, but ol' Gert's not getting around as well as she used to." His look told me to open my eyes and look.

Fucker. I knew that. I paced away, but the kitchen was

way too tight for that. "Fine." I pulled my fingers through my hair. "I'll take Whomper."

"In this weather?" Fox's face crumpled in a how-stupid-are-you look that also called me cheechako—someone who hadn't wintered over yet.

"I can take you," Leah said.

Over my dead body. "No."

"I open the door." She mimed a box with her hands. "We do the thing. We come right back."

"We're in," Fox said with real animation. "We're out. And this thing is taken out for good this time."

It sounded good. "How are we going to do that?"

"You said you created it."

I nodded. Though, how still didn't make a ton of sense to me.

"So, it's karma."

I nodded again. "So that means that *anything* you do to it could return at you three times as hard."

He raised a hand. "Then I'll just be super careful."

I looked at Leah, her face eager. I couldn't bring her into this. She wasn't my daughter to sacrifice.

She reached out and touched my chest, her eyes unfocusing. Then, she turned away and cut a door open.

A blast of icy air cut at us. We weren't exactly dressed to be out there for a long time, so if her door magick failed for whatever reason, there was a very good chance we'd die out there or lose fingers or toes.

But I had to do this before I lost the courage, dressed in normal winter gear that would have been okay if we'd just been hopping from the store to the car and back again. But out here? That wind cut through my jeans and my jacket, making me really wish I'd brought a hood.

She'd done really well, dropping us somehow directly in front of the cave I'd trapped the demon in.

It looked abandoned, as if no one had lived there for years.

Fox stepped out behind me, hunching his shoulders against the cold and surveying the area. "It's here?"

I shook my head. I didn't know what I expected to see, but... nothing wasn't it.

There were no blood stains. No foot prints.

There were no karmic smears. "If that was the demon, it didn't return here."

Fox turned in place. "Something isn't right. I can feel something."

I followed him up the side of the mountain, looking with my magick to see what I could see.

My protections were still up. The prison should still be in place.

Leah walked up to me as I stopped, her entire body shivering so hard it looked like she was almost in convulsions.

"We can't stay long," I told Fox. It was *certainly* cold. Below zero temperatures weren't pleasant to even the most seasoned Alaskans, but I'd forgotten what it was like for first timers.

He gestured for Leah to join him in the cave's mouth. "The wind doesn't get you here."

She pushed past me with an even bigger shiver.

I needed to hurry this up. Either the demon was still trapped there and whoever was killing wasn't it, or my demon had escaped and I had no way of tracking it. I stopped beside Leah and stared into the cave, but I couldn't see hardly anything.

Fox pulled out a flashlight and shone it around inside.

The sigils were still in place and strong. The demon shouldn't have been able to get out. "I don't think—"

"What's that?" he asked, focusing the light on a pile of leaves.

Except it wasn't a pile of leaves. It was roughly the same shape of a man, and a very tall one.

He made a move to check it out.

I stopped him. "It might be dormant right now. It might be dead. I don't want to jinx it or trip something."

"But that's your demon?"

I stared at the shape with my witchy eyes and saw a body made of karma, sleeping, dormant. "Whatever's killing people isn't my demon," I said quietly, that statement shocking me to my core.

Fox nodded.

What it meant, it wasn't good? "We gotta get Leah back to the house."

He nodded again, but still looked like he was intent on checking out the body, going against what I'd just said.

Leah just shivered, her face tough like she was just going to weather the storm.

You didn't *weather out* twenty below wind-chill. "Make the door," I told her. "Before you pass out. I take a body back to your mother and she'd gonna kill me."

Leah shiver-snorted and cut a rather jagged door.

Her doors were always rigid and straight, which to me was a sign that I'd pushed her way too hard. I shoved her through the door into Gertie's warm living room.

Fox followed and the door closed behind us.

The first order of business was to make sure Leah was okay.

The second was to figure out who the hell was killing people if it wasn't my karma demon.

Who had I nearly sacrificed my daughter to in order to save the valley if it wasn't the monster of my own creation?

18

P aige decided she couldn't just wait to handle the Blackman coven. She understood they weren't leaving, and they hadn't made any plans to do so yet. But if a better offer came up...

So, she didn't allow herself to wallow in the fact that her daughter was growing up much too fast. She asked Derek to take her to see his leader.

He opened a door into the main house.

A group of kids screamed by, laughing and hollering at each other.

Derek twisted to be missed, tucking the tails of his coat behind him. "Watch it!"

A couple of the kids shouted back that they would.

Whatever that meant. Paige was fairly certain it meant absolutely nothing.

The house was an open-spaced farmhouse with exposed beams, hardwood floors covered by homemade rugs, and was sparsely furnished. Where the Whiskey house was *over* furnished with couches and comfortably chairs, the Blackmans had decided to go with seating that took up less space and was less comfortable. They had folding chairs tucked into the corner. They had a bevy of wooden kitchen chairs and stools.

And no tables.

Lamps were hung from the ceiling instead of rising from tables or the floor. Herbs hung from the ceiling as well as silk flowers, giving the place an almost cheery feel.

This was much different than when Eldora had run the coven. She'd been strict, no-nonsense—which was probably the reason for the chairs—but with Phoebe in the lead, at least there were flowers.

The coven leader appeared around the refrigerator, stepping out of the semi-closed off kitchen with a dishtowel in her hand. She smiled at Paige, tucking a strand of her dark hair back into her loose ponytail. "Please tell me there isn't another emergency."

There'd be plenty more as the days progressed. "Not today, but I've got to talk to you about something. You wouldn't happen to have any coffee on, would you?"

Phoebe nodded largely and stepped back into the kitchen, setting the towel on the peninsula that separated the two rooms, her head barely clearing the overhead cabinets.

They exchanged pleasantries while she made coffee and then they both sat on stools on either side of the counter.

"What's up?" Phoebe asked, getting to the point as she sipped her coffee.

"Blueberry?" Paige wasn't certain what her nose was smelling.

Phoebe nodded. "Wanted to try it. You're my guinea pig. What are you doing here?"

"Right." Paige took a sip and turned up her nose. She wasn't certain this was going to be a favorite. "I had a thought and I need to address it."

"Okay."

"One of the things that keeps coming up in negotiations with people is transportation and supplies. Everyone wants access to your door magick."

Phoebe grunted.

"Which made me realize that without your coven, we're sunk. Not... sunk. We'd figure something out—"

"You've seen a potential weakness."

"Yes. Walton could potentially start targeting you and your family. Also, anyone providing door magick would probably be targets of violence."

Phoebe nodded, blinking as she set her cup down. "We realized this a while ago. Derek's been teaching everyone how to create spelled objects. So, that's helping. Also, Lovejoy and General Saul have been sending us with a protection detail. Not with you because you're the protection detail, but I think we're okay."

"Mm. Good." It was nice being surrounded by people who knew what they were doing who didn't *rely* on her to come up with all the decisions herself. "I need to know if this is going to be a problem."

"Huh?" Phoebe looked caught off guard.

"If you're being pulled in too many directions."

"We know what's at stake."

"I understand that, but..." Paige stopped, paused, and let her mind be still a moment to regather her thoughts and to give this conversation the direction it needed. "There are a couple of things. You're being actively entered into each of these negotiations with the states, so I think a representative of your coven should be present in those negotiations."

"There's... you." Phoebe gave Paige a look that said she should have thought of that.

"I'm in everyone's coven right now. And in everyone's pack. And... I can't have allegiances."

214

Phoebe pulled back a little, frowning heavily into her coffee cup.

"Someone who only has your best interests at heart should be in every negotiation. Just to be fair."

"Okay." Phoebe's tone said she was trying to figure out who that person would be.

"And I need to know if you're going to want some power investment in the new government we're creating."

"Huh?" This time when Phoebe asked that, her face was twisted in confusion.

Paige gave her a look that told her to think about it for a minute.

Phoebe's ears pulled back. Then her eyebrows lowered and her eyes narrowed. Then they relaxed as she raised her head and straightened. "Like what?"

Paige shrugged. "We're creating this as we go. I know that we need a cabinet of leaders who can advise the person making the decisions."

"So, you."

"Currently, yes, but when this is all said and done, we'll have a leader who's been voted in and the cabinet will have to support that person. So, not just me."

"So, for the future."

She was getting it. "Not just today. Not just you and me helping each other out. For the long-term."

"You're really serious."

Paige faced her cousin squarely. "We are becoming very dependent on you. We're keeping Alaska right now *only* because of your family's ability to bring in supplies."

"Oh."

"Yeah. Leah's up there right now."

"She's a good kid." Phoebe's tone was distracted.

"Super proud of her. I'm headed to Colorado. They're going to want access to your door magick too. If we lose

Colorado, if we lose any of our states, we lose power. If we lose power, we could lose this war before it even begins."

"And this is all just… juggling before the fighting starts? When that happens, you're going to need us for that, too."

"Yeah." Paige sipped her coffee and let the flavor sit on her tongue. It was surprisingly *more* bitter for some reason. She thought it'd be smoother with the addition of the berries.

"I could really ask for the world, couldn't I?"

"Probably." Paige hoped she wouldn't but understood that Phoebe had to at least bargain for something that would garner the worth and value of what the Blackman coven was providing. "Think about it? In the meantime, I need someone to come with me to Colorado."

Phoebe trailed her hand along the dark granite counter as she sat up straighter. "I'll… grab a bag."

"Great." Paige gave her a smile that she hoped looked warm enough. "I look forward to a healthy partnership."

"Yeah." Phoebe got up and left, her steps still hesitant as if she was still thinking things through.

One step at a time. They'd win this war one small step at a time. Paige just had to make sure the steps she was taking were the right ones.

"What's your name, what's your power?" Dexx let his brain run on autopilot for at least a half hour. Immigration intake was *boring* beyond the norm. The rest of Red Star had their own lines of people, but Dexx felt like he had the job all by himself.

"I catch cars and spit acid. Hero track, right?"

Dexx snapped his eyes up to the nondescript man and

looked closer. No, not faceless, but average, with a scruff on his face, and light blue eyes and a chiseled chin.

"Did I really go *Sky High* on you?"

The man smiled and nodded. "Yeah, you really did."

"Damn. Sorry. I've been taking names down so long, I just let my mind go."

The man shrugged at him. "I get it. We're bored out of our skulls, too. Baker, Simon. Vampire."

Dexx took half a step back and pulled Hattie up in case he went vampy. He must be more tired than he thought. "Simon Baker. Vampire." He tried to sound like he hadn't just made a complete ass of himself. No use. Ugh. He had to set things right before it became a real issue. He let his clipboard fall to his side. "Okay, I'm going to start over. Pretend you just came up to me."

Simon put a half smile on and glanced at Dexx side-eyed.

"Welcome to Troutdale and Parawest. I need your name and para-affiliation." The clipboard rose so he could take the information down. Dexx waited expectantly.

"Um, Simon Baker. I'm a vampire?" He looked less sure this time.

Dexx should have looked at the man before he'd even asked his name. The lack of infra-red signature was a dead giveaway. "Excellent. As a vampire, you will be expected to either ask permission to feed or hunt wild game. Also, *no* turning. As I understand it, you have regulations on turning. Correct?"

Simon eyed him with more interest. "I wouldn't— how do you know about... things?"

"Had a friend. Boss. Tony Guerrerro. You know him?"

"You know we're not a totally exclusive club. Never heard of him."

Dexx's head bobbed with a frown. "Fair enough. Just so

you know, if you want to be in the para militia, we have a sign-up. It'll be a little different from the *other* Army."

"Good to know. Thanks." Simon walked by Dexx, his head swiveling back and forth inspecting his new city and country.

Dexx blew out his cheeks. With so many paras mixing there was bound to be issues. But so far, the overwhelming feel of the paras and normies who walked through the intake was of anticipation of a new life. Dekskulta had built something similar in Kupul, but it ultimately had failed. Would they make it past the initial conflict and make something of the brave new free country of Parawest? He hoped so. For his kid's sake, he *needed* to make this work.

I got Leah wrapped in blankets and hunkered down in front of the fireplace with a hot cup of cocoa. She hadn't been outside long enough to really worry, and she'd been shivering, which was a good sign. But if that girl really was staying here, she needed tougher skin—which a good weathering would give her—and better clothes. Namely socks, boots, gloves, and hats. The weather up here might not be as terrible as everyone liked to claim it was, but it could kill. That was a fact.

Also, survival training. That kid needed to know how to survive in the woods, in the snow, what to do if she came in contact with a moose, gun training. The works.

But not at that moment. I pulled out my phone to call Paige, but the phones weren't working. Great. The screen came up, but there were no bars. How long would they be down this time?

I went up to Charlie's room and knocked on the door, pushing aside my fear of her reactions. If I just treated her like a stranger—which she was—then it'd be cool.

"Yeah," she called.

I opened the door to a small disaster. Yeah. It was kinda creepy to see that some things were probably genetic. "Leah got super chilled and could use a buddy. You busy?"

Charlie's pale blue-almost-teal eyes met mine and then skittered away as she scrambled to her feet. "Yeah. Sure. She okay?"

"Yeah. Just cold."

"'Kay." She pushed around me.

"Char," I said quietly.

She stopped, but didn't look at me, her attention focused on the stairs she was about to go down.

"I know I'm not your mom."

She flinched.

"I don't have that right. I get that. But could I..." What the hell did I even *want?*

I *wanted* to be a part of her life. Realizing that I might not have actually put her life in danger, that maybe I wasn't *that* horrible, took a little pressure off. Reality, though, I had still possibly endangered her and that was still bad.

She put her hand on the rail and stepped on one of her feet.

"Can I just be your Wy?"

She looked up at me, meeting my eyes. "I don't know."

"That's fair." I didn't know what else to say. "I had my reasons for leaving and I really thought I was doing the best for you."

"I heard," she said quietly, looking away again.

Right. We'd had that conversation nearly right outside her door. "And I was right. You turned out okay."

"You don't even know me."

I snorted. "I read karma, kid, and you don't have the bad stuff rolling around you. So... that's pretty good in my book."

She opened her mouth to say something, but then nodded and headed down the stairs.

Well, that was a start. At what, I didn't know.

But that also needed to get set aside for the moment. I went back downstairs and gestured for Fox to join me in the plant room. Not that the girls wouldn't hear us in there. Both glass doors were open, and sound bounced off the walls even *with* all the plants, but I still didn't want to discuss dead bodies in front of two impressionable young girls.

Fox shook his head as he pulled me closer to the monstera, ducking under one of the leaves. "So, if this wasn't your demon, we're still trying to figure out who did this."

"Yeah." I calmed my heart and eased my head back into problem solving, which wasn't super easy. I'm a feeling kinda girl, not an overly thinking one. But I still was wondering if going down this path was even the right thing to do. We were preparing for war. Did we have *time* to catch killers on the side?

He stared into the living room, but I knew he couldn't see the girls. They were by the fireplace which we couldn't see from this corner of the other room. "Whoever our killer is was *here* fourteen years ago."

"You think it was one of the kids in class?" Our graduating class had been pretty big though. I know what you're thinking. We're in Alaska, sure, but we're not all villages. Wasilla and Palmer are pretty big. We can't all be Nome.

"No. I widened the search, trying to see if this went back further. And it does. Just not here. It started *here* our senior year. So, no. It wasn't a student."

I ducked in under the massive plant as well. It gave me the feeling that we were being secretive even though I *knew* it was just a potted plant. A gigantic one, but still just a potted plant. "How far back?"

"Hundreds of years." He pressed both hands into his forehead and scrubbed before flinging his hands down. "It's spotty in places, but yeah. There's just enough of a trail to follow. It was down in the lower forty-eight for centuries, then moved up here almost two decades ago. It seems to look for power and then feeds on hearts. If there was a gathering of witches, there'd be several murders with hearts missing. A gathering of alphas. Same thing. Then our senior year, it started the killing spree. But then it stopped at four bodies."

If I separated my dumb decision and the decade of blame I'd lathered on myself—you know, just set that chunky weight of guilt aside like it was nothing—and looked at it... "Do you think he was drawn here by the power of the prison?"

"I do. I think it drew him in and he's... I don't know, trying to get it?"

"The power or the gods?"

"Uh." Fox shrugged, shaking his head. "But here's the thing. When this thing was killing before, it was random. Five people in one place, then three months later, it could be twelve, or a year and a half later, it could be three. It was just random."

Random turned karma-specific? "Huh." Well, hundreds of years. That... meant it had to be— "So, an immortal? Vampire? Do they eat hearts?"

Fox tapped his lips with a finger. "No. There *are* vampires, I guess? I mean, at least from what I found. But no. Werewolves, though, will sometimes eat hearts."

"They're not immortal." I'd met a pack of those, so I knew. "They're hot. Damned fucking sexy, but they really don't live long though."

"So, they're real."

"Super real. And great kissers." I pushed away those happy thoughts to sustain me later. "Maybe some other kind of paranormal?" Honestly, before Paige Whiskey had burst onto the scene, telling the world that other paras existed and that everything was okay with that, I hadn't paid that much attention. I knew of other witches. Sure. I dated a super-hot werewolf and half his pack for the hottest summer of my existence. But anything outside of that?

"Why is he still here, though?" Fox asked. "That doesn't make any sense. In the past, he'd moved on at max a couple of years. It's been fourteen."

Huh. There'd been a *reason* I'd thought I'd actively endangered my daughter's life.

In the battle where I'd lied to save Fox's life, when I'd tried to impress him rather than truly do the right thing, I'd... caught something. It'd been this super highly-intense surge of energy. It'd been laced with enough bad karma that I'd just assumed it was me and my big dumbness.

That was when I'd first seen my karma demon.

What if when I'd performed that spell, karma *had* kicked me in the butt, but more creatively than I'd thought. What if she'd created a karma demon using the bad guy's magick?

But then, as the murders continued, and as I tracked down the karma demon because it was tangible and I could see it and track it, I'd been chasing the wrong thing?

But no. The murders after that point—after that fateful night as we stood over the body of the first victim, the people who'd been murdered had been tied to me. They were either close to my sister or to my daughter. That couldn't be coincidence.

Maybe this paranormal guy was after the power I'd stolen from him. Maybe he was using my karma to track me, which is how... Okay. That didn't quite make sense. No.

I was close. I was *close*.

In the ceremony—honest to gods ceremony—I'd performed to *trap* my demon, I'd *felt* another huge power surge. I'd... collected... something.

I'd *thought* it'd just been my demon.

Which had made sense at the time, but now that I was thinking about it, looking at it differently—

Yeah. Okay. I'd made a dumb mistake. I'd *lied* to karma.

But I was a karmic witch. Karma and I had a different understanding with one another. I'd *thought* that was the *reason* I'd been treated so badly, that karma was trying to make a poster-child of me, to teach me a lesson, to get at me through Evie's teachers and friends, through my daughter's babysitter.

But... karma wouldn't have to *search* for me. Karma had a direct line to me. So, if...

If the people who'd been killed after that first night had *actually* been someone trying to find *me*, then...

First, there had to be a reason why someone would be searching for me.

Like that initial power surge had been me catching the real enemy's magick?

Like, what if this murdery person's bad magick plus my stupidity in trying to get Fox back after having some dumb jock's baby while still trying to graduate high school had worked together to create a demon?

That kind of made sense.

I had a much better understanding of karma now, though. I knew that, yeah, sure, it could be a mean beast. But its *intent* was to *help* people do *better*. Sometimes by punching you in the face with your own actions.

But ripping hearts out of people's chests?

That wasn't karma.

That... wasn't... karma.

But I *had* seen a demon and it *had* reeked of karma.

What if that demon had been *trying* to help me?

What if I'd listened?

What if I'd been able to stay?

What if I'd been able to marry Fox and raise Charlie and not have Evie pissed at me?

That was a road I couldn't travel. Because, you know, if I hadn't left, I wouldn't have gained the treasure trove of life experiences I now had that made me the amazing person I was. So, cool thought, but really dumb.

However, I was pretty sure I'd landed on what this murdery person was after. "I think I stole his magick."

"Hu-what?" Fox's expression said I'd left him behind about eight what-ifs ago.

"Back before, we were chasing down someone who was hunting us."

"Yeah."

And he had been, leaving messages and really gross stuff for us to find. *Maybe* the power of the prison had drawn him in, but he'd been *hunting* us. If what Fox said was right, we might have been what'd brought him. A meeting of alphas? A meeting of witches? We'd been a supernatural hunting team.

That time had been a dark point in our school year, to be sure. Dead pets. Broken friends. One of the kids at school had been admitted to the psyche ward and, as far as I knew, was still there. "That night I cast that spell—"

"That did absolutely nothing but fireworks?"

Maybe for him. "Oh, it did something. I'm still not *entirely* sure what, but that demon we saw in the cave, it was born that day."

"Oooookay?"

"I felt... something. Super powerful. I thought it was just karma. I used it. I used more of it to contain the demon in that cave."

"Okaaaaay." He looked away in thought. Confusion laced his features with the thinking.

"What if it wasn't all karma? What if was magick? But, like, so deeply twisted in karma that it looked like karma to me, and I was able to use it. What if I stole it from this... guy, whoever or whatever he is, and he's still here because he's trying to get it back?"

"But what's with the yearly thing?"

"Well, I don't know. Maybe his magick is something blood related or death related." Karmically created? "So, he needs all year to build up for the kills? And he's trying to..." The thought fizzed because I seriously had no idea on how that would even work.

Something clicked into place for Fox though. "If he can kill the right people in the right order and collect the right 'ingredients' for lack of a better—yeah. That makes sense."

"It does?"

He nodded, his dark eyes flitting as if he was reading something. "I hadn't been able to figure out the connections between his victims, but now?"

"Well, before, it was me."

"How so?"

"They were either close to my sister or Charlie."

His eyes latched onto mine.

"He was trying to hunt me down somehow." That had to mean something. "What if he's still trying to do that now? But he's... lost my trail?"

"Because you left?"

Yeah. Because I'd left. This really wasn't my fault. I stared at the wall keeping Charlie and Leah from my view.

If I came back, she really could be safe.

From my demon, but what would happen if I came back and this guy got my scent again, came after Charlie again?

Did I want to? Come home?

Fox opened his mouth to say something, but Whomper came staggering in holding my phone awkwardly in three bristles of his right "foot."

I grabbed it and stared at it. It had reception and was

getting a call, but there was no information on the number. I answered. "Yeah?"

"Wy," Veronica said breathlessly. "I'm in trouble. Help me."

And then the line went dead.

19

W hat was I supposed to do?

"Who was that?" Fox asked and then frowned. "I didn't realize cellphones were working."

They worked so randomly. It was as if someone was at the control desk somewhere was trying to figure out what was wrong and how to fix it, but instead of actually fixing things, they were flipping a bunch of switches. "That was Vee— Veronica. My girlfriend. She says she's in trouble."

"Do you know where she is?"

I had no clue. I went to into the room where Leah and Charlie sat on the coffee table in front of the fireplace.

Charlie slipped off the table and onto the floor like an eel.

I didn't care. That coffee table had seen a lot worse when *I'd* been a kid. I offered the phone to Leah. "Veronica called and said she's in trouble."

The girl reached through the opening in her blanket and took the phone from me, looking really confused.

"Is there any way you can get the location from the call?"

"I don't think so. Did she give you an address?"

"It was too fast. She called. Said she was in trouble. And that she needed me to come help her."

Leah shook her head and handed me back the phone. "I'm good, but not like that."

"You pulled the location to the cave out of my chest."

She shrugged and shook her head. "That was different. It was like you were shouting it at me."

Magicks were weird and didn't work the same all the time, probably because they were emotion-based. "I had to check." I stared at the phone in my hand trying to figure out how I was going to figure out where Veronica was.

Or if I even should.

Leah shed the blanket and stood.

I waved her back to the table.

She waved my waving off. "What was she doing? Do you know?"

I appreciated toughness like anyone else, but we couldn't afford to be stupid. I picked up the blanket and gave it back to her. "We'd have to check the cameras, but I'd bet she was tracking down that demon that can touch your mom's magick."

"What?" she asked in surprise.

"What?" I asked back. She'd been *helping* me track down the demon, but I'd forgotten I hadn't told her *why* we'd been doing that. Besides the fact that we were trying to save my girlfriend. "I didn't say anything."

Her brow furrowed in a teenaged face of you-better-tell-me-now.

Damn it. "Threknal is tied to the demon who's got the contract on Veronica's soul. So, yes. We are tracking him down for that, but..." I pulled a long face, wishing I was better at keeping my mouth shut. "...he can also touch your mom's magick. And we've determined it's not good. He works for a really bad demon."

"She's the demon summoner," she said as if that meant something.

"Agreed." I wanted to keep her in the know, but I didn't want to freak her out. "And his touch-her-magickness is the reason she wasn't able to unsummon him."

"Oh." She blinked and relaxed like she'd been defused. "Well, that makes sense now."

Why hadn't I told her this already? But a lot had happened. "I need to figure out how to find Vee, and how to save her."

Fox narrowed his eyes. "Does your magick work better in a fight now?"

Than when we were kids? "Meh. Not really. But I can use sigils and lay those down. That helps." But not always because sigil work took time and that wasn't something I could count on having in the middle of a battle.

"So, even if we get you there somehow, *you* won't be able to do much."

I hated it when he stabbed me with the truth. "Yeah."

"Okay. So, we need a different plan."

"We could talk to Ty—Remix." Leah narrowed her eyes at me as if to tell me to learn their names. "Check out our—" She paused to finger quote with her blanket-filled hands. "—cameras."

Fox frowned as if wondering why that needed to be air quoted.

I shook my head and winced off his questions. "Yeah, yeah. But, uh, how do we we—"

"I could call my dad," Leah said.

"What's your dad gonna do?" Charlie asked, rising to her feet.

"He's the local police captain," I said.

Leah scrunched up her face and shook her head. "He just runs Red Star."

"Oh," Fox said with a tone that said he was impressed. "He could definitely help with things. But how do we call him? Will your phone work again?"

I tried, but I had no signal. "How'd she get through in the first place?"

"Trap?" Charlie asked, keeping her gaze focused on my phone.

I didn't like that idea, but it had merit. If they hadn't been working and then suddenly did for one thing? But it could also mean that Veronica'd done a spell and made it work. "What would he gain by luring me into one?"

"You're... karma?"

Well, there was that, but there was also the fact that Veronica and I had created an elaborate plan where I would be used to kill Valfire. If Threknal was luring me out, that might mean they knew.

"What's going on?" Fox asked, his voice low and rumbly.

I hated it when he used that voice on me but only because I couldn't resist him. "Nothing."

He narrowed his gaze as if able to see right through me.

I hated that about him too. "We're—Vee and me—working to take out his boss."

"To help Mom?" Leah asked.

"Sure."

Fox raised an eyebrow. "So, no."

"No." Of course not. "Look, we're trying to save her from a soul contract. But," I said, looking to Leah, "we are *also* helping your mom."

"That's real?" Charlie asked incredulously. "Soul contracts?"

"Apparently." I let my head fall back and stared up at the ceiling for a moment, then brought it back down. How much time did we have? Was she really in trouble? Was this a trap?

Was this a lie? "He's collecting the souls of witches and creating very powerful demons from them."

A light lit in Fox's eyes. "That explains a lot."

"Of what?"

He shook his head. "Stuff that doesn't matter to this. Are you going?"

Yes. "Maybe?" No.

I had to go because I loved Veronica. I was mad at being played and for playing myself, but at the end of the day, I really did love her. At least, I was pretty sure. But with this much distance, it was hard to say. Was it really love or were my feelings for her the biproduct of whatever effect she had on me?

I didn't *know* if it was a great idea to go after her. I was needed here. My family needed me here. There was some prison that needed protecting. And, of course, Paige... needed me... here. Yeah. That one was still a bit of a stretch for me.

I definitely *shouldn't* go because the risk was too high, and the intel was so low. I couldn't take Leah into more danger. I'd *just* nearly killed her with snow.

So, there were my yes, maybe, and no reasons. What was my decision, though? "Okay. Okay. Is there a tree out here who can talk?"

Leah leaned back but all the windows were either stuffed with plants or had black out curtains keeping the cold air out.

"Talking trees?" Charlie asked her.

Leah nodded and straightened. "Dryads. But would they be frozen out here?"

I shrugged. "I don't know how they work. We can dial up a door or we can try to find a tree or..."

"Or find a witch who can scry?" Charlie asked like I was stupid.

Oh, right. Gertie could. "Or do that." Right. Well, we'd

impart the information, but I didn't feel great about leaving my family knowing a killer was on the loose still and I didn't feel great about running away to save a girlfriend I'd been tricked into loving.

Somebody needed to give me a direction, though.

Quinn stared at the message and read it again.

Invasion force imminent. Recommend manning borders.

Which borders? All of them?

She got up, went around her desk, left her tiny office, and went directly to Lovejoy's, knocking first, but entering before she was cleared.

Lovejoy was on her earpiece communication device—there were so many different kinds out right now and everyone just had what they could get—so Quinn set the message down in front of her and waited.

Lovejoy closed her eyes and nodded once. "Yeah, I've gotta go. Just got something that came in. Yeah. Yeah, you too. Yup. Thanks. Bye. You, too." She tapped her earpiece and took it off her head. "How credible is this?"

"Very." Quinn trusted Gardner with her life.

"Couldn't be a bit more specific?"

"Probably couldn't, sir." Quinn clasped her hands behind her back. "Not without blowing his cover."

Lovejoy nodded as if she understood. "Okay. Looks like it's time to see if all those plans amount to anything. Let's go."

Quinn followed and hoped like hell she was on the right side of history. Only time would tell.

Phoebe looked around the ornate room, one eyebrow raised. "Who are we meeting again?"

Paige was starting to get used to being in rooms of people who made way too much money. She went to the bar along the back wall and helped herself to a glass of something dark. She raised her glass and took a sip. "Don't really know, but it's someone with power over Colorado, so..." She shrugged.

"And that's..." Phoebe pointed to the glass in Paige's hand.

She shrugged. "Stealing? Too early in the day?" She shook her head. "With the days we're having and are about to have? I think it's okay."

"It's also," a refined and male voice said from the doorway, "the very reason it's there." A tall man in a business suit walked in with a smile. "Please, by all means, help yourself."

Phoebe raised an eyebrow and tipped her head to the side, but didn't make a move on the liquor stash.

The man did, however, and poured himself a glass. "To what do I owe this great honor?" he asked with a charming smile as he turned to us.

Paige regarded him, trying to get a bead on who he was, what he was, and what he'd want. "I heard you're the person I need to talk to about keeping Colorado."

"Ah." He sipped his drink and sat, pushing his jacket tails out of the way first and crossing his right ankle over his left knee, lounging back in his white chair. "I feel, then, I am doomed to disappoint you."

Paige took a seat opposite him already frustrated with this conversation. He was wordy. "Why?"

"So blunt." He took in a breath through his teeth and ravished her with his dark eyes. "Let's savor this moment a while."

"Let's cut the crap instead." Paige leaned back, crossing her legs similarly. "Are you the man in power or not?"

He shrugged with an impish look on his face.

If he was *doomed* to disappoint as the man in power, then that only meant he didn't think she'd be able to meet his price. "Then what do you want?"

All pretenses slid from his face as he studied her. "You're quite good."

That didn't answer her question.

His eyebrows flicked and he smiled. "Fine then. There's an artifact and a book that I require."

So, a treasure hunt in the middle of a war. Perfect. "Do you know where they are?"

He gave her a cool look. "The library."

Phoebe glanced at Paige, opening her mouth as she took a seat.

Paige knew what library he was talking about. The very one with an entrance guarded by Cyn's family. It wasn't even in this dimension. "If they're there, it's for a reason."

He nodded. "I do not doubt that."

"What do you want it for?"

"Do you really need to know?"

Not really. "Will it be bad for us?"

He snorted. "Not for years to come."

"But it will be bad for us."

"Will it? Or will it shape you in ways you didn't understand you needed?"

Paige wasn't going to be tricked into philosophical discussions. "What are they?"

He studied her as if weighing her. "The Stone of Albrec and the *Tome of Souls*."

Paige hadn't heard of either of them. "I'll talk to the librarian."

"Oh, please do." He sat up, setting his glass down like a giddy school child. He looked Phoebe up and down like she was a treasure to collect.

She gave him a look that told him to stop or she'd bless him with baldness. "What?"

His smile cocked to the side as his dark eyes lit up, the coveting zeal toned down minutely in his eyes. "It always a pleasure to meet something new."

She bristled.

"Mr..." Paige hadn't gotten the man's name.

He gave her a twinkling smile and extended his hand. "Steven Odison."

Paige took his hand and electricity buzzed up her arm. "It's a pleasure," she gritted out, "to meet you."

He chuckled and released her hand, then relaxed in his chair. "So, you want Colorado, and you don't bore me. Let's talk."

Paige wasn't sure what The Stone of Albrec and the *Tome of Souls* was going to bite her in the butt, however, she did know that Colorado *would be* a key state in the fight for independence. She wouldn't sell people's souls.

But she might get dangerously close. She needed to talk to Cyn's parents and figure out what secret power Mr. Odison was seeking.

I stepped through the door with Leah, Charlie, Whomper *and* Fox coming through behind me.

The magick door closed with a zippering whisper. "Do you need me right away?" Leah asked as if in pain.

Technically, I had access to cars here. I mean, kinda. Sure. I might have to beg, borrow, or steal, but there was zero need to be carted around by a door witch. "Yeah. We're good."

"Great." She exhaled a burst of air and dashed up the porch stairs to her house. "Have fun. Don't die."

Remix nearly collided with her on his way out. After

saying something I couldn't understand, he fell out the door and landed awkwardly on his feet in front of me. "Wy." He grinned and waved. "So, cameras. Things happened. Great stuff. Need to fill ya in."

"I was only gone a couple of days."

"I know," he said, pulling his head back until his double chin appeared. "Crazy, right? So, anyway, like I was saying, we found another of those fingers. Right here beside the house. Took us forever to find it. Don't know how they did the whole digging thing and foundation—yeah, I don't know. Backhoes, man. They're amazing."

"Thrill," Charlie said with a tip of her head.

He smirked at her with a nod. "Anyway. Did my own research, thank you very much, and the symbol means delta. Okay. So, it *is* a delta and it means—" He shrugged floppily. "Wet?"

In relation to leylines? "If leylines are rivers of magickal energy, then a magick delta would be kind of cool." Because it meant it was a meeting place of ley-lines or earth's energy rivers.

"Pog. And, also, our house is built on top of it."

I had no idea what pog meant. It sounded like someone was making up the language again. But whatever. "Anything else?"

"That's pretty good," he said, his tone asking why there needed to be anything else.

"It is." I moved the party toward the house. "But I was *asking* if you'd seen anything on the cameras and maybe like where Veronica would be."

"Veronica?" Remix wrinkled his face. "Dude, she's home. Er, I mean, in your cabin."

"Are you..." That didn't sound right. Did it? "...sure?"

"It's a trap," Charlie said.

236

"Definitely," Fox agreed, looking around. "What kind of protections are in place?"

I wasn't going to list them all. "I'm going to let your witch eyes see and tell *me* what protections are in place. We literally landed in the most safest place on the face of the planet."

"Ms. Hunt," a female voice commanded from a distance.

I turned, trying to figure out who was using that tone on me. I found a woman in a business pant suit and sensible shoes walking with purpose in my direction. I looked around to see if she was really calling me.

"Ms. Hunt," she said again, raising a hand as if to signal where I should look.

"Give me a sec," I told Fox. "Keep her out of I trouble," I told Whomper and then walked to meet up with the blonde. "Yeah? What's up?"

The blonde stopped. "I heard about Veronica."

I didn't know *how*. "I heard it on good authority she's in the treehouse."

"She is not." The woman tipped her head to the side, her pale eyebrows rising. "I intercepted their video feed days ago."

"How?" And did I need to be worried?

"They're very innovative, but I can't have them meddling in affairs of national—" She held up her hands and shook her head as if unsure if she's used the right word. "—security."

"So, Veronica? You know where she is?"

The woman nodded. "Director Lovejoy." She offered her hand. "I need you to take care of Threknal once and for all."

That wasn't going to go over well with Veronica. "We need him to bait a trap."

Director Lovejoy shook her head. "He's a direct threat to the leader of our new nation, so he needs to be eliminated.

He was captured and contained once before. I cannot risk him being released again."

"She was the one who released him."

Director Lovejoy bit down on her lips and rocked her head back, the expression in her amber eyes dry. "I'm only too aware." She looked at the team who'd followed me here from Alaska and back at me. "I'm going to need debriefed on your situation."

"Uh, it's a work in progress." And I didn't know who this woman was. Where the hell was Paige?

"Understood. But take a moment, fill me in, and then I'll let you go again."

I'd said I'd needed direction from someone. If this woman was *here*, it was because Paige trusted her.

And she knew where Veronica was.

What did I have to lose? "Yeah, okay. But let's make it fast. Vee sounded urgent when she called."

"Ah. She called you." Director Lovejoy narrowed her eyes and blinked as if she was staring into the sun. "Then we have another situation. Come on. We don't have a lot of time."

Great. What the heck was going on here?

20

Lovejoy took the information I gave her—which wasn't a ton because I didn't know how much I was supposed to share about Alaska's unique situation. They didn't appreciate people who blabbed. Then she gave me Veronica's location and what little she knew.

Threknal had taken Veronica to a remote location in the Wyoming Rocky Mountains and she was being held in a warehouse. However, none of Lovejoy's agents had been able to get inside. If this was a trap for me, there was a very good possibility that only I would be able to get in.

So, I armed myself with my karma blades and ring spells, and pocketed a few sigil spells as well. Then, I'd gathered Fox and had tried to talk another door witch into helping me.

But Leah'd pushed her way back through saying that all she'd needed was a hot bath to unfreeze her bones and to "get over" myself.

Kids, man.

I stepped through the door Leah cut open and took in my surroundings. Rocky Mountain forest surrounded me with the tall, beefy spruce trees and shorter quakies. I couldn't tell exactly where we were, and didn't see any recognizable mountain peaks anywhere. But if Lovejoy had said we were in Wyoming, then I guessed that's where we were.

Fox stepped out and surveyed the area, a stick with runes in his right hand. It looked like a bad-boy sex toy or an Agiel that the Mord-Sith carried around. Cara Mason was still the sexiest woman in red leather—or white leather—that ever lived.

That only made me think "sex toy" even more as I tried *not* to look at his...stick.

Leah closed the door behind her. "What do we do now?"

Anger shot through me. "You open a door and head back, that's what."

"Gertie said that where you go, I go."

"And in Alaska, what she says is the rule of law, but here?" In these woods with who knew how many bad guys who could also be demons? "Your mother is going to kill me and I don't like that." I also didn't want to put yet one more kid in danger.

Even if I *hadn't* before, I *felt* like I had because I'd *believed* it. And that mattered.

And I wasn't doing that again. "So, go home."

"No." Leah gave me a tough-luck look and took a step forward, looking around.

"Leah," I said with a hint of warning.

She tipped her head to the side. "You'd actually have to be willing to follow through. That's what makes Mom and Aunt Les terrifying. They say they're going to do something, and they do it. I mean, most times. Not always. But like...okay almost half the time. Sometimes, they're just really tired. Anyway, you're not willing. So..." She held her hands out on either side of her and looked innocent. "Make me."

I was ill prepared to face this particular enemy. "Fine," I said quietly. "Then stay behind where it's safe."

"Unless you're attacked from behind."

Dear gods, I wanted to strangle that girl.

I'd left Whomper to look after and protect Charlie, which made me feel a little better. Also, there was the fact that she was quite literally in the safest place on the continent. "Okay. Well, if you die, you killed you." I had no idea what I was even saying anymore. "Lovejoy said the warehouse'd be over here."

"And we're supposed to just kill this guy?" Fox asked, frowning.

"What?" No. "Sure. She sends two people she barely knows and a kid to go up against a demon who needs destroyed to protect our new powerful leader. Yup. Sounds perfectly... legit."

"Okay," he said dryly. "When you put it like that..."

Yeah, when I put it like that, I had no idea what we were doing out there. "We're to grab Vee and get out. Nothing fancy. No going after Threknal. Or...anything else."

Fox narrowed his dark eyes and then slid them away with a nod, gripping his stick.

I had a dirty, dirty mind.

"How far away are they?" Fox asked, pulling another rune-covered stick out of his belt.

"Just over that hill?" Leah said in more of a question than an answer.

Pressure built in my ears and Whomper wizzed past me, standing on two bristled feet in front of me and just stopped.

Oh, no he didn't. He was being a *very* bad broom. "I left you at home protecting Charlie," I hissed at him.

"Yeah," Storm said behind me. "Well, Oracle said you needed help of the us kind so we're here."

I spun around so fast I twisted my ankle. Not badly, but it did hurt. "What..." I couldn't believe I was staring at so many kids. Including Charlie. "...are you doing here?"

"O.ra.cle," Storm said slower, using her fingers to punctuate the word, something I'm sure she'd seen her mother do. "Remember, the kid with visions?"

"I know who you're talking about, asshole."

Storm jiggled her head from side-to-side as if trying to figure out a witty rejoinder.

I probably shouldn't have called her an asshole to her face. "What are you guys doing here?" I knew what they were doing there. Putting themselves in danger. "What did he see?"

"Oracle?" Fox asked, looking at me out of the corner of his eye.

"Yeah." I gestured toward Storm. "The kid who has visions." I shared an exasperated look with the girl. "What'd he see? How're we about to die?"

"Uh, no," Storm said, holding up a finger. "You survive. *He* dies and then you release a karmic storm and then we all get sent to prisons and camps and we're slaughtered. But *you* live."

That was... that sucked. "I hate your brother's visions."

"Yeah." She reached in her pocket and pulled out a stick of gum, popping it in her mouth. "Anyway. We brought the squad."

It was just her, Whomper, and Charlie so far. "This isn't..."

Another door opened behind the kids and the rest of the squad plus a few poured through, the final one through closing it behind her.

Fox folded his arms over his chest and gave me a hard stare. "This is what you do? Collect kids to relive your past?"

"No." Though, this was giving me flashbacks a little. "No. Guys."

Storm walked forward like a force to be reckoned with. "You lived. We're fixing this."

"Okay. So, if I die here?"

Oracle stepped up, his blue eyes narrowed, his brow furrowed. "We don't need that. We just can't let you kill Threknal."

"But *how* do I kill him? He's a demon."

The boy just shrugged. "Just don't do it. If you feel like you're about to, maybe stop. I guess. Yeah. Don't. I don't know."

I released a long breath and waited for the kids to march past. I reached out and almost snagged Charlie's arm, but stopped myself. I wasn't her mom. Not really. I was as responsible for her life as I was for all the rest of them.

"What's going on here?" Fox asked in a low voice.

I shook my head, trying to come to terms with the feeling of relief swimming through me. That's *not* what an adult was supposed to feel when a bunch of kids came swooping in to get themselves killed. "Just trust me. Okay? Those kids are... it's gonna take a lot to take them out. And if Oracle is here —" I paused and gestured to the boy in question. "—he'll find a way for this to work." I hoped.

Fox shook his head and followed the kids. "For the record, I am *not* okay with this."

Leah gave me a cocky look on her way past me. "Still want me to hang back?"

I flipped her the bird.

Then followed the kids who'd come to save the world I was about to destroy.

Paige left Phoebe at her place then took a car to Cyn's mansion. There were very few people who knew about this place and Paige wasn't going to change that. The entrance to their own version of *Warehouse 13* was nestled in the master bedroom, tucked in between the shoe rack and the sweaters.

This wasn't a conversation Paige was looking forward to, largely because she didn't know if she wanted to know what these two artifacts could even do.

Cyn and Lynx were nowhere around, so she let herself into the mansion, walked through the modestly furnished-for-a-mansion foyer, up the wide and sweeping staircase, and into the master suite. There, she went straight for the closet, touched the safety panel and stepped through the portal.

If anyone else followed, they would be treated to something rather unpleasant, though Arthur never gave her details of what that would look like.

Paige was almost certain that the castle on the other side didn't like her. It felt like a living, breathing entity. It would open doors. Close them. It could get a person totally lost if they didn't watch it, something she'd had the pleasure of experiencing.

So, when she stepped into the hallway the portal now dumped new arrivals, she put her hand to the wall and waited until the stone warmed under her palm. "I'm here to see Arthur and Charlotte. Are they available?"

The stone cooled to the touch and the air went silent. Paige's hearing had decreased considerably since losing her shifter spirit, but nothing moved. No mice. No doors as the building shifted. No... buzzing lamps.

Finally, something wisped in front of her, but kind of far away.

Paige watched it for a long moment.

It danced toward her and then kind of chirped at her, bouncing up and down like it was trying to get her attention.

She put her hand on her chest. "Me?"

The chittering sped up and then the wispy light bounced all over the place and then headed back the way it'd come.

Paige took that to mean that she was supposed to follow it, whatever it was. "Thank you," she said to the walls and moved as quickly as she could after the glowy thing.

Eventually, she was led into the most massive library she'd ever seen. The ceiling was several stories up. The books went from the floor all the way to the domed glass ceiling in rows and rows—or stacks as they were called.

The bouncy light led her past several flights of stairs and moving staircases that had oddly been grouped together and finally stopped at a table stacked high with books. It chittered incessantly and then disappeared.

Great. Paige looked around. "Charlotte?"

"Be there in a moment," a woman's voice called from somewhere overhead.

Paige looked at some of the books. They were pretty cool for old books, though, to be honest, she just didn't really care about most of them. Maybe if she had some spare time—

No. She'd still rather read something else, something like sci-fi, flying around in a spaceship with a quirky AI and a gun that never ran out of ammo. Yeah. That sounded like a good time.

In a steaming hot bubble bath.

Oh. Now she was talking.

"Paige," Arthur said, coming up one of the many aisles, wiping his hands on a rag. He was a portly man with a balding head, but his smile was always genuine. "It's good to see you. How're the twins?"

As the guy who'd raised her twins from the age of a couple of weeks to teens, she was more than a little jealous of him. But she bit that off. "They're good. They're good. Hey, uh, I've got a strange request and I need to know how bad it is."

"Paige?" a familiar male voice said.

She winced and then forced herself to relax as her grandfather walked up to them. She didn't know how long it was going to take her to get used to the fact that Father Reece was her mother's father, or that he'd abandoned Alma to raise Rachel on her own while he'd followed the Lord's path, whatever that meant. But she forced a smile and turned to him. "Father Reece."

He raised his bushy eyebrows at her but didn't verbalize the chastisement. He'd been trying to get her to not be so formal with him since she'd discovered his truth.

She wasn't going to let up though. He wasn't a part of her family. He hadn't been a part of her life, or her mother's life. Maybe if he'd been around, Rachel wouldn't have abandoned her and Leslie when their gifts had bloomed. Or she might not have taken Leah. Or she might not have unleashed heaven's hounds on Leah in order to get her back.

There were... a lot of reasons Paige struggled to be okay with that man, most of which was the fact that her grandmother had sincerely loved that man and had never wanted another.

Charlotte came swinging in on a rolling ladder in complete Belle-style. Minus the singing. Paige'd heard that woman "sing" once before and it was... bad. Like, really bad. Charlotte laughed as she hopped down, her blonde hair in a slight disarray. "I love my job."

Paige was glad for the woman. She'd sacrificed a lot to be here, so knowing she was okay with it only made the entire situation better. "So, my strange request."

Arthur led them over to a free table and gestured at something Paige didn't see. "As you said."

Paige grunted as glasses appeared filled with a honey-colored liquid. "What can you tell me about the Stone of Albrec?"

Arthur narrowed his eyes and pulled his head back as he sat forward over his glass. "Where did you hear that name?"

"It came up in negotiations."

"Hmm. What kind?"

Paige filled them in on what had transpired in Colorado.

"Steven Odison, you say?" Charlotte shook her head, her thin lips tight. She made a tsking noise and then shook her head again. "He's Loki's son or grandson? I don't know exactly. Or, at the very least, I'm not quite sure which texts to believe on the subject."

So, a demigod. "What does he want with the stone and the book?"

"Well, if it was one or the other?" Arthur shook his head and shrugged. "But together?"

That wasn't giving Paige *any* information.

"The stone," Reece said, glaring at Arthur, "grants people the ability to see beyond the veil. It was named after the person who it was said created it in the fit of a great vision."

"I don't need the details." And she didn't. Reece might be a priest, but he was a historian at heart and loved to go on and on about things that didn't help the present situation. "So, it sees the dead."

"Well, yes," Charlotte said in a tone that said *not really*. "The unclaimed souls, the ones that could still be stolen."

"Let me guess." Because Paige was starting to see the connection. "With the help of the *Tome of Souls*."

Arthur nodded grimly. "We cannot allow both to leave the safety of the castle. They were both brought here for very good reasons, Paige."

"I understand that, Arthur, but I *need* Colorado."

He grunted. "At what cost?"

Paige leaned back in her chair. They were the high-backed wooden chairs she'd seen in several medieval movies, and they weren't comfortable. "You said you couldn't allow them *both* out of here." She sighed, trying to find a compromise that wouldn't break her soul. "What about one of them?"

Arthur shared a pinched look with his wife. "How many more of these negotiations do you have?"

"I have no idea." But she did have a slight clue. "States. Countries. Probably a lot of people."

He rose to his feet. "Then you're taking Reece with you."

Paige opened her mouth to protest.

Arthur held up his hand to stop her. "He knows what these things do, what can be agreed to and what can't." He looked at Reece and nodded. "You can take the stone, but the tome stays here."

Reece bowed his head. "I will have my things gathered."

This was unnecessary. "Arthur—"

"Don't argue, Paige," he said gently, yet firmly. "You needed a solution. This is it. We're done here." He smiled at his wife who rose and took his hand. "Have a good day, Ms. Whiskey."

As much as she didn't like being dismissed, she did appreciate winning.

And that had been a win. "Thank you."

She said to an empty room.

21

So, this was Leslie's life now, not being able to find any of her kids and heading off to some war front to protect people she didn't even know. Like *she* was some big, dumb hero.

Well, she wasn't.

But Angela Blackman closed her doorway behind her, leaving Leslie little choice but to stand there with the rest of Dexx's pack. She didn't want to stand there, waiting on Dexx.

It feels good, Robin said in Leslie's head.

Yeah, sure, she grumbled back to her pea-brained gryphon buddy. *This feels great.*

He was quiet for a moment, still churlish over the ghost attack.

Which was fine because she was supposed to be off searching for trouble, which meant that if he was sulking, she was free to work.

Relax, Robin said.

Easy for you to say. She shifted into hawk form and beat her wings until she found a current she could ride upwards. *You nearly got us killed.*

She still didn't know if she was okay being saddled with Robin. She wanted to be, but her job in this world was to help ghosts.

And Robin didn't do ghosts.

I'll do better, he said, sounding pitiful.

She'd tried being supportive of the big bird. She'd tried being a mom. She'd tried being his friend and everything else Dexx had offered, but in the end, they'd still nearly been taken down by ghosts when she'd tried to handle a situation that should have been under her control.

A lot of townsfolk had *died* because their in-town medium had been taken down by a scared bird.

He whimpered and retreated.

If he wanted to do better like he said, he'd have to prove it to her because Leslie... didn't believe him. Not one bit.

Movement caught her eye to the east. *Dexx.*

I see it. He was in cat form and moved in the direction she'd given.

Leslie appreciated the ability to change shape, but she knew that DoDO had found a weakness in their defenses. She also knew they wouldn't hesitate to use it again. She had to make sure they were ready next time.

But she had to figure out a way to get Robin prepared.

Or she'd have to find a way to let Robin go.

Thanks to Oracle, we located where Veronica was being held with relative ease. We hunkered down along a hill and peered over, trying to see what we could see.

Karma vision isn't showing me a whole lot, I said to the mind meld.

Fox wouldn't stop giving me death glares.

What are we even looking for? Storm asked.

Anything demon related?

Well, Blaze said, his inner male voice lower than his physical one, *I see... something. Here.*

My eyes got this overlay effect on them, like the world darkened to allow the burning outlines of runes or sigils that flamed along the walls.

You can see that? This was cool, but if this was related to his abilities, if each witch could see with the help of his or her own magick, then this had something to do with fire? *Pyro, what do you see?*

She snorted beside me. *Nothing followed by nothing covered with nothing slimed with... nothing.*

Okay. So this had something to do specifically with him. *What's your shifter animal?*

Fox gave me a look that demanded to know why that was even a question.

Rajasi, Blaze grunted.

Yeah. That didn't tell me anything because I still had no idea what that had to do with anything.

Can you read them? Remix asked.

Not super really. These were... really old. Maybe not quite as old as the stones, but it was if the sigilwork was interlaced with some kind of language. Well, sigilwork *was* a language of sorts. So, it was as if whoever had created these had written them in different languages.

I've seen this, Storm said. *In the library.* She shifted around beside me like a cat excited to pounce. *Okay. That?* She pointed.

I couldn't tell what she was pointing at.

That's something like door or... something.

Great. *Okay, Oracle. What did I do wrong the last time?*

He pushed his tongue to the roof of his mouth, which

gave him a dumb look on his face as he looked at me with his blue eyes. *You killed Threknal.*

So… I had to go in and rescue Veronica and *not* kill the demon we were trying to trap? *How did I kill in the first place?"*

He shrugged. *Karma, I guess?*

Fox narrowed his eyes and tipped his head to the side as if wanting to know what the hell was going on.

He could wait.

I can open a door, Leah said. *Drop us inside.*

Probably not, Storm said. *There's something I there that would blow us up.*

I wanted to know what kind of language this was and how I'd been able to get in without Storm reading the sigils only Blaze could see. However, I also made a mental note to ask Storm where she'd seen this before because this might help me with my own sigilwork. *Here's the plan.*

I raced through a rough idea of a plan as quickly as I could, which wasn't a great one. But it did work to all of our strengths.

Once we were all clear on our goals, Fox led the way to the door—which happened to be the *only* door, which was probably the reason I'd been able to open it without Storm and Blaze's help in the vision version. He crouched low, checking the door for more traps, but since none of us really knew what we were looking *at*, it was kind of a mute move.

I stepped into a wide space with big industrial shelves filled with things that seemed… forgotten about. From the outside, we hadn't been able to determine what this building was. A big shed? A warehouse? A home? Who knew?

It looked like a storage locker and my karma vision showed that some of the things stored here had considerable karma attached to them.

We've gotta let Arthur know about these, Storm whispered telepathically.

I had no idea who Arthur was, but the kids could handle that.

Fox's job was to handle Threknal along with Storm and Blaze. The other kids were to handle any kind of other troops or opponents we might come up against.

And I was there to rescue my girlfriend.

So, knowing that they were all set on what they were supposed to do, and with Charlie sticking close to Leah, I went in search of Veronica.

But not before I drew a sigil of protection on myself. Not against damage.

Against manipulative magicks.

Like Veronica's.

I slipped past the last set of shelves and stepped into an open area, the concrete floor clean of debris. However, there were more sigils painted onto it, ones I could see with my naked eye.

Veronica was held in a silver stasis field in a floating position. Her eyes were open and wide, and her mouth moved as if she was trying to tell me something, but her hands didn't move.

I knew what she was trying to tell me though.

This was a trap.

Well, no shit.

I held out a hand palm down to let her know I knew that already and looked around, trying to make sure that Threknal wasn't in the immediate area. The only truly crucial part of this particular plan I really had to follow was not to engage with Threknal. As the karmic witch who wasn't super great in battle anyway, I was super okay with that. I had no idea how I was supposed to kill him in the first place.

Well, I did. Using the same theory I'd come up with in order to save Veronica from Valfire...I could, in theory, use my karmic magick powered by love to... kill a demon.

But this time, I was going in with my memories, loving Veronica, but also knowing the trick. I didn't think it'd work because I *understood* the lie I'd woven, the karmic trick I'd laid.

I just had to hope Charlie remained okay. Whomper and Leah were both protecting her, so...

It was still a battle with a demon.

This whole thing was dumb.

So, instead, I went to the stasis field around Veronica and tried to figure out how to take it down.

The sound of something metal hitting something electrical filled the air followed by Fox's grunt. Clashing sounds screamed "fight!" in another part of the warehouse.

Well, someone had found Threknal. It was time to get this thing down and get her out of here.

But there weren't any sigils or... any things I could use. There was a lacework of karma, but it wasn't enough for me to use to unravel this.

"What's that?" Charlie asked.

Something crashed followed by a yip.

Charlie flinched.

We didn't have a lot of time. If I couldn't get this thing down, then I'd have to abandon Veronica.

Maybe that was the reason I'd killed Threknal in the vision-version. If Threknal, the caster of this spell, died, then his magick died with him.

I needed solutions that didn't involve killing the demon.

Charlie gestured toward the silver column surrounding Veronica.

"It's a field." I didn't know much more than that.

"No." Charlie pointed, glancing with fear in her teal eyes to our left as the sounds of battle went quiet. "This."

The fighting had paused and they were now talking, so

that was good. Maybe Fox was buying me time. But I didn't see anything special where Charlie pointed. "What?"

She looked at me like I was dumb and flared her fingers as she gestured to whatever it was again.

Shaking my head, I called on my karma vision and looked where she pointed.

A faint, smoky outline of a sigil line of text appeared over the rippling blue-white surface of the cylindrical containment wall. It was so pale though. I reached behind me to use some of the karma attached to a few of the objects stored behind me, transferring it to the sigils in front of me.

They lit up with a pop, dark smoke spilling around us.

Dark smoke. That couldn't be good. I grabbed Charlie's shoulder and pulled her back.

"What's that?" she asked, fear rising in her voice.

"I don't know. I couldn't read the…" Fuck, fuck, fuck. "I'd only meant to read it."

My ears struggled to pop as a hand grabbed my shoulder, pulling me through a doorway. I spun as the doorway closed in my face.

She'd brought us to the fight. Away from the smoke, which was great, but right into the fight. Which wasn't great.

Leah spun, opening another doorway behind a falcon with lightning coming off its wings—Storm. Leah closed it behind the bird as another opened in Storm's flight path, letting the falcon through.

I pulled out one of my karma blades. If I could get close enough, I could cut him and it'd be deep. That demon had a lot of really bad karma coming off him.

Crap. Veronica.

But if she was still being protected by the force field holding her in place, she'd be fine. Though, we still might be fine. It was black smoke. It might not be anything.

Suuuuure. Black smoke in a demon trap might not be anything. Riiiiight.

Oracle surrounded the demon with a golden cocoon of light, but Threknal was able to keep it away with some sort of shield.

Blaze hit it with a fire that ate the shield away like acid.

Fox searched for weaknesses in the demon's defenses and shot magick through the holes Blaze created.

They were doing good against the demon, but we needed to do what we'd set out to do.

I crept forward, grabbing Charlie's hand and bringing her with me. It certainly seemed like we were headed away from the greatest danger. The industrial shelves stood just on the other side of the non-magickal door. I didn't see any of the black smoke, didn't hear any coughing or sputtering.

"Do you see anything?" I asked.

She didn't say anything as we continued past one row and then the last.

The light in the middle of the room was gone, meaning the containment field had to be down. I peered around the end of the last shelving unit.

Veronica knelt on the concrete floor as if gaining her bearings.

I didn't see any other traps.

"We need to be careful," I told Charlie.

She nodded and together, we crept forward.

Veronica raised her head. "Is he still here, *chèrie?*"

I nodded. "We've got him busy, but now that you're safe, it's time for us to get out of here."

Veronica looked at me and then reached over and touched my face, bringing me closer to whisper against my lips, "We need to trap him. Do as I say, please."

I wanted to see what she did, wanted to see the affects, watch it, study it.

I didn't feel anything.

Maybe she hadn't tried anything, but maybe this was just the sigils working, too. "No," I said, pulling away from her. "He can remain here, but we're not capturing him."

She stood up, advancing on me. "I can hear them. Why wouldn't we?"

"Because they're kids, Vee." I straightened, turning on her. "It's time to collect the kids and get out of here. Now."

Oracle stumbled into the area, his arm out and glowing gold. "Wy, stop."

Veronica clenched her hand into a fist and pushed it at me, flinging her hand open.

Her violet-colored magick sent me hurtling backward into the shelves.

She wanted to play dirty, did she? I picked myself off the floor and reached for some of the karma magick clinging to the objects on these shelves.

Charlie frowned and took a step forward.

Veronica advanced on her, her dark eyes twinkling, her mouth set and grim.

No! I didn't even think. I just took the magick I'd gathered and wrapped it around Charlie as if to protect her.

At the same time, an explosion reverberated through the warehouse.

I spun around, looking behind me.

Oracle held out his hand, his blue eyes wide as he started to shake. "N-n-no!"

I caught him as he slid to the ground.

Veronica raced to the back where Threknal lay still.

"He's dead," Bobby whispered.

"Threknal?" I asked.

He nodded. "Fox killed him."

"Okay." Was everything okay?

Bobby's blue eyes turned gold and then he convulsed.

The next conversation with Steven Odison went much better with Reece *and* Phoebe there to work with negotiations. By the end of an hour, Paige and ParaWest not only had Colorado back, but also South Dakota, and the entire Four Corners. Steven also said he would talk to the leaders of Texas and the Confederation of Southern States.

And that was all *very* good news, especially with the information Lovejoy was feeding her about the potential conflict at their borders, which, apparently, was all of them. Lovejoy was sending people to the hottest points along the border, hoping to quell things there. And meanwhile, there were still people flooding in, trying to escape the Registration Act that *still* hadn't passed.

Paige wanted to cripple Walton before he could get started. She wanted to end this before it became a full-fledged war, before missiles and fireballs could fly.

Dawn didn't agree this was a good idea, but Paige didn't particularly care. She'd asked Dawn weeks ago to pull a few strings and to get a meeting of the generals anyway. Paige got the text saying they were ready to meet, but that it had to happen as soon as possible and she was given a location to meet.

This could be a trap. Paige had to know that.

However, the location was in Missouri, a state that hadn't declared itself for or against either side, so it was a neutral state.

That had to be a sign. Right?

Paige let Lovejoy know so she could make the arrangements.

The intelligence director seemed stressed. "What's going on?"

"Just a lot of stuff," Lovejoy said gruffly. "The border is

heating up. We don't have enough men on the ground to manage it. We've got a demon on the loose and a witch to chase it down. There're uprisings all over the place in Denver. The vampires are in revolt."

"Oh." Tony Guerreros was in Denver. Hopefully, he could help calm them, since Troutdale was such a bad idea for them with the Eastwoods.

"And those are just the big things."

"Well, I managed to get Colorado back."

That put on a smile that faded quickly under Lovejoy's stony expression. "Great. Maybe that'll quell the uprisings back down there."

Paige tried again. "Yup. Also got the Four Corners back."

"Don't count on that lasting long."

Okay? Was there something more Paige needed to know? "Am I okay to meet with the generals?"

Lovejoy paused and read a message that flashed across her modified tablet. "It's fine. Doesn't look like a trap. You should be good."

"Great." That was another bit of good news.

"Bring me back some troops. For fucks sake. Please. General Saul's doing everything she can with the resources we have, but we need actual troops."

Paige would see what she could do, but she didn't actually think she'd get any.

When Derek opened the portal to the meeting, she stepped into a hotel conference room, filled with people in uniform. These were generals of all the branches of the military and leaders of the intelligence agencies, including a few of Lovejoy's old bosses. They all mingled, and Paige was on a time crunch. Lovejoy had seemed *stressed,* and Saul hadn't even been around, meaning she'd probably been busy. With the borders heating up, that meant Walton was preparing to make his move.

So, she got up in front of them started right in. She shared her intent with them, and tried to make her case on why this was the right action to take at the right time.

"I cannot stand by while my nation attacks its own citizens."

That seemed to resonate with a few of them as she talked to them after her speech.

But she was focused on General McConnel. He was the one she wanted.

"The answer's no, Ms. Whiskey," he said firmly as they gathered around afterward. "I don't agree with what he's doing, but I will not actively agree to go against the country I swore to protect."

"Did you swear to protect your country or your president?"

"You know the answer to that already." He slid his narrowed gaze to the side with a shake of his head. "I won't actively engage against our citizens. I will, however, protect us against outside threat."

"Because you think that'll happen." Paige had already heard this from Dawn. As soon as the U.S. showed signs of weakness, the other countries would come in looking to gain power.

"Of course. And you'd be stupid to—" He stopped himself as soon as he saw her face, which meant that her expression showed she understood what he was saying.

Good. "That's fine, general. I have no answer to missiles."

"Oh, you do." He clamped his lips shut and raised his chin. "I'm withdrawing our troops."

"To the south." And if the southern states withdrew, they'd have all those troops as well.

His jaw clenched. "They're being remobilized."

Well, crap. There went that instant win.

"Don't become the threat I have to fight."

Paige waited until his blue eyes settled on hers and then she held his gaze. "Same."

He was still for a long moment. Then he nodded and left.

Dawn came over, maneuvering through the gathered military leaders. "We've gained several of them." She gestured to the room, her blue suit jacket sleeve rising to expose a bruise on her left wrist. "That went better than I thought it would."

"I didn't get McConnel though." Paige looked at the bruise and then raised her gaze to Dawn's significantly.

She tugged on her sleeve to cover it and then shook her head. "Yet. Give it time. You'll see."

If Dawn didn't want help with whatever that bruise represented, Paige would let it go. She had too many other things on her plate as it was. "Do we have troops?"

Dawn nodded. "Saul's coordinating with Phoebe to allocate them along the borders. Then it's all about supplying them and making sure they're taken care of."

And hopefully that was something Paige—ParaWest could accomplish. "Thank you."

Dawn shrugged. "You did this. I just hope it's enough."

"Me, too." Wars with humans were a bit more complicated than wars with demons. Though, after what she'd learned with Ez'gizol, she wasn't certain that was the truth. The wars she'd fought previously with the limited knowledge she had had been easy. Now, she wasn't even sure she had the full story.

Hell was an entire *world*. That still hadn't quite hit her.

She'd traveled to a different...world.

Did that—that didn't... make her an astronaut.

She almost snorted a laugh right there which would have been very bad. Instead, she straightened her mask and her shoulders and smiled at Dawn. "This is a start. In the right direction."

With the states she wanted back under her control, with

demon negotiations started, and troops and weapons being negotiated under their command, Paige felt a lot more comfortable heading into war.

"Bring it on," she whispered too low for anyone else to hear. She'd stand up for those who couldn't.

That didn't mean she felt any better about it.

22

Oracle was awake and only shivering hard by the time we all made it back the Whiskey house.

"What's wrong with him?" Fox asked, blood running into his eye.

"I don't know." I half-carried him to the couch and propped him as if having him sit up would make things any better. It didn't. I *knew* that, but I'd also broken someone else's kid and I didn't know how to fix him. "We should call Paige."

"Call her what?" Paige asked, walking through the front door.

I stood, the phrase, "Don't be mad," at the tip of my tongue. I bit it off. "Need help," I said instead.

She looked at the couch which... she could probably only see the top of his shaking head—and she came flying into the room, around the side table, clearing the table lamp, and pushed me out of the way to get to her son. "What happened?"

Storm looked at me with an accusation in her lightning eyes and looked back to her mom. "He's in a vision loop."

"What do you mean?" she growled threateningly.

I didn't know why Storm was pissed at *me*. Oracle had told me not to kill Threknal, so I hadn't. That he was still dead wasn't my fault. "I went to get Veronica. Threknal had her. Orac—" I stopped myself. While *I* thought the code names were cute, Paige didn't find a lot of anything cute or funny, but I honestly could *not* remember the kid's name. "He arrived with his sister—" I gestured to the little lightning twerp trying to get me in trouble. "—and told me that we had save her but I couldn't go up against Threknal because I'd kill him."

"And *when* she did," Storm said, advancing a step, her hands fisted on either side of her, "she'd unleash the end of this war. The *losing* side."

"I didn't kill him," I yelled back at her.

"He's still dead!"

Paige shot to her feet and got between us. "Stop it!" She looked at me then at Storm and said quieter. "Killing Threknal wouldn't lose us the whole war."

"That's not what *he* says, Mom." Storm did a wake-up-and-listen eye roll.

"And now he's stuck?" Paige asked.

"That's our best guess," I said. "He was staying out of the battle until…"

Paige looked up at me, not quite pissed enough to devour my soul, but not calm enough to trick me into thinking we were safe, either. "You killed Threknal."

"No, *I* did not. Fox did, but yeah."

Paige's eyes narrowed as she looked from me to Charlie to her son and back again. "Everyone's safe?"

"Yes," I said firmly. "Except… when we were done… I don't know. He just fell to the ground and started convulsing."

"And you *think*—" she said, turning to her daughter behind her, "—that he's stuck in a vision loop."

"He was giving us directions as we fought, telling us what to do to—" Storm took in a deep breath, releasing her fists. "We've been practicing this, Mom. We know what's going on. We know we're gonna be needed at some point and he figured out a way to do that."

"By…" Paige shook her head.

"By visioning while we're fighting," Storm said, her look telling us both she knew she'd be in trouble.

"And you allowed this?" Paige asked, turning back to me.

"I was there to save Veronica who managed to get a message to me that she was in trouble. I went in on my own —well, with Fox, and Leah was supposed to come back after dropping us off, but without all of them. Your kids. They all —*all*—" Except Leah who would have stayed behind. I'd've made sure of that. "—weren't a part of the plan."

Paige cupped the boy's cheek and stood. "Bring him into the kitchen."

I went in to grab him.

Fox pushed me out of the way and gathered the boy in his arms.

That man had great muscles even when he was pissed off at me and bleeding. "Do you have a first aid kit or something?"

Paige gestured to her right. "Bathroom under the stairs. Bottom drawer."

I went and retrieved it but paused with the door closed as the moment washed over me. I was a disaster of a mother. First, I would sacrifice my own daughter to save the world and now I was endangering other moms' kids? What was *wrong* with me?

I met my own gaze in the mirror.

I screwed on a strong-girl face and stepped out, grabbing Fox and directing him to one of the dining room chairs.

Paige was doing something in the kitchen, but her son was in her care now and there was nothing more I could do. So, unless she asked for help, I'd focus on what I could.

Charlie sank down in the chair beside me, her knees touching my leg. Just barely.

I made sure not to move away. She'd been scared out of her life. It was probably the first real magick fight she'd seen. I barely remembered my first time. Fox'd been there to support me. Well, we'd supported each other. I did remember it'd been hard on us though.

"Where's Veronica now?" Paige asked as she prepared tea or something.

"Still at Threknal's warehouse thing?" I focused on the cut above Fox's eye, wiping it off with an alcohol wipe.

He hissed and pulled back.

I grabbed the back of his head with my free hand and jerked him back. My nursing skills weren't great. "Stop being a baby."

"Why?" Paige asked, bringing a banana to her son who sat on the other side of the L-shaped table.

The cut was deep, and he probably needed stitches. I wasn't great with needle and thread, so I dug around looking for a butterfly bandage. "He had a bunch of stuff there. Boxes of stuff. It was just... I don't know." Finding what I was looking for, I unwrapped it and applied it to his head. It should work. "They were wrapped in karma magick."

"A magickal collection?" Paige stopped in her tracks on her way back to the kitchen. She turned around. "Where's Leah?"

"She stayed back, I think." I honestly hadn't heard much after Bobby had gone into convulsions.

Paige bit back something and pulled her phone out.

So, *her* phone worked?

Which kind of made sense. She was our acting president. Queen? What were we going to call her? I searched Fox for other wounds. There was a lot of blood on his shirt and when I lifted the grey material away from him, I looked up at him in disbelief. How was he still standing? "Do you have a doctor around?"

Paige nodded, but her attention was on the floating head above her phone. "Hey, we have something I think you need to see. Can you come to the house?" She glanced at me. "Quickly?"

The hole in Fox's abdomen was deep. "If that phone works, we need to call an ambulance."

"It's not that bad," Fox said, pushing my hands away.

"Like hell it's not." I shoved his hands from mine and tucked the bottom of his shirt into his neckline. There was a gaping *hole* in his side.

"It's stabilizing," he said calmly. "Just sterilize it and it'll heal."

I pulled away from him, leaning into Charlie who was looking around me to get a better view. "What are you? A werewolf?" He didn't come off as a werewolf and I had it on good authority that when a witch or warlock was bitten and turned, they lost all their magick. They could be a werewolf *or* a witch, but not both.

He shook his head but lifted a hand. "It's a spell. A healing spell. It just takes time. I *will* be fine."

A *healing* spell? I'd *never* heard of anything like that.

Paige came over and inspected the wound. Her lips pulled down and she said, "Huh," like she was stunned. "I may need a few thousand of those."

Fox grunted with a frown. "I don't—"

"We're going to war, Mr. McMillan. Against men with automatic weapons. Do you have a magickal answer to that?"

He grunted again, but with a shake of his head.

"Me either." The front door opened, drawing her attention. She turned it back to him. "You're really okay?"

"I am, ma'am."

"Good. You rest here. Charlie, you stay with him. Get Bobby to drink that tea. Wy, you're with me."

Charlie got up and went to the stove, muttering something.

I didn't catch it, but I got to my feet, silently asking Fox if he *was really* okay.

He released a tight breath as if saying, "For the thousandth time, yes."

Fine. I followed Paige down the hall and to the front door where an older man in a priest's collar stood.

Paige had her phone out and another head appeared above it. This one was male and had long, wavy hair. "Hey. I need a door, but just a quick one."

"Sure—" A door opened beside them. "—thing." The floating head disappeared and the man himself stepped through his own door. He smiled, but it wasn't a full or genuine one. "Where to?"

Paige gestured toward me but frowned at his legs. "Where's the coat?"

"Left it behind." He looked at me. "I need an address."

I gave him the same information I'd given Leah.

He got us close.

We walked over two hills that didn't look big enough to hide anything and then topped another.

In the bowl was the warehouse. "There."

The man—Derek—opened another door.

"Don't!" I smacked his arm before he could try to make a door to the inside.

Paige looked at me, her face folded in a frown. "What?"

"The place is... warded. Blaze—uh, your boy twin—" I

shook my head, realizing how dumb I sounded. "—is the only one who can see it. Speakeasy—the kid who reads minds? He's down for a nap right now? I guess? And so we're not in communicado."

Paige narrowed her eyes and glanced over at her brother. "Where did you go in? The exact place."

I directed the door witch to create his portal next to the door we'd used.

"When this is done," Paige said calmly, "you and I are going to have a long talk."

"Won't that be fun," I said, leading the way into the building.

The kids were milling around the place, looking in some of the containers on the shelves.

Pyro closed a lid and came over. "Aunt Paige. Hey, how's Bobby?"

Paige growled at the girl, then waved her hand. "He'll be fine. What are you guys doing here?"

"Well," Pyro said, turning around and gesturing to the room. "We got to thinking. The first time Wy came in, saved Vee, and killed Threknal, they all left. Didn't come back."

"But *we* thought," Remix said, popping out from behind one of the containers up on the third shelf, "that maybe *this* was the reason the world came to an end the first time."

"The first time?" Paige shook her head.

"Ora—Bobby," I said, trying to be helpful, "can share his visions in such a way, you live it."

Paige nodded, her expression saying she was quite familiar with that. "So, you think," she said gesturing to the boy above our heads, "that the enemy gets their hands on these and... destroys the world?"

"Well," Pyro said, drawing the word out, "the world doesn't *end* end. It just...it's not super great, is all. We all go into prisons—you know, if we *survive*. It's all very dystopian. I was kinda hoping we'd go that route and then I could find a couple of boys to moon over and save the world with my heroics." She met Paige's gaze and nodded, her lips pushed to the side. "You know. Like you said."

Paige grimaced, glancing at me and shaking her head.

This has to be some inside joke between the two of them. "What do we do with these then?"

The priest walked over to one of the containers and pried off the lid, peering inside. He made a sound of exclamation and stepped back, a smile on his face. "We need to get these to Arthur."

I looked around. That was the second time that name'd come up. "This place is huge. This is going to take a lot of time."

Paige nodded and waved me off. "Go take care of Veronica. And—"

I stopped and met her gaze.

She held it for a long measure. "Since Threknal is dead, you're no longer needed. It might be time for you to go home."

Ouch. I nodded and went in search of Veronica.

She knelt beside Threknal's body, her eyes closed. I could feel magick pouring around her. I just didn't know what she was trying to do.

"Vee," I called.

She didn't answer immediately, but she released her magick, the temperature rising minutely as she let it go. "How are we going to get Valfire now?" she asked harshly.

"He's a bad guy, Vee." She didn't get to throw this on me. "Fox was trying to... I don't know, save kids, save himself, save my daughter? What the hell did you expect him to do?"

"You—" She stopped herself. "Daughter?" Veronica stood. "Charlie's *here?*"

I nodded. "Long story. Went to Alaska for treaty stuff. Came back with my daughter and my old boyfriend."

"You're old—" Realization crashed over her gorgeous face and her lips rounded. "Fox."

I nodded and took a step toward her. I didn't know how we were going to capture Valfire—or if I even still wanted to. *She'd* been the one to sell her soul to a demon. Mama Gee had. They *all* had. That was their cross to bear. Karmically speaking, I was well within my rights to walk away. "I'm not going back under again." To have my memories locked away. To try to go along with the ruse again.

"I know," she said quietly. "I… don't want you to."

I stared down at Threknal's prone form, my heart twisting with guilt and regret and love and worry. And wondering why I felt all that.

"Do you love me?" she asked, her voice barely above a whisper.

I could pretend I hadn't heard, but… I sighed and looked at her, not sure what to tell her.

She took my hand. "Valfire is still collecting the souls of witches to create more demons like Threknal, threats to the most powerful witches this world has. Witches like Paige. Like you."

I snorted. I was *not* as powerful as Paige Whiskey.

Veronica took a step toward me, her head bent, a sultry look entering her eye. "If we don't stop Valfire now, he will take me—he will take many more witches, and then he will release us on you, on anyone who stands against you."

I didn't have an answer for that, but I got the sense that she was *trying* to magick me back. And that pissed me off. More than a little.

She closed her eyes, licked her lips as she breathed through her nose, and opened her eyes again. "Do you love me?"

271

I still thought she was the most beautiful woman on the face of this planet. "I don't know."

She swallowed and squeezed my hand. "Well," she said, her voice shaky and thick, "I love you. And..." She paused, swallowing hard as she bit both of her lips before starting again. "I'm going to keep trying, *ma cher*. You are mine and I am yours." She cupped my cheek.

Her hand felt so good, but what was this? What was she?

"I will find a way to earn you back," she whispered against my lips. "I swear it."

I let her kiss me, wanting to melt into to her, to find our remembered friendship, to fall back into the bond we'd fought so hard to forge.

But I wasn't sure it would work this time.

Time would tell. But not here because we'd worn out our welcome here.

23

T hanksgiving and Christmas both flew by. Both of them were just days ending in Y.

Between them, there were smaller skirmishes here and there, but we maintained our borders. Walton retained his.

And Veronica refused to give up on her attempt to reanimate Threknal in order to trap Valfire. I was doing my level best to find another way around the trap without needing the witch-demon.

Fox helped when he could, but he, Leah, and Charlie were spending most of their time in Alaska. I saw Charlie for an hour on Christmas, but it was while business was conducted at the house.

The other codename kids had moved their finger-stone research to the northern country as well, where the research was hopefully helping the eclectic coven up there to keep the gods contained whether or not Paige won her war.

The Confederacy did indeed split, thankfully taking a large chunk of the Navy and half of Walton's remaining land troops. I had actually started caring because things were getting scary. Dangerously scary.

We'd drawn the attention of the other countries.

I wasn't actively a part of any of it. My active participation was sitting around, doing my thing—mostly in Alaska, but also on the Whiskey lands because Veronica refused to leave —while reading headlines. My greatest skill was not losing it while reading the Dryad News.

Walton had a handful of ships left at his disposal. But he maintained control of *all* the launch codes, which was terrifying. China and North Korea made their intentions clear about making a move on the North American continent, trying to find a weakness. Somewhere. Anywhere.

Russia made moves to creep into Alaska. They'd had more than one scare-up there in the past month alone, but the witches of Alaska had come together with Leah's help.

And it was working.

The world was on fire in a way that made me super uncomfortable in staying this focused on saving my girlfriend.

Well, I really wasn't. I was just making sure that Paige didn't have to deal with a reanimated demon or a crazy Voudon witch who, apparently, made bad choices when she got scared. Not that I could talk, you know. But... I just had to keep Veronica from doing anything stupid.

Sex was still rockstar amazing with her. She was still drop-dead gorgeous and in those super rare moments when she let her hair down and just unwound, I was irresistibly drawn to her.

But I kept that protection sigil on me at all times. I didn't know *how* she affected people. I did, however, watch it in action.

I felt like I was being used. She quite literally needed me for one thing and one thing only; to help her break her contract with Valfire because she didn't want to pay up on the contract she'd signed.

And the more I thought about it, the harder it was for me to get behind what she was doing.

It took us weeks to relocate all the magickal artifacts in Threknal's warehouse to the library, which was a *castle* in another dimension. Yeah.

That's how I discovered Threknal's study books. It turned out, that sigilwork was actually a really ancient language, which told us just how old Threknal was. He'd been a wizard long before Merlin, back when the world had been "connected" to other worlds and…

It all sounded very Norse, very One Tree or… Yggradasil? Yggydreesal? I could never remember the name of it. It was spelled in another language and it didn't particularly sound the way it was spelled. That's what I remembered. But it was the tree that connected all of Odin's kingdoms or… something. I didn't really catch it all.

We weren't alone. *That's* what I got. We weren't alone. We just didn't have anyone particularly interested in helping. You know, like gods. Which, apparently, *were* a thing. Who knew?

My whole world was opening up around me.

And I was focused on trying to figure out what to do about Veronica.

The sigilwork I was learning from Threknal's personal grimoire was mind blowing and it was bringing my A-game up to whole new levels. That, along with an entire section of books devoted to sigilwork in the library, was helping more than I could have imagined. I could create sigils—complex ones—on the fly now.

But it still wasn't going to be enough to bring Valfire in— if I still wanted to. I'd tried to ask Paige, but she was still a little miffed with me. She hadn't told me I *had* to leave, but I wasn't allowed to be alone with the kids anymore.

That made sense.

I knew I could lay a trap for the demon. I'd done that with my karma demon *before* I'd learned all this other stuff. I could kill him with what I had here if I double-dosed my new knowledge with karma.

But we couldn't reel that fish in. Not without bait.

I didn't really understand how *Threknal,* of all people, was going to *be* that bait. From what I was reading in his grimoire, Valfire had made Threknal, but didn't particularly *like* him. I was pretty sure I could send an invite to Valfire asking for a reward and he'd probably honor it. Well, probably not. According the journal entries, Valfire was... a dick.

But it also sounded like Hell wasn't a pleasure cruise either. I didn't *wish* Veronica to go there. I didn't. But... she was the one who'd agreed to it in the first place. Originally, I'd thought her reasoning outweighed the consequence, which was the reason—or so I thought—I'd agreed to help in the first place.

I was starting to realize that part of Veronica's magick had something to do with attraction. I didn't know what it was. Maybe it was voice? Maybe she was part siren or succubus? I didn't know. Or maybe it was the touch of her skin? Whatever it was, when she was near, I had wanted her. Badly.

Until the implementation of the protection sigil.

Now, under the protection of my sigil, I didn't want her. She kinda really irritated me. I was actually a little repulsed by her. More so when I was in the castle or the library. I wasn't *allowed* anywhere in the castle *besides* the library. It was magick in a Harry Potter kind of way, which was cool until it trapped you in a broom closet for hours when all you wanted was a sandwich.

Fox came with me occasionally, helping me research. He was looking for his own stuff, anything that would help him track down the guy terrorizing the valley. The murderer had gone back to ground, meaning he wouldn't be back again for another year. Well, less than that, but that gave Fox time to look into lore he hadn't had access to.

He released a long breath and leaned back in his chair, letting his arms fall on the old tome he'd been reading. "This is some great stuff."

I pulled my thoughts back and focused again on the page in front of me. I'd found something I *needed* to tell Paige.

But if I did, it'd derail everything Veronica was trying to do.

I needed to know if I cared.

Fox moved his arm toward me, palm up, his fingers relaxed.

Him, on the other hand, was driving me nuts in a soul-craving kind of way that had me wondering if there was something broken in me. Was I so easily led? Was what I felt for Fox really crazy love? Or was this me being needy and being unable to live without another human being?

I moved my hand a toward his but didn't touch. I needed to distance myself from both of these two and get my head on straight. "Valfire has a small army of demon witches."

"Ew." Fox pulled a face and slouched deeper in his chair. "An army? That implies he wants to release them and go to war."

The grimoire didn't say, actually. The only thing I did know was that... "He can't *get* them over here because some-thing's wrong with the gate. Threknal didn't know what." But it was all multi-dimensional bull crap I didn't understand on a good day.

"What do you want to do?"

I met his gaze and just held onto it like it was a couch and I was hanging out in it. "I want to lure him in and kill him."

Fox nodded. "Veronica wants to do that too."

"Yeah. But." I chewed on that little flap of cheek on the

left side of my mouth, not quite sure I wanted to admit this out loud or not. But this was Fox. He'd seen me at my dumbest already. We'd survived high school together. You didn't get much dumber than that. "Veronica's contract is coming up."

Fox raised his head, but with the way he was sitting in his high-backed chair, he was pushing his body up. "You...." He sat up fully and leaned in, looking at me through his short, but thick lashes. "You know what that means, right?"

That I was offering Veronica up as a sacrifice?

I'd done that already with someone I'd been deathly terrified of loving.

Was I hesitating because I might not be able to save Veronica?

I'd faced that already with my daughter.

Or that I might not have the power to save Veronica the same way I'd saved Charlie because... I just didn't *love* her the same way anymore?

I ran my tongue along my teeth. "Yeah."

He ducked his head and then fell back as his mouth ripped open in a wide yawn. He rubbed his stubbled head with his right hand, leaving his other on the table beside me. "Is that what you want to do?"

I shook my head and stared emptily at the pile of books strewn around us. "Yup." But by committing to this, I might be setting myself to be a murderer.

He didn't move for a long moment, and then he turned his hand over and clasped mine. "Okay. I've got a few ideas. You've done this already. What do we do?"

When we'd started this journey, I in no way thought I'd be setting up to kill the woman I'd loved.

And yet here we were. But if it kept the threat of an army of demon-witches out of our world? I couldn't ignore it.

I'd just have to bear the karmic consequences when they came.

———

Paige staggered through Derek's portal and nearly fell onto her desk. That battle had been hard, but they'd won.

Barely.

The office door burst open as Ishmail directed the normal team of healers to take care of her and Derek.

It gave her the time she needed to realize what'd happened.

Walton wanted Colorado and, it seemed, he didn't care the cost. That'd been why Paige had fought so hard to get it back in the first place. But because she hadn't been able to give Steven Odison the stone *and* the book, he wasn't in the mood to help. He'd told her that he'd be able to weather out any storm. He was, after all, Loki's grandson.

Great. What did a demigod need with a magick stone *and* a book in the first place?

Once the healers had stepped out, after telling her to be careful, to get rest, to not break her newest set of stitches, she met Ishmail's gaze. "I need Saul."

He nodded and disappeared, closing the door behind him.

Paige and Derek had an after-battle ritual. He went for the whiskey. She made a pot of coffee.

He poured two shot glasses and offered her one. "That one was close."

It had been. They'd found an answer to the automatic situation. It wasn't a *great* solution, but they could, for short periods of time, put a barrier that would suspend the bullets, giving the paranormal forces time to hide.

They'd come up with their preferred battle styles. They still lacked numbers and were still out-armed. Walton had most of the arsenals, most of the planes, most of the missiles. Fox had not come through with more healing rings, saying they were nearly impossible to make.

Which sucked.

General Saul walked into the office in cammies and battle boots. "They have a new weapon."

Paige had kinda thought so. She just didn't know what it was. "Do we have intel?"

"Not a lot." General Saul walked up to Paige's desk and set down her tablet, flicking her fingers so a holodisplay projected up and outward. "Brack and Zoe already have a counter-agent to the magebioweapon we know they're planning to deploy. As soon as they launch it, we're ready with a reply."

That was great news. Bobby hadn't come to Paige with any more visions of losing, so she had to hope that meant they were on the right path.

Derek grabbed another shot glass and handed it to the general.

She took it and knocked it back, setting it on the desk with a clunk. "However, the *newest* weapon. We had Walton's forces under control. As we planned. Here and here." She put her finger in the middle of a hill on one side of the display and at another on the other. Red heat signatures blazed along the green typography showing the people who had been on the battlefield.

This was dryad intelligence as interpreted as best as it could be. But it left a lot to be desired. This wasn't like some sci-fi film where it looked like the actual terrain. It was sculpted how a root would see it, or how leaves would interpret it. People who burned hotter—like shifters—were bigger. Bigger things that ran cool—like tanks or big trucks—were smaller and orange or didn't show up at all because there was nothing *living* for the trees to *read*.

"Talk to me, general. What are we up against?"

Saul leaned on one hand, shaking from side to side as if trying to figure out how to say what she had.

That gave Paige time to get up and pour everyone a cup of coffee. The whiskey had taken the edge off her nerves.

It was time to get her head back in the game because she couldn't *afford* downtime.

Saul took her cup and nodded at the same tempo she'd been swaying from side-to-side earlier. She licked her lips and straightened, turning back to the poorly shaped holodisplay. She moved it around until she got to a big dark spot. "This."

Paige stared at the lack of information, her mind racing. "Are the dryads in that are okay?"

"No." Saul blinked furiously and gritted her teeth so hard Paige heard her teeth grind. "They're husks. Like the life was sucked right out of them."

"What do we think happened?"

Saul flicked her fingers down and the display disappeared. She perched on the edge of Paige's desk and sipped her coffee. "A couple of people said they saw what happened. A *man* tried to *open* a portal."

Paige didn't understand why Saul was emphasizing those words. "What am I missing?"

The general pressed her white coffee cup against her chin. "They didn't all describe him as a man. Some described him as something evil, something twisted. Some called him a demon. Merry even said it was Phoebe." The look on General Saul's face it was most definitely *not* Phoebe.

"Okay." But who could open a door if not a Blackman witch? Paige would have to go talk to Phoebe and see if she was missing anyone in her coven. Maybe shield them somehow from possession?

"The door opened to what they're calling Hell."

Paige knew Hell wasn't fire and brimstone.

But she didn't know that the fire and brimstone part of Hell didn't still exist. Maybe there *was* a pit somewhere. Afterall, Earth had Death Valley and some place in Kuwait that looked like Hell's armpit. But she also knew that the doors to Hell were all but closed. *She* could get there. It took a lot, but she could get there.

She was the demon summoner, though, with a direct line to Hell. And, while, it was no longer branded to her bones anymore, it still belonged to her like the blood in her veins. "Did anything come out of it?"

General Saul shook her head. "Not successfully, at least. But *someone* is *trying* to bring something over from... Hell?" She shrugged, turning her head to the side. "Is that something we should be worried about?"

Yeah. It certainly was.

It was time for Paige to initiate her talks with Ez'gizol and hope she wasn't starting another kind of war she wasn't equipped to handle.

24

War wasn't simple. That was the first thing Paige was learning and each time she thought she fully understood that, she'd get yet another reminder.

Walton had stationed his people at fifty-eight different locations. Which one was she supposed to focus on?

Her gut told her that Walton was planning something big and she needed to have an answer for it, that these fifty-eight locations were only strategic in the fact that it was keeping her spread thin, and not on preparing for the future when he got really serious, when things he was putting into motion now came to fruition.

She was starting to feel a little experienced at this point, but she was by no means a veteran of war. Her skin was still a little thin, her nerves still a little rattled. Her head was screaming at her to be on the battleline. Somewhere out there, fighting with everything she had.

Instead, because her wounds from the last battle were enough to keep her off the field for a while, she was headed to Hell to see if she could speak with Ez'gizol again. She needed to know what had taken out those dryads, what invading force was coming, and if she could rely on Ez'gizol for backup.

Creating the door to Hell took a lot more effort than she wanted to admit. Derek didn't say anything as she struggled, the outline wavering, the black inkiness failing to spool out and actually form the door. He couldn't get them *to* Hell and she couldn't get them *from* Hell, but his doors always went up faster, neater, and with a great deal less effort.

For all that she was the demon summoner, she didn't seem to be super awesome at it.

Maybe she *was* wounded more than she let on even to herself.

Finally, her door popped into place and she and Derek trudged through.

Stepping through the door felt... icky. Her stomach threatened to heave. Her toes tingled, and she started to sweat on the back of her neck.

Her portals didn't always show where she was dumping people out. Not like Phoebe's and Leah's and Derrick's. So, she had no way of knowing where her door was even opening to. She just had to hope it was on solid ground. She wasn't as good at location as everyone else, and had no idea where Leah had gotten the ability to land where she needed to. Paige just opened the door, focused on Hell, and trying to find Ez'gizol.

She stepped into what looked to be a demon bazaar.

Which, oddly, looked like any other kind of bazaar with merchants lining the streets and hawking their wares. It actually reminded Paige of some of the sci-fi shows where the teams would land on other planets.

By the time she closed the door behind them, they were surrounded by horned demons wearing a red and gold uniform and pointing spears at them.

Paige held up her hands. "I'm here to speak with Ez'gizol."

No one answered right away. Finally, someone pushed through the circle of demons. She was shorter than the others and the only way Paige could tell the demon was a woman was because of her finer bone structure. She wore jewelry made out of living plants and her clothing didn't seem quite as practical as the others. She reminded Paige of an elf. Kind of.

Paige tried to keep all judgement from her expression. "I'm Paige Whiskey from… Earth." That sounded weird being said out loud. "I'd met with Ez'gizol a few weeks ago. I was wondering if he was around? Can I speak with him?"

The woman came closer, leaning in and sniffing with her concave nose. Her red eyes studied Paige. "I know who you are," she hissed, and then she pulled away. "Are you the reason he was killed?"

"Killed?" Paige had no idea what this demon was talking about.

The woman snarled and took a step back. "Take these two under custody," she said, putting extra emphasis on each syllable. "I will have their truth."

This really wasn't the way Paige had seen this meeting going.

Derek made a move to open another door.

Paige gestured for him to stop. She needed answers and the only way that was happening was if she stayed. So, that's exactly what they were going to do.

"I figured out what we did wrong, *ma cher*," Veronica said as she breezed into the treehouse, a huge, beaming smile on her face.

I was on my way to the border of Colorado and Kansas. Where exactly on that border, I had no idea. The door witch would drop me and the rest of us off. We'd battle if it came to that.

I'd been practicing with the sigil magick and I was getting good. Teaming that with karma, and I could finally be useful in a fight. So, I'd gone to General Saul and had been intercepted by Lieutenant Silver, and had volunteered for duty. I was now on rotation.

"I got deployed."

Veronica waved me off. "We are not going to war, *chèrie*. We are reviving Threknal and bringing an end to Valfire."

This had to stop. "Babe," I said as forthright as I could stand it. "This is not the way."

"Valfire is a grave danger to Paige and to everything she stands for." Veronica stood beside the bed, a frown marring her face. "Do you think we should let that be?"

No. I didn't. But I'd *hoped* I could put off my plans of using her as bait a little longer. I didn't feel incredibly comfortable with the idea of sacrificing *anyone* to a demon in order to hopefully, maybe kill him. "Vee, please. Can we..." I massaged my temple. "Let's talk about this after I get back. Okay?"

She gave me a grim look and then shook her head. "I'm sorry, *chèrie*."

Something hit me over the back of my head and the world went dark.

The hairs on the back of Leah's neck stood on end. Something was wrong. But what?

She looked up from her homework, staring at the plants.

This was her favorite room in the house even though it was freezing.

The house was silent.

"Gertie," she called as she pushed away from the tall table tucked near the drafty window, letting her afghan fall to the floor. "What's going on?"

No one answered.

Leah had been helping in Alaska working on her own pretty much for a few weeks and was starting to get a bit of confidence finally. That didn't mean she wanted to face off against monsters on her own though. "Gertie!"

Charlie's head popped out from around the top of the stairs. "She went to the store. What's up?"

Gertie had gone to the store hours ago. Okay, so granted, Leah understood that a "trip to the store" was a couple of hours at the very least. She got that. She didn't quite understand why, but it was a thing. Ask for a soda and you didn't want it by the time someone finally got round to bringing it over.

But this was... excessive. "I got a bad feeling is all."

"Okay." Charlie slid down the stairs on her socked feet. "Did you call Bobby?"

No, but that was the next thing to try.

Before she had a chance to, though, a portal opened in the middle of the kitchen and Bobby and Bonnie stepped out. "Someone's after you," Bobby shouted and grabbed at Leah's hand.

She pulled away. If she was leaving, she needed shoes and that was something they didn't wear inside the house here. "What's going on?"

He shook his head and waved hurriedly at Charlie. "Where's Whomp?"

As if called by a whistle, the broom whizzed into the room and came to a screeching halt.

"Hey," Bobby said to it with another wave. "Come on. They're nearly here."

Leah ducked into the artic entry and grabbed her boots, jamming her feet into them. Then, she reached over and grabbed her coat.

Charlie followed suit, being a bit more deft about it. "I gotta leave Gertie a note."

"Hurry," Leah said, tugging a hat onto her head.

"We're going home," Bobby said, giving them both a weird look.

"It's cold outside," Leah said, brushing past him and opening the top junk drawer to grab a piece of paper and the second junk drawer to grab a pen. After trying to write, however, she pulled open the third junk drawer and grabbed a Sharpie. *Bobby came and got us. Will be back soon. Leah and Charlie*

Bonnie flared her hands as if trying to get them to hurry.

Charlie shut the arctic entry door. "Let's go!"

Bonnie relaxed and moved her arms to cut open the door.

Someone kicked the front door.

Leah'd been keeping it locked. No one used it anyway because the front stoop slanted and people slid on the ice all the time.

But the back door wasn't locked because that door was broken. And if these guys were local, they'd know that. If they weren't, they'd be circling back around anyway.

Leah waved Bonnie to stop and cut open a door. She was faster than most of the other Blackmans. Distance and location seemed to effect everyone differently, but not Leah.

Bobby shook his head. "Too close. Too close."

Leah punched the door through, opening it to the backyard of their house. "Come on! Let's go!"

Sagging with relief for a moment, Bobby leapt through the

door, landing on the other side, his feet touching the grass poking through the January snow.

Bonnie gave Leah a wide-eyed apology and the walked through.

Charlie followed.

The back door slammed open. They were out of time.

Leah stepped through and closed her portal behind her.

"Hello," Veronica said with a smile, clasping her hands in front of her. "I was looking for you. Come. We have things that must be done."

The look on Bobby's face told Leah that they were *not* safe.

She reached for her door magick again.

Veronica slapped something around Leah's wrist and then wagged a finger. "Nuh-uh-uh. None of that now." She sighed and smiled. "We are saving your momma. Do not fight me, *bebe.*"

If they were saving Leah's mom, then why did Bobby look absolutely terrified just now?

Dexx prowled in front of the Jeep, studying the line of armed men several hundred yards away. He didn't like this. Not one bit.

They'd had plenty of skirmishes, with clear victories and losses, but they hadn't had a full-scale fight with missiles, UAV's, tanks, and the whole bit.

To say the shifters and witches with him were scared wasn't even the tip of the ice burg.

The Federalists were out there, but they were just so much better at the fighting thing. At least with conventional weapons. And those had the nasty habit of killing paras as easy as it did normies.

All the waiting was... stressful. What were they waiting for? At least the other side looked nervous, too. Maybe the soldiers were aware that they had weapons pointed at other Americans, no matter their special abilities.

Hopefully that kept fighting down to skirmishes. Dexx could deal with raids. Paras fought best that way. Those rules were easy. War was... messy.

Movement on the other side drew his attention. A six-wheeled armored carrier stopped at the line of soldiers. A short flurry of activity calmed, and a stick raised with a white flag out the passenger side. The wheel-tank thingy drove slowly, waving the white flag in wide arcs.

"What the hells are they doing?" Not surrendering, for damn sure, but why wave the flag?

Dexx waved for Alwyn. He didn't respond quick enough, so Dexx shifted and ran to the ex-DoDO witch. "We got a request for parley. I don't trust these fuckers any farther than you can throw 'em. I want you to target that thing with everything you got. Everyone else, pick a section and be ready. If this goes south, take them all."

He wished he had Rainbow. She'd been his all-time favorite ranged attacker. Tarik would have been good, but he'd removed himself from fighting and stood by for healing.

"Margo, Garek, Alex, with me." He shifted and trotted out to meet with the armored truck.

The federalist truck stopped in the approximate middle ground. The doors popped open and soldiers ran around the back. One stayed out front with the flag.

Do we trust them or not? I mean, I'd like to believe they're honorable, but I can't reconcile that with all the evil shit they've done.

We will be ready. Leave it to Hattie to be... ready.

Dexx shifted, walking the final few yards to the front of the truck. He motioned to the Army rig. "Like the wheels. What's it called?" At least he could act human to these people. Might make a few of them less willing to shoot citizens.

The man with the white flag stopped the waving. "It's a... uh... you can talk?"

"Yeah." Oh, boy. "Even have a pretty good vocabulary when I want to use it. Sometimes 'ugh and goo' just aren't descriptive enough."

The boy's eyes hardened a little.

"Sorry. Sometimes I speak in front of my thoughts. But I like the ride. What do you call it?"

The back of the vehicle whined, dropping a ramp. Armed soldiers? Seemed like a waste of an ambush.

"Got a seventy Challenger myself. I call her Jackie. Passes anything but a gas station."

The boy's eyes shifted, and his mouth worked. He was obviously shaken, and worried over talking to the enemy and giving away information, but he had a sense of humor. "It's a, um. It's a light combat reconnaissance vehicle. LCRV or *lacrov*. Sir."

"Sir? Nobody calls me sir. What's your name, soldier?" Dexx didn't get an answer.

The ramp at the back had folded down, and several DoDO agents pushed a cart around the LCRV.

The cart wasn't a cart. It was a wheelchair. Dexx stepped back from the red robes out of reflex. Shit. He wasn't prepared for *this*.

Shit, we gotta move. They're going to—

Relax your young body, Colt. Bussemi's voice rang in his head.

Fuck you and the spinster demon you rode in on. Dexx took several more steps back, and put his arms out, pushing his pack back too. *I hope Alwyn has a good shot. It'll only be the once.*

Your pitiful band of mutts won't save you. The wheelchair stopped, and the old man looked up, several folds of the robe falling back. "I just wanted to see you before the start of hostilities."

Dexx mashed his brakes hard as he tried run away, but he was also too afraid to turn his back. "Why're you here?" His mind spun as he tried to think his way out. Bussemi was a *bad man* and if he was here, then things were a lot worse than he'd thought.

"I told you to relax. I'm here to offer you one last chance. Willingly come over to this side. You know you have no chance, and I have walled your pitiful allies in. Come with me. I am God, and you'll soon know the truth of it one way or the other."

"You're *God*, huh? I guess then that makes me *Godhunter*."

For the merest instant the fires of the bahlrok inside the ancient man lit. He furrowed his brows and turned his head to the DoDO agent behind him. "We're leaving." He turned back to Dexx. "I will have you. Dead or alive. Better alive and willing, but either way." The DoDO agent turned the wheelchair and pushed him to the rear of the LCRV.

Margo stepped up to his ear. "He just wanted to look at you?"

"What? No. He just threatened me. Didn't you hear it?"

Margo twisted her head in front of his eyes. "No, he was wheeled out, paused, and wheeled back."

Dammit. He'd done the time thing on him. *Again.* "Let's move. There isn't going to be a fight today."

"Where's Mom?" Rai asked, bursting into the attic bedroom.

Mandy looked up with a huh-what?! look from where she laid on her bed on her stomach reading a book.

"Mom," Rai said again, gesturing with her hands, waiting for her cousin to catch up. "My mom. Where's she at?"

"How am I supposed to know?" Mandy scrambled off the bed, pulling her pink quilt to the floor. She stumbled as her feet twisted up in it. "Doing leader-y things, right?"

Rai *knew* that was probably the case but... "She hasn't checked in and Ishmail's looking for Leah to go get her. He completely forgot she's with Char this week, so he came to see me, thinking I'd somehow know. And I talked to Kam, and he's got nothing. So, I looked for Bobs, thinking he might have some vision or something and he's completely missing, too." Rai held her hands out on either side of her. "Ideas?"

Mandy shook her head, then narrowed her eyes as her mouth fell open. "She was supposed to go talk to some demon about some guy about a thing."

"Right." Her mom had said she was going to go see Ez-g-something because he hadn't sent a messenger. "Thanks, Pan."

Mandy thumped after her on their way down the stairs. "Do you need me to come with you?"

"No." More couldn't hurt. *All* the kids did better when they were together.

"You're going after her, right?"

"Yeah."

"Okay, then. I'm going with you. Who're we getting to take us there?"

Rai turned around and gave Mandy a look that should have screamed duh because all of her inside voices were. "*Leah.*"

Mandy gave a yeah-that-sounds-right shrug and nodded as they continued down the stairs. "Wait. Hold up. Kam just said Lee came back but's gone already."

Rai stopped at the bottom of the stairs beside the front door and turned on her cousin. "What do you mean, gone already ?"

"I mean…" Mandy shook her head before she repeated herself. "What do we do now? Kammy says Leah needs our help."

"More than Mom?"

Mandy shrugged the corners of her lips pulled way down.

Rai didn't think Mandy was getting it. "Who's probably in Hell right now?"

"Isn't she the demon summoner and stuff?"

Okay. So, point. "Yeah."

"And isn't Leah a kid?"

"She's our age."

Mandy jutted her head forward and nodded. "Exactly. Well, I mean, older because you're like, what? Not even one?"

Rai rolled her eyes. *Daina, what do I do?*

Her thunderbird rumbled quietly within her. *Let the drums roll. It is why I was summoned to you.*

Rai didn't feel *entirely* comfortable with her thunderbird all the time. She was a little too blood thirsty.

But if Leah was in trouble, then maybe that's exactly what they needed.

25

"We are doing this to save Paige and everyone else." Veronica walked quickly across the clearing, her hands moving excitedly. *"Ma chèrie*, please understand. I do this to help us all."

I didn't know this woman.

Leah was bound and laid next to a boulder in the winter snow. I hoped she'd be okay, but at least she was dressed for snow. Living in Alaska these past weeks had at least taught her that.

Charlie was being held at knifepoint by some guy I'd never met before. Anger shot from her eyes as she glared spite at Veronica, but Charlie didn't do anything irrational.

There was a lot to Veronica I didn't know about Veronica. "Babe, don't do this."

She giggled. Honest to the gods giggled. "This solution is even better than ours, *chèrie*. We can put an end to all of this. We can free all of the souls they trapped."

From what I'd been able to translate in Threknal's grimoire, there were quite a few souls they'd been able to capture. Not, like, hundreds. Just maybe a dozen or so, but they were all powerful.

Like Veronica and Mama Gee.

The protection sigil was still on me, so I didn't have to worry about her getting too close and possibly changing my mind. That was good. I had to buy time, though. I didn't know for who or for what, or what I could do. I needed to think of something though. "Baby, talk to me." I pushed more desperation into my voice than I felt. The Veronica I knew wouldn't be able to hurt my daughter. But this one? Would she?

The guy holding the dagger to Charlie's throat snorted and turned his head so I could get a better view of his flaming yellow mohawk. He grinned at Veronica, showcasing three missing teeth. "You really got this one, didn't you?"

She gave him a look that told him to shut up but continued to place black candles around Threknal's body, using the snow to hold them up. "There is no need to talk. You and the necromancer will bring him back to life and then we set the trap."

The cold of the melting snow had seeped into my jeans and was sinking into my bones. "That'll take days."

"Nah, *chèrie*," she said with a shake of her head, meeting my gaze. "I've already set up the time-consuming pieces for you. All you have to do is care enough and find the karma to make your trap work. And I have the thing that will make it happen."

Charlie.

Veronica nodded as if she'd heard me, her expression settling into a kind of calm resignation. "I know you will not love me in the way you must. You can't, not now. Not after you've learned so much. I know this. I do." She came to me and knelt down, cupping my face with her hand. "I do love you."

Meeting those dark eyes, I almost believed it. "Then, let Charlie go."

A sadness filled Veronica's eyes. "No."

Leah made a startled sound as she woke up.

Veronica stood and turned toward the girl. "Here is what I need you two to do." She smiled and clasped her hands together as if she was teaching a class. "David is going to hurt Charlie until you use your karma and your necromancy," she said, pointing to each of us in turn, "and bring Threknal back."

"But he's a demon," I said, my eyes going to Charlie as David pressed the knife into her throat.

"Wy," Charlie shouted. "Don't."

Big words. "Where do demon souls even go?"

Veronica shook her head, her face folding in frustration. "Where all souls go." She turned to Leah. "You two have become close, yes?"

Leah's blue eyes were super wide. "Yeah."

"Leah," I called to her.

She wouldn't take her eyes off Charlie.

"Necro," I barked.

Her gaze shot to mine.

I'd been prepared to go to battle because there were things I'd learned. I wasn't completely useless in a fight. I *could* do things that would help us. But I couldn't have Leah breaking down right then or flaking out. "Do your best. Okay?" I needed a few minutes to set up the trap I'd already designed.

She closed her eyes but nodded.

"I do need you to understand that I will be hurting your friend even while you help me, so please do not stop."

Leah's eyes shot open. "What?"

Veronica shook her head helplessly. "Wynonna's karma

magick is a delicate affair and cannot be tricked. She *must* feel as though her daughter's life is in grave danger."

"But it's not, is it?" I asked. "You're not *really* going to kill her."

David snorted. "Lady, you don't know Vee." He said her name like the name itself was a drug. "Back in the day, we killed lots o' people. Didn't matter how old they were. Got us power. Got us an audience," he said, gesturing to Veronica with his knife before returning it to Charlie's throat.

What? I stared at Veronica like she was a complete stranger because she was. I'd known she'd done some shady stuff in her past. She'd summoned a demon and had made a deal with him, but this? Killing people the way Mohawk Guy said? That didn't make any sense.

Veronica came up to me and breathed in my face. "Just do this for me, *chèrie*. Please."

As those words touched my lips, something inside me shifted, wanting to help, wanting to do whatever it took to make her happy.

"Scream for your mom," Dave said.

I looked away from Veronica, my fingers tracing the first of the sigil pieces I'd decided. My hands were tied behind my back, so I was free to do that without Dave or Veronica seeing.

"She's not my mom," Charlie growled.

I latched onto Charlie's teal gaze, my fingers still moving.

She held mine with a deep resolve. "You're," she said through clenched teeth, "not my mom."

What was that kid saying because there *was* a coded message in there somewhere.

Veronica pulled away and slapped her thigh. "David, please."

"It'd be my pleasure." He slid the knife along Charlie's shoulder.

She bit back a scream until it strangled out of her.

"Char," Leah cried.

She wasn't my daughter. I hadn't raised her.

I closed my eyes and breathed.

I didn't have a heart-claim on her and so I didn't have the right to focus on saving her. I needed to set and bait the trap.

She screamed again.

Veronica wasn't the love of my life. She was *playing* me. Her voice or her breath or something *did* something to me.

She was the villain.

She was the villain. It hit me suddenly, why Bobby had seen a much different world after I'd rescued Veronica. It might not have been about the artifacts. Well, I mean it might have. But if I'd rescued her the way he saw originally, I might have stayed closer with her. I might have been the one to capture Leah, maybe do something to her to make her follow along? I didn't know.

I didn't... know.

But that feeling of completion I'd felt when she would whisper her love against my lips.

All the other times we'd gotten into a fight flashed across my mind. One minute, I'd been mad. The next, I'd been in love.

I closed my eyes and focused on the karma twisting around her, karma I'd given her a charm to clean.

I opened my eyes, listening to the screams and cries of the daughter I couldn't claim in my heart as my own. My soul didn't care. Her blood called to mine.

The karma of Dave's actions alone was enough to power the sigils I needed. I slid a smile on my face and tipped my head to the side. "Babe, I've gotta do this right. I need my hands."

Veronica turned to me with a radiating smile. "I love you."

In that moment, I actually believed she did. "I know." I got to my feet and turned my bound hands toward her, faking the loving look as best I could. "Let's bring him down once and for all."

She scrunched her face and moved toward me. "I do so love it when you come back to me."

Except I wasn't this time. Or ever again.

I was going to offer her up as a sacrifice to Valfire.

And I was ready for her death to be on my hands.

Rai let her senses leach out of her through Daina, trying to find anything she could track. Ember was totally gone. Probably out with Dexx or something. And Tyler was out on patrol with Alex and Garek. Kate was off busy doing elfy things with a dryad or whatever, which just left Rai alone with Mandy looking for Bobby and Leah.

Without Kamden's help.

Sleep, his tired voice said.

They're lost, Rai answered. She didn't get the whole being two excuse.

'Kay. Find them. His voice winked out.

Crap. Could she do this on her own?

Mandy frowned, thought for a second, and then grabbed Rai's hand, dragging her into a room she hadn't been in before.

A big, wooden table reigned superior over the whole middle and there were really old cabinets and stuff along the other walls. Well, and dressers. Plants. Herbs. Lots of herbs.

Mandy grabbed a map. "I… think I might be able to do this," she said with excitement. "Without Mom." She let go of a terrified chuckle as she gathered a bowl, a map, and then paused before grabbing some herbs. "Yeah, okay. So, I don't remember it all, but I'm pretty sure this'll be close enough. You ready to witch with me?"

No. No, Rai was not, but she also didn't think she'd get much say in the matter. So, she just nodded and stepped up.

Mandy mixed some herbs in the marble bowl thingy and smashed them with the blue marble stick thing. When she was done, she sniffed loudly and nodded, wiping her palms on her pink pants, her eyes dancing across the map. "Okay. Uh, okay. Yeah. Repeat after me?"

Rai would've felt a whole ton better if she'd sounded just a tiny bit more confident. "Have you ever done this before?"

"On purpose?"

"Sure."

"No."

"Not on purpose?"

Mandy winced. "Still no." She shook out her fingers and held them out over the map, closing her eyes. "I now invoke the laws of three, make Bobby return to me."

That was actually going to work? Rai shook her head, ready to tell her that this was dumb.

Mandy shook her fingers and repeated the incantation. "I now invoke," she said, her tone implying Rai *really* needed to join in, "the laws of three."

Against her better judgement, Rai joined in. It was simple enough to remember at least, even if it didn't make a ton of sense. "Make Bobby return to me."

They repeated it three more times, and each time, Rai dug a little deeper into her magick, pulling on Daina's power rolling off her spirit wings to feed the spell. No matter how lame it might be, it was still better than doing nothing and she had to get her brother back.

Something popped behind her and the sound of stumbling feet heralded the arrival of someone before Bobby plowed into Rai's back.

She spun around, forgetting the spell and grabbed him. "Bobs." Was he okay? His arms were so limp, and he seemed like he was barely conscious. "What's wrong with him?"

Bonnie released a squealing cry as she fell against one of the cabinets. "Veronica," she said, shaking her head in disbelief. "She kidnapped Charlie and Leah."

"What?" Lightning fury swirled inside Rai's chest. "Take me to them."

"But Bobs," Mandy said, scurrying around the table to catch him on the other side.

"She's gonna kill her," Bobby moaned, his voice filled with pain. "She's gonna kill her."

Rai had no idea who was going to kill who, but it sounded bad. "Pan, take him to the kitchen and do the... the tea thing. That worked last time."

Mandy nodded, taking most of his weight. "What're you going to do?"

We're going to war, Daina said contentedly.

"Don't worry about it," Rai said, resting her hand on Bonnie's. "You okay?"

"Will be." Bonnie straightened. "You ready?"

Nope. "Will be." Rai swallowed and set her shoulders. "Let's go."

Leah didn't know what to do. Her hands were still bound and she was still cut off from her magick, but she didn't think she could do what Veronica was asking her to. She could make zombies. She could talk to spirits. But to raise a dead demon who had died *weeks* ago? That wasn't something she'd ever done before.

And Charlie just kept screaming.

Leah understood why. She did, but she didn't know how

302

much more she could take.

Wy kept walking around Threknal's body doing some slow blink-slink thing that probably looked pretty cool, but right then it was just kinda creepy and Leah didn't know if Wy was the good guy right then or the bad guy. Because Veronica was definitely the bad guy. One hundred percent.

She turned toward Leah with a smile that wasn't really a smile and advanced. "It's your turn to play your part."

Leah held up her hands, letting Veronica take the magick dampener-whatever things off. "Can you make her stop screaming?" she whispered as tears threatened.

"Make her stop?" Veronica asked, both bracelets in her hands. "No. Your magick can be used under great duress, but hers? It becomes worthless without the right ingredients."

Leah's breath hitched.

"You make her stop screaming by doing as I ask you to do."

Leah moved away from Veronica, trying to get circulation back in her fingers.

Wy gave Leah a long look as she continued to circle, her fingers flicking regularly.

Leah didn't know what Wy was trying to communicate. Do bad things? Don't do bad things? Raise a demon? Keep him dead? What?

Wy came close and whispered, "On my mark, get Char out of here."

Oh, thank the trees. Leah nodded barely, fighting to keep her reaction off her face, but she sucked at that and she knew she'd failed because everyone could read everything on her face because she couldn't hide—

Wy stopped, one knee tucked in, the other foot out, her hands cast out in front of her.

Snow spat up from the ground and settled around them as a wind rose.

Leah ran to Charlie, screaming her magick at Dave. She didn't *know* what she was doing. That whole magick in battle training hadn't gone over super well with her because *she'd* been in Alaska studying her lessons and passing math for the past few weeks.

Charlie growled and punched upward with her bound hands, knocking the knife out of his hands as Leah plowed into him, knocking him off his feet and onto the ground.

Leah didn't wait. The best thing they could both do for Wy was to get the flock out of there and let the adult witch deal with her adult and crazy girlfriend.

"Get Fox," Charlie yelled, pushing Leah away.

She shook her head. This was a bad idea, but her hands were already clawing at the air, creating a portal to get them out of there and following the pull of Fox. She stepped out of the cold and into a blazingly hot coffee shop.

Fox sat at a table, a cup of coffee in one hand, a smile on his face.

Leah rushed to him. "Wy needs you."

He dropped the cup on the table and stood, grabbing his coat which was draped over his chair. "Let's go."

Leah opened a door back as the coffee spilled, drenching the person he'd been talking to. As soon as she was on the other side, she searched for Charlie.

She was busy fighting Dave.

She wasn't winning.

Leah rushed forward, letting her portal close behind Fox on its own.

Fox grabbed her shoulder and pushed her back. "Get out of here."

Like craps. Leah wasn't leaving her family and she wasn't leaving her friends.

Fox surged forward, pulling something out of his pocket and slammed his fist against Dave's face.

Dave went stumbling back, but at least he forgot about Charlie for the moment.

Leah ran to her, slipping on the snow, the cold making her toes freeze to the point where balance was dumb.

Charlie held out her hand to stop Leah. "Go," she whispered.

Then she took a step backward as an opalescent wall filtered between them.

What was going on?

Charlie just shook her head in warning and then spun around.

Wy wasn't alone. A well-dressed man floated down, his feet finding purchase in the snow.

No. No, no, no. Leah beat against the wall, trying to get inside. What was she thinking?

A hand landed on her shoulder and Fox leaned down to hiss, "Stand down. Stand...down."

Leah didn't know what was going on, but she'd be ready.

For whatever was about to happen.

Listening to Charlie scream drove me crazy but watching her fight Dave and *not* going to her rescue was even harder. I'm not saying I had a mother's instinct. I'd obviously proven I didn't.

She was a smaller human being, though, and she was in trouble.

But Veronica was the bait in my Valfire trap. And I couldn't let her escape.

Valfire settled onto the snow as my protection sigils snapped into place. He looked around with a smirk. "Got your hands on Threknal's work, I see."

I shrugged.

"Veronica," he said dryly, advancing on her slowly. "What's the plan here, love? You really think you can get out of your contract?"

Her smile was smug as she raised a single, dark eyebrow. "Now, Wy."

I took in a deep breath and closed my eyes, sinking in the karmic energy flowing around me. I was surrounded by the bad—Vee, Dave, and Valfire—and the good—Leah, Charlie, and Fox. I hadn't actually counted on the good, but I knew how to use that.

Pulling on the energies, I let the dark karma flood through me, feeding me like fried candy bars. This was the stuff that needed to be balanced, brought back, realigned and made right.

Then, I pulled on the good karma, letting it roll around, meshing with the inky karma, reminding the energy what it felt to be good, to be right.

But karma didn't need to be right. It didn't need to be good.

It just needed to be balanced. In harmony. A little bit good. A little bit bad.

But not disastrously in either direction.

With a large, empowering breath, I exhaled the gathered magick outward, letting it fill the sigils, remaking them one line and curl, one letter at a time.

Valfire made a noise of alarm.

Opening my eyes, I smiled. He saw what was about to happen. He saw the trap for what it was now.

He growled and gathered magick of his own.

I didn't need to answer it. I just had to feed the sigils and let them to do the work I'd designed them to perform. I just needed them to trap him.

Or kill him of needed.

Veronica threw her head back and laughed.

Valfire roared in rage and slammed his magick into her. Hard.

She flew back, hitting the magick barrier I'd thrown up, and then slid to the ground, blood trailing from her nose.

The karma swelling in me merely shrugged. Karma begat karma. One action demanded an equal and opposite reaction. The deaths she'd caused would not be answered with one death, but by many. But this one was a good start.

I funneled the karma through the sigils, the magick carefully lighting each line a single mark at a time.

Valfire charged me, gathering more magick toward and around him.

I might not be able to complete this. I stepped out of the way, drawing and casting a hasty deflection sigil.

It didn't deflect a whole lot. I went stumbling backward, landing on my butt.

Charlie was already advancing, her dark hair fluttering around her shoulders with each step. She looked down at me on her way by, shaking her head, her expression serious and grim.

I scrambled to my feet, the cold making my fingers stiff, my legs sluggish.

She threw something at Valfire, getting his attention.

He spun around and grabbed hold of Charlie with one magick hand. "Your daughter."

"Yes." I stood on my feet, the karma still clutched within me, still releasing slowly, so ever slowly.

"Stop and I will let her go."

"No." But I didn't' have another solution. I didn't have a way out of this.

And I wasn't willing to sacrifice her. Not fourteen years ago. Not now. Not ever.

Charlie smiled painfully, clawing at her neck and mouthed, "I'm not your daughter."

Rage filled me. The anger and guilt of abandoning her so many years ago fueled my karma with a karmic debt I'd carried for over a decade. It raced out of me with a guttural roar.

The karma flew through the remaining sigils, reaching out to him with silver karmic tendrils, grabbing onto his magick, fighting to force him to release Charlie, dragging him down into the very soil.

He fought back, but the rage of my karma and the weight of his own, he was faced with a power he couldn't withstand.

Charlie stumbled backward as his magick released her.

I grabbed her, wrapping her in my arms as the power built, as the karmic blow back raged like a water balloon ready to burst. I spun us around, shielding her with my body.

As the karma enveloped Valfire and Veronica, consuming them both in a powerful rush that ate away the protective barrier I'd created.

A fine and silvery mist fell over us in the gathering silence.

Charlie and I breathed, holding on to each other, her back pressed against me, her freezing hands wrapped around the arm I had slung over her chest and shoulders.

She pulled away slightly and turned around, her teal eyes alight. "You didn't do it," she whispered.

She wasn't talking about what'd just happened. She was talking about the crime I'd committed against her fourteen years before. Tears filled my eyes as my whole heart twisted with that whispered truth.

I *hadn't* nearly killed my daughter all those years ago.

But I'd carried the price of the actions as though I had.

And now, gloriously, I was free. I wrapped her in my arms and held onto her like she was a lifeline. I was free.

And Valfire, the threat to the Para War had been dealt a blow he couldn't return from.

26

Paige turned away from the massive window of the posh bedroom suite she shared with Derek in frustration. She'd been trying to get out of there for over two weeks while Queen Mavofne's court investigated Ez'gizol's murder. Paige'd tried to offer her assistance, reminding them that she was a detective and had been on the police force for nearly twenty years.

She didn't want to think about what had happened in her absence. Had they lost the war? Had states pulled out because no one could find her? What was going on? Were the kids safe? Leslie? Dexx? The pack? Ishmail? Her staff.

Derek had gotten good at ignoring her. He sat in the chair designed for people with wings and read a book.

That was written in demon tongue. She'd given him a basic decoder of sorts and he had been applying it religiously since they'd found themselves trapped.

She'd managed to read quite a bit while she was there as well, but there was only so much she could take in before she went absolutely stir-crazy.

She was nearly there.

The double doors of their resplendently furnished room opened and Queen Mavofne swept in, her violet cape-skirt fanning out behind her magenta pants. She stopped, rolling her head around majestically, a headpiece adorning her head making her horns look more intricate than they actually were.

Her eyes were a vibrant amber. "You have been..." Mavofne let her violet tongue poke out of her white teeth as if tasting the words. "...cleared of all charges again you."

Paige bit off the retort that came readily. Instead, she straightened and clasped her hands behind her back so they didn't do things to tattle on her emotional state. "What a relief."

"Indeed." Mavofne lowered her head and let her weight settle into one hip as she looked up. "I am willing to hear your negotiations for our service in your war."

That was fast. Paige had been gathering as much information as she could about the political situation in Hell, which was indeed a rather large world. Surprisingly, Lucifer was a very small person on this place and very few people actually cared about him. He might have been a problem on Earth, but not here. "What can we offer that would interest you?"

Mavofne raised her head, resituating her weight more evenly on her cloven feet as she crossed her arms over her armored chest. "Keep the angel gate away from your world."

That wasn't a problem. Paige wasn't certain they could fix *either* gate. "Okay." She hadn't been able to glean a lot of information about their war with the angels, but she did get the distinct impression that there had been a *war* unlike anything humans understood. "What else?"

Mavofne shook her head and gestured vaguely with one long-fingered hand. "Whatever else you think we might need. I'm sure our soldiers will find things of value as we... assist you."

That sounded like a loaded statement. "I'll discuss it with my people, and we'll come up with a firm offer. How many troops can you spare?"

A smile slithered across the queen's face. "A few thousand should suffice, I would think. Don't you?"

That would be... great. "If Ez'girzol's killer is on the other side, I will, of course, bring—"

The queen waived Paige off. "His death has already been accomplished. Another thousand troops will be offered to complete the debt I owe you for bringing that justice to bear."

Really. What *had* happened while Paige had been away? "Okay." Why did Paige feel like she was missing something? "When can we expect the troops?"

Mavofne leaned in, taking in the briefest of gasps and held it for a dramatic pause. "When you fix *our* gate so it is stable enough to support the transfer of men." She reached up and touched her ornate headdress and turned as if she'd just won. "You're free to leave," she said at the door. "Please do so." She paused before leaving. "Immediately."

Derek stared at the open door, his eyes narrowed. "That didn't go as I'd expected."

Paige understood what was being said. The queen had offered her help *knowing* Paige would be unable to stabilize the gate between their worlds enough to bring the promised legions of demons to join in the war. "Fuck." Shit. What a waste of fucking time. "Let's go."

He gathered his coat, draping it over his arm and let Paige lead the way.

The demons had a gate room that was supposed to be used by all travelers in and out of their realm. Once inside the multi-arched room, Derek spared little time in creating a door that took them to the Whiskey house.

Paige stepped into organized chaos. People filled her

kitchen and living room, some getting magickal medical attention, others making dinner as the sun set.

Rai's eyes widened from the dining room table as she came over, maneuvering through the people to get to her mother. "Hey," she said, hugging her. "I was just getting people together to rescue you."

"Got that handled." Paige moved her daughter to the right so they could walk through the living room.

"Headed home," Derek said.

Paige waved at him over her shoulder. "Take care."

"Yeah." The air popped and he disappeared.

"What's... all this?"

Leah stood and stopped mid-step. She pointed a finger, winking in pained thought, and then continued. "Wy killed Valfire, so that's one threat we don't have to worry about."

"Really." That was a relief. "How?"

"I can give you details," Leah said with a sigh. "But with things under control here, I gotta get Fox and Charlie back to Alaska."

She was so grown up. Paige nodded, not knowing what else to do. "If you need anything..."

"I'll let you know. Oh!" Leah snapped and pointed at her. "I aced math."

Paige grinned. She didn't know how normal things like that could still be a thing in the middle of a civil war, how schoolwork and grades just kept going when the whole world was almost literally on fire. "Well done."

"Thanks." Leah grabbed Mandy and headed upstairs.

"What happened?" Paige asked the room at large.

Rai pulled away and went to grab a plate, dishing up something that looked like sausage and taters. "A lot. But we're good."

"And no one hounded you for me?"

"Just me," Rai said, looking pained and affronted. "But

Leah needed me more. I made a call. You're safe. We're all good."

Leah had needed—Paige was going to need to put on her detective mask and get some answers.

Two hours and a full belly later, she got the full story about how Veronica had turned on them, trying to resurrect Threknal to get Valfire to get her out of her contract.

"She was out of control," Bobby whispered. "All the paths led to bad."

He still looked shaken. "Yeah, well," Wy said grumpily, "maybe next time lead with something more than 'she kills her' because that was super unhelpful."

Bobby grunted by didn't move from his slumped position in his chair.

Paige would have to find someone who could help him with vision interpretation. She understood there was a science to it. She'd tried to dreamwork before when she was a teen. Not successfully, but she'd tried. But she put that on the list of things to do.

Later.

For now, her family was safe—mostly. Dexx was still out there. She knew she couldn't count on everyone around the table remaining alive through what was coming.

She'd treasure each moment she could *while* she could.

Several hours later, Wy, Leah, Charlie, and Fox left for Alaska. The dinner dishes had been washed and put away.

Paige discovered that while she'd been away for two weeks in Hell, she'd been gone less than a few hours on Earth. So, she had nothing to worry about, as far as time.

How was she going to make the demon gate stronger without strengthening the angel gate so they could get some reinforcements? She had no idea if that was even possible. So, chalk up one loss, but one they didn't have before. They just had to continue on.

Lovejoy walked through the living room in the midst of Paige shuffling everyone off to bed.

Paige met her back at the floral couch. "What's up?"

Lovejoy smiled tiredly. "The Confederate States officially pulled away and are making a hard stance along their border."

That... was a relief. With Walton now facing a two-front war, the pressure would be off ParaWest for a bit. "Good."

Lovely nodded and turned away. "Don't get used to it. There's more coming. I can feel it."

As could Paige, but she'd take the wins she could for as long as she could.

And she'd keep her family as safe as possible while doing it.

It was the best she could do.

THE END

This concludes Book 5 of the Whiskey Witches Para Wars.

Join us for the next book in this saga as Dexx leads the battles, Paige fights for freedom, and Wy tries to save her home from a godly break-out in the middle of a world-changing war.

Be sure to order it now!

Pre-order now at: https://www.fjblooding.com/preorder

We hope you enjoyed *Slipping on Karma Peels*.
Be sure to visit my site, fjblooding.com, to sign up for our newsletter, get free books, join the forum discussions, and find out more about on our latest books!

And please leave reviews where you buy books. You can also leave reviews on FJBlooding.com.

ALSO BY F.J. BLOODING

Whiskey Witches Universe

Whiskey Witches

Whiskey Witches

Blood Moon Magick

Barrel of Whiskey

Witches of the West

Whiskey Witches: Ancients

Desert Shaman

Big Bad Djinn

Lizard Wizard

Whiskey on the Rocks

Double-Double Demon Trouble

Mirror, Mirror Demon Rubble

Dead Demon Die

Whiskey Witches: Para Wars

Whiskey Storm

London Bridge Down

Midnight Whiskey

International Team of Mystery

Slipping on Karma Peels

Pre-order now at: https://www.fjblooding.com/preorder

Other Books in the Whiskey-Verse

Shifting Heart Romances

by Hattie Hunt & F.J. Blooding

Bear Moon

Grizzly Attraction

Here's the reading order to make it even easier to catch up!

https://www.fjblooding.com/reading-order

Other Books by F.J. Blooding

Devices of War Trilogy

Fall of Sky City

Sky Games

Whispers of the Skyborne

Discover more, sign up for updates and gifts, and join the forum
discussions at www.fjblooding.com.

WHISKEY MAGICK & MENTAL HEALTH

Sign up to learn more about our books and receive this free e-zine about Whiskey Magick and Mental Health.

https://www.fjblooding.com/books-lp

ABOUT THE AUTHOR

F.J. Blooding lives in hard-as-nails Alaska growing grey hair in the midnight sun with Shane, her writing partner and husband, his two part-time kids, his BrotherTwin, SistaWitch, TeenMan, and SnarkGirl, along with a small menagerie of animals which includes several cats, an army of chickens, a rabbit or two, but only one dog.

She enjoys writing and creating with her wonderful husband and dreaming about sleeping. She's dated vampires, werewolves, sorcerers, weapons smugglers, U.S. Government assassins, and slingshot terrorists. No. She is *not* kidding. She even married one of them.

Sign up for her newsletter, get free books, and join the discussions on the forums when you visit her website at FJBlooding.com